A Sunset Touch

Also by Marjorie Eccles:

Cast a Cold Eye
Death of a Good Woman
Requiem for a Dove
More Deaths Than One
Late of This Parish
The Company She Kept
An Accidental Shroud
A Death of Distinction
A Species of Revenge
Killing me Softly
The Superintendent's Daughter

A SUNSET TOUCH

Marjorie Eccles

Constable · London

First published in Great Britain 2000
by Constable, an imprint of Constable & Robinson Limited
3 The Lanchesters, 162 Fulham Palace Road
London W6 9ER

ISBN 0 094 80460 5

Printed and bound in Great Britain

A CIP catalogue record for this book is available from the
British Library

PROLOGUE

Early autumn, a little Indian summer. A dancing wind whirling the yellow and copper leaves, the sky crisp and blue and a hint of coolness lying on the edge of the air. Memorable evenings, Technicolor skies that made you itch to get them down in paint. And woodsmoke, she thought. Nothing was more evocative. Could you capture the smell of woodsmoke in colour? It was an interesting idea.

Watercolours were much in her mind – those painted by her, though she never attached overmuch significance to them. A late-flowering ability she'd discovered in herself, they were done purely for personal satisfaction, but if one of them sold occasionally, who was grumbling? And last week someone, dropping into the interior decorating shop she ran with her sister, had liked them enough to shell out good money for *two* of them!

Her eyes on that incredible sky, Alex Jones walked home in the early dusk, feeling good.

Then gradually, she became aware that the wisp of smoke lazily curling upwards had become something more, a dark shadow between herself and the sun, that the sweet woodsmoke smell had changed, too, turning acrid and unpleasant. She heard the clang of a fire engine, then another . . . She began to run.

The house was beyond hope of saving by the time the fire brigade arrived.

Flames were shooting sky high, the heat could be felt from a hundred yards away, though the fire was concentrated on one small, shabby house at the end of a run-down row of identical houses, its other side abutting the Royal Oak car-park. A typical Black Country terrace house, common enough in Lavenstock, its front door opening directly off the street, the garden behind no more than a narrow plot of sour earth. Neighbours had been evacuated and the street cleared of the beat-up cars normally lining it, but knots of people still stood around, craning forward, ignoring warnings to disperse, jostling and shoving further for-

5

ward in the hope of some excitement. The frisky wind was a cause for concern. British Gas was standing by.

A commotion started at the edge of the crowd, where a fat young woman in black stretch leggings and an oversized, grubby white T-shirt had managed to get through the cordon. She was running forward, screaming above the noise, grabbing the arm of one of the firemen who was training his hose on the roaring flames.

'Get back, missis!' he bawled, over his shoulder. 'I'm telling you it's dangerous!'

'And I'm telling you as there's kids in there!'

The fireman swung round as that got through to him, and met eyes wide with horror under a ragged fringe of unevenly dyed blonde hair. '*Christ*! Yours?'

She shook her head violently. 'No, no! But what's it matter whose they are? Get 'em out, can't you?'

He cast a look back at the raging inferno. Kids in there? Bloody hell. Not now, there weren't. Not alive. No chance. 'Dave!' he bellowed. 'Get the chief, sharp! And you do as you're told, missis! Get out the road – *now*!'

His attitude was maybe rougher than he intended, hiding the sickness that the thought of small charred bodies brought to his soul. People thought you got used to it, that it was all part of the job, like being a doctor . . . they didn't know about the memories, the waking nightmares that came on you when you least expected it.

Something crashed inside the house, probably the bedroom floor. With a roar, the flames whooshed even higher, sparks flew. The dry leaves of a sad-looking urban cherry planted into the pavement caught alight, giving it its moment of glory, but the fireman, whose name was Andy, immediately trained his high-pressure hose on it, leaving it dripping, sadder than ever.

Dave was back, shouting something about the next-door neighbour's pigeon loft, an old boy who refused to leave his birds . . .

'Never mind the bloody pigeons, what about the kids?'

The woman was still there, shrieking, refusing to be put off, though she, like everyone else, must see the impossibility of anyone still being alive in there.

A young police constable came to the aid of the firemen and

tried to hustle her away, not unkindly. 'Come on, m'duck, they're doing all that's humanly possible.'

She struggled for a while but then, with a last despairing look back at the conflagration, allowed herself to be led away. When they were at a safe distance, he began questioning her. He was big and unflappable and said his name was Dawson, and presently, she began to calm down.

'They're foreigners,' she told him, sniffing. 'Russian or Czech or some such. I don't know what they was called, they haven't been here more'n a week or two. Two kids, boy and a girl –' the tears threatened again – 'and their Dad. Very quiet, kept theirselves to theirselves, didn't hardly speak to nobody.'

'How do you know they're in there?'

'I saw him go off on his own this morning. He's left them before . . . not right, is it? I took mine to their Nan's after school and when I got back smoke was pouring out the window. I shouted and knocked and no answer. So I tried to get in but the door was locked, and the back entry gate was bolted shut.'

'Likely he came home and they've all gone out together.' Dawson was only trying to reassure her, but she looked disbelieving, and he added, 'It was you called the fire brigade, wasn't it? What's your name, m'duck?'

'Parkes. Debbie Parkes.'

She was still crying, her mascara had run and her lipstick had been licked off. Her fat cheeks wobbled. She sniffed again.

'You've done great, Mrs Parkes. Pity there aren't more like you.'

'Mebbe I should've made more of an effort to get to know them, like, but he – their Dad, I mean – didn't make it easy. Not that they was standoffish, mind, just shy, I reckon. I saw them all in the street once and spoke to them and the girl curtsied and the little lad bowed. Lovely manners, they had. Likely they couldn't speak English – the kids, any road. Their Dad could, but you could tell he was a foreigner . . .'

Dawson understood what she meant. Not just a foreigner as Lavenstock usually meant it, *anyone* from more than ten miles away, but somebody not English . . . 'What made you think they were Russian, then?'

'Dunno,' she said vaguely. 'They just had that look. And who else but foreigners would live in that dump?' She threw a scathing glance at a woman who'd just arrived at the scene and was carrying on loudly and at length about why no one had done more to save her property. 'That's the landlady. What she's got to create about? It was a rat hole, that place, beats me how she had the face to charge 'em rent at all. She should've been paying *them* to stop there.'

'Yeah, I reckon.' Dawson knew Bessemer Street, he'd been inside several of the houses more than once in the course of duty, and thought he couldn't have found a better description, himself.

He glanced back at the burning house. The fire seemed to be under control now. They'd stopped it from spreading, it would soon be over. It didn't take long for little houses like this to end up as a heap of ashes.

1

A few days before the fire, in a house that was only a couple of miles west of Bessemer Street, yet half a world away, Cecily Haldane had been hanging a picture. She pulled a stool forward and climbed on it – though she'd been told often enough that she shouldn't, at her age – firstly to lift down, with a great deal of satisfaction, the dim sepia print of Wells Cathedral she'd disliked for years, and then again to replace it with one of the water-colours she'd bought yesterday. Definitely an improvement, she thought, stepping down from the stool to appraise it, though she'd have to be tactful about the replacement, the last thing she'd want to do was to hurt Edgar. He'd spent several years as chaplain to the Bishop of Bath and Wells as a young man, and still had a great fondness for the place.

However, a picture that did the magnificent cathedral more justice than this dreary old thing shouldn't be hard to find, one he could hang in his study. That would go a long way towards mollifying him. And she could instruct him how to look at this new picture so that he'd eventually believe he'd always liked it and that placing it there had been his own idea.

The other watercolour would be an ideal special present for someone. Julia, perhaps, whose fortieth birthday was imminent, and who would appreciate it, Cecily knew. Which couldn't be said of her other two children: Olivia would think her mother ought to have given the money to the Overseas Relief Agency, and would probably say so – really, Mother, fancy wasting all that money on a *picture*! She would never admit that the money stood more chance of being wasted by falling into the wrong hands when it went abroad, Cecily thought, with that streak of toughness and scepticism which constantly surprised those who didn't really know her. As for Jago, he would only look down his nose and murmur something derogatory about 'talented ama-teurs'. And then blush with embarrassment and fall over himself to apologise for putting his foot in it, because of course, he wouldn't have *meant* to look down his nose, not Jago, her vague, good-natured and talented youngest child, it was just that he was so used to dealing with the very best of art treasures that it would never occur to him to give anything less than a true opinion on any work of art.

Never mind, thought Cecily, *I* like the pictures, and maybe I'll keep both, after all. Although she'd have been the first to admit she was no expert on art, she instinctively felt they had an originality and a calm, understated quality one didn't often see, a coolness that held a hint of sensuousness, rather like a reflection of the artist herself. It had been such a delight to talk to her, a pleasure all of a piece with the delicious September weather, with finding in the library several interesting books for the coming week, having her hair done, and the feeling that life wasn't over, yet. Before the day had been dimmed, that is, by what had happened later. She would have to consider very seriously what was to be done about *that*. The possibility that she might not be able to find a solution to the problem never occurred to her, but if she had learned one thing over the years, it was not to rush decisions, even one as pressing, as devastatingly upsetting, as this.

She lit a cigarette, trying not to notice how her fingers shook, and stood back again to admire the placing of the picture, remembered that she'd given up smoking – yet again – and put it out, went to open the window. Edgar might not notice the picture for quite a while, he was notoriously unnoticing, except in matters concerning his church, but he would certainly smell cigarette smoke. And then he would look wounded at her lack of moral fibre, though Cecily was not unduly worried about nicotine in her lungs, not when she'd smoked for over fifty years without so much as a cough. Nevertheless, the thought was yet another intimation of mortality, and such intimations had occurred to her with increasing frequency over the last year: the urgent feeling that affairs must be set in order. However painful that might be. Things to be put right. And as to what that would mean, she was much exercised in her mind.

A graceful woman wearing expensive clothes, Cecily was far from beautiful, she never had been, and had settled for elegance instead. Her hair was discreetly tinted and cut in a short, plain style that suited her strongly boned face, she had a generous mobile mouth and a fund of energy that belied her years, and indeed had reluctantly retired only a few years since. She had married late, though not by today's standards, already established in a career in the Civil Service when she and Edgar had met, and she had kept on working throughout her marriage, except for the short periods when she'd had the three children. She'd reached a responsible position on the ladder and besides, her work had enabled her to escape the usual role that befell clergy wives of her generation, that of being a mere second thought to her husband's profession, nothing more than Canon Haldane's wife. Or worse, turning into one of those other wives, whose every effort was directed by the assumption that their husband was entitled to become a bishop. All the same, although she had believed passionately that a career was worthwhile and fulfilling to her as a woman, it had added another layer to the usual guilt of the working mother, and to that other guilt she had for so long resolutely buried.

As her hand lifted to the window catch, she saw that opening it wasn't going to be a good idea. She'd been so preoccupied that she'd failed to take into account what they said would be only a blip in the lovely weather. Yesterday's bright, crisp day had given way to rain, blustery and unpleasant. She leaned her forehead against the sash of one of the two tall, graceful windows. Rain blew against the panes as she gazed unseeing along Folgate Street. The traffic swished past on the narrow road between the vicarage and the impressive bulk of the Norman church of Holy Trinity, built on the foundations of a Cistercian monastery, Lavenstock's largest church and one of its greatest treasures, over which – and his flock – Canon Haldane so selflessly, yet so uncompromisingly, presided.

She finally admitted that she couldn't put off decisions much longer, after receiving yesterday what had almost amounted to an ultimatum, but of one thing she was very, very sure: she wasn't about to give in to such.

So why had it been such a body blow? Why did she feel such dread? She had, after all, been bracing herself against that knock on the door for over fifty years. But, dear God, she'd never expected it to take this form.

On the day of the fire, Piotr Kaminski's home help was late

again. He was waiting impatiently for her to make his coffee, and cursed her slackness roundly. Shifting his heavy bulk in his sagging armchair, he wondered if it would be yet another new help who would appear today, though whoever it was, it was a sure thing she wouldn't know how to make coffee properly. They never did, these women sent by the council. A spoonful of Nescafé in a mug of hot water, with cold milk added. None of them lasted long, they complained that he pinched their bottoms, or any other part of their anatomy he could grab from where he sat, more or less immobilised in his chair. The last one had threatened to slap his face and called him a dirty old man.

You'd think they could at least humour an old fellow who couldn't move an inch without the aid of his frame, but they'd no sense of fun, young women today, not like those he'd known in his heyday. Ah, those lovely girls! He sighed, drifting easily back into the past. His window overlooked a dusty north London street, but he could always close his eyes to the rubbish-filled gardens and the row of wheelie bins waiting on the pavement for the municipal dustcart, and remember better days. Especially those wartime ones, when he'd been serving in the Free Polish Air Force, God's gift to lovely young Waafs, plump and bosomy in their blue cotton shirts, pleasantly rounded with starchy wartime food and Naafi snacks.

Sunny summer days, evenings in dance halls and crowded pubs. Crazy, madcap antics with old cars and motorbikes, if you could scrounge the petrol. And popsies galore, smiling, compliant, all agog for those mad Poles, dashing and different, with their foreign manners, their growing knowledge of English all mixed up with RAF slang. Ready for anything. You went along with all that, along with shooting a line about the daring night bombing missions, although if truth be told – which it never was – those raids, at the mercy of German flak, with the ever-present possibility that you might never return, scared the hell out of anybody with any imagination at all.

But ready for anything, yes, that at least was true, anything to shut out what they'd left behind as darkness descended over Europe, and he and Jerzy escaped over the mountains, with nothing but a handful of zlotys in their pockets, and in their rucksacks some black bread and cheese, a lump of garlic sausage and a few hard, unripe apples from the tree at the back of the house. A photograph of the Black Madonna for him, and for Jerzy, his own secret, hidden between his shirt and his skin.

It had been autumn in Krakow, beautiful as only the old city could be, the sun sparkling on the Vistula as it curled round the castle mound of Wawel Hill, that day they'd eventually made up their minds to go, two hot-headed young students in their last year at university, but it had taken months to finalise their plans, to reconcile their families to their going.

Who had mentioned escape first, the chance to hit back? Jerzy, without a doubt. He'd always been a daredevil, and a bit of a joker, but he'd been as deadly serious about that as Piotr himself. From the very first days of the war, when a disbelieving world had watched Poland being attacked on both sides, the Germans marching on Warsaw from the west, and the Russians, in accordance with their secret pact with the Nazis, descending from the east, and Poland forced, unthinkably, after a short, bitter and courageously hopeless struggle, to capitulate.

An underground army had immediately sprung into being, but it was the chance to strike oppression from outside that moved Jerzy and himself, the heady sound of freedom that rang in their ears. A new Polish government-in-exile had been formed and most of the Polish Air Force had escaped to form crack fighting units in France and Britain. He and Jerzy had been fired with the determination to follow suit. By the time of the Battle of Britain, in which Polish pilots were playing such a heroic part, they were ready to kiss their mothers and their sisters goodbye. Jerzy, solemn for once, had shaken hands with his father, that old rogue Jozef, differences forgiven if not forgotten.

Kaminski's own beloved father had not seen the day of his departure; along with almost five thousand other Polish cavalry officers, regarded as a potentially dangerous political force, he had been rounded up and later shot by the Russians, *pour encourager les autres*. Kaminski crossed himself, as he always did whenever the memory of that appalling massacre at Katyn, that place in the forest, came back to him. How far away now it all seemed, a dream: the forests, the flat Polish plains, the mountains over which they'd finally escaped.

A heavy lorry passed, laden with materials for the washing machine factory at the bottom of the road. The floor shook, the window frames rattled. Kaminski opened his eyes, pushed an overflowing ashtray and his bottle of tablets aside as he reached for one of the many framed photos on the cluttered table by the side of his chair, polished the glass on his sleeve and stared at it intently, familiar though it was. Dear God! how young they all looked, he and the rest of the two bomber crews, standing in front of their Wellington aircraft with the PAF red and white chessboard markings on the fuselage, still in their flying jackets after a training session: Rajewski in the front row, trailing his Mae West; Bics the bomb-aimer; Liebert; Dejmek; Czerminska the rear gunner, whose remains had later been swilled out of the gun turret. Himself, their pilot, big, blond and handsome, half a head taller than Jerzy, navigator with the other crew, though he too was tall, and equally good-looking, in a darker, thin-faced way. More than half a lifetime ago!

He sighed and replaced the photo next to the posed, oh so English wedding picture of himself and Muriel. He and his best man – Jerzy, of course – both of them ultra correct, impeccable and polished in British RAF uniform, but with 'Poland' emblazoned on their sleeve and the Polish eagle on their cap. Muriel in a blue suit and a strange hat, begged or borrowed from someone, a wedding bouquet as big as a cartwheel hiding her already swelling stomach. He should have been warned, even then. Out of her WAAF uniform Muriel looked quite different, all traces of the pert, pretty girl he'd chased wiped from her face, her mouth disagreeably pursed in that way which became so familiar later. She'd been trying to keep back tears of emotion, or so she said when the photographs were developed, but Kaminski knew it was because this wasn't how she'd envisaged her wedding at all, this hurried and shameful affair with no white satin, a cardboard replica cake and few guests or presents because it was wartime.

He coughed and lit another cigarette. Poor Muriel! He kept their wedding picture on view from a sense of guilt, because although the baby had died and he'd stayed with her in England after the war and tried to do his best for her, he'd never succeeded in making her happy – nor she him, if it came to that. He'd watched her die, painfully, of cancer ten years later, and after that he'd stayed unmarried until he was well over forty – until his next wife came along, that is, young enough to be his daughter. Lovely blonde Sirkka-Lisa, dancing into his life for so

14

short a time that he barely remembered her now, bearing him a son and then skipping off back to Scandinavia, leaving him to bring up Stefan alone.

Both his marriages had left scars, but he had come through the war physically unscathed. He'd abandoned his ambition of trying to get into an English university to continue his scientific studies as being too difficult, the scramble for places being what it then was, and had contented himself with a job flying commercial aircraft, until he became too old and was grounded and given an administrative position in the same company. He had thought about going back to Poland more than once during the years following the war, but nothing he'd heard from his native country had persuaded him to do this. His family, like many more, had become dispersed and disintegrated, and communism and all its attendant woes, and the years of unrest, shortages and strikes, had made even post-war Britain seem like a very desirable place to live.

He had to admit he hadn't had a bad life here, all in all, better than Jerzy for sure, who'd been shot down over Germany and had spent the rest of the war, despite daring attempts to escape, in a POW camp, where he'd contracted TB, from which he'd died shortly after the war. Impossible to believe that Jerzy, at first full of life and fun, his eyes dancing, was now dead.

No, his own life hadn't been so bad, Kaminski repeated to himself . . . until now. Now he was lonely, damned lonely. He had his books, of course, books had always been a lifeline. But he had few visitors; he hadn't seen his son for months.

Damn that woman, where was she?

He was thinking he was going to have to make the painful effort to go into the kitchen and prepare his own coffee when the doorbell rang. At last! They'd been given a key, but it had been known for those in charge to forget to give it to whichever woman they sent.

He heaved himself with difficulty out of his chair and, moving slowly with the aid of his walking frame, manoeuvred himself down the passage to the front door and opened it awkwardly. For a moment, he stood there, immobile, unable to believe what he saw, and then his heart began to bang painfully and unevenly against his ribcage as he confronted the evidence of his own eyes: the man he had thought dead for over forty years.

* * *

Later that evening, as the misty autumn darkness fell, and Alex went to draw the curtains in the house on the hill, she fancied she could still smell the smoke from the fire. The roaring flames were imprinted on her retina, and she couldn't get out of her mind the horror of what it must be like for those who'd lived there, suddenly to lose all they possessed. Like every other woman she'd ever known, she'd wished, from time to time, that she could set fire to her entire wardrobe – but that was just something you said without much thought, not really meaning the whole shebang. Not *everything*, and absolutely not in a fire like that . . . not just clothes, but everything else, too. She shivered, visualising this newly furbished kitchen going up in smoke, and the rest of the house, too, so recently bought from their erstwhile landlady, furnished and decorated with such love and care. Then felt ashamed, despising herself for being so trivial . . . what was that, compared to the danger to human life . . . people having to jump out of windows, or suffocating, sometimes whole families burnt to death?

There'd been a traffic jam of fire engines and police vehicles and the like around the entrance to Bessemer Street when she'd reached there, already knowing by then there'd been no need to run. The fire was well below her own neighbourhood on the hill. When she saw the traffic hold-up, she'd been glad of her decision to walk to work that morning and leave her car at home. She skirted the jam quickly, and the crowds of gawping onlookers – what horror were they hoping for? – but also because, as an ex-police sergeant herself, she recognised how much worse their presence was making an already difficult and crowded situation. As she left, a television camera unit screamed round the corner, hot on the trail of a scoop for the evening news.

A demented shriek issued from the sitting-room. Perhaps the cat was killing the parrot – or the other way round? No chance, it was only Bert complaining that he was hungry. She grabbed the packet of bird seed, wondering, as she did sometimes, why she'd got herself into all this, a life punctuated by the striking and chiming of – was it twenty-seven? – clocks, she'd lost count, plus the demands of a jealous cat and a parrot with attitude, when all she wanted was peace and order. Then she smiled, her stomach did its familiar little flip. Gil Mayo was why, and there was no answer to that.

After she'd replenished the bird seed in the parrot's cage, and received an ungrateful nip for her pains, she went back to the kitchen, sucking her finger, then busied herself in getting the evening meal ready. She turned the oven on and scrubbed potatoes for baking, prepared a salad for tossing, set the steaks ready to grill. The phone rang.

Mayo said, 'We've got problems. Carry on with your supper, I'll grab something here if necessary.' Long experience had taught him that he was in no danger of being accused of spoiling any attempts at *haute cuisine*. Alex's cooking skills – and her inclinations, apart from the sweet tooth that was her Achilles' heel – were directed towards food that was plain, quick and non-fattening. As if food was merely a matter of survival. She tried valiantly to steer him in the same direction, for the sake of his weight and his cholesterol, but it was a losing battle. She more than suspected he'd secretly be glad of the opportunity to tuck into off-limits steak and kidney pudding from the canteen, or sausage and chips.

He was explaining about the fire – 'I passed it,' she said. 'It looked horrendous, Gil, from what I saw. I hope no one was hurt?'

There was a pause, which probably meant yes.

Something serious, at any rate. It must be, if he was staying on because of it, though it didn't take much for him to find reasons why he should be there, in at the sharp end of any investigation, preferably before anyone else, Detective Superintendent though he might be, and never mind the almost permanent, crippling work overload that ensued as a result. He expected the same effort from the disparate bunch of men and women who worked under him, too, and though they grumbled under their breath when their private concerns were disrupted, they took it as an insult to be removed from the team. He demanded a lot, but he was known for never forgetting a face, a name, or an achievement.

'It doesn't look good,' he replied eventually. 'Anyhow, I'll see you later. Don't wait up if I'm very late, love.'

She turned the oven off, put the steaks back in the fridge, tried to eat some salad then pushed it away. She thought of the cheesecake, but left it where it was, guessing what Mayo hadn't said. She had years and years of police work behind her, but nothing had ever accustomed her to certain aspects of things. It was why, in the end, she'd packed it in.

He came in a couple of hours later, looking tired.

'Have you eaten?' she asked.

He shook his head. His clothes smelled faintly of the fire and the chemical odour of the extinguishers as he bent his head to kiss her. There were worry lines between his eyes. But he was still deeply tanned from a recent walking holiday, and looked reassuringly healthy, solid and dependable: he would, as usual, take whatever had happened in his stride, though any feelings he had about the case he'd keep to himself, in his non-committal Yorkshire way, until he felt ready to talk. Without being asked, Alex poured him two fingers of scotch. He touched her cheek briefly with the back of his hand, drank half the scotch, then went to change.

When he came back, showered and in his favourite old out-at-elbows sweater and comfortable slacks, he was looking more relaxed.

'Out, Moses!' he ordered peremptorily, turfing the cat out of the comfortable basket chair, settling himself and sipping the rest of his drink and watching Alex while she poured herself a glass of Chardonnay to keep him company. The grey lump of fur who more usually responded to the name of Damned Cat, sensing a unique opportunity, jumped back up, landing heavily in his lap. It was a measure of how he was feeling that Mayo actually let him stay there. He didn't like cats, he repeatedly told everyone, this ugly old brute was only here on sufferance, having once belonged to his landlady while nourishing a deep feline conviction that he was rightly meant to belong to Mayo. Circumstances had worked in the animal's favour, Miss Vickers having left him behind when she moved. He settled now on his new master's knee, looking smug with forgiveness for the years of unrequited affection.

Mayo reached for the bottle to freshen his whisky. 'We thought there were two children in there.'

Something caught at the back of Alex's throat as the word 'children' registered shock before the sentence came together, with its past tense.

'It's OK, they weren't,' he reassured her quickly. 'There *was* a body though.'

In the act of taking the steaks from the fridge, she changed her mind. Grilled steak no longer seemed like a good idea. Instead, she got out the cheese, and eggs from the rack for an omelette.

'We think he's a Pole called Tadeusz Siemek,' Mayo went on, absently stroking Moses until the animal vibrated with pleasure under his hands, 'arrived here a couple of weeks ago with his two children.' Such was the power of the computers he'd once so distrusted! Information in a flash that would once have taken days, weeks, to compile. 'The good news is that the children weren't in the house when it went up. The bad news is they've apparently disappeared.'

'Disappeared? How come?'

'You might well ask. We've a witness, a young woman who lives opposite and doesn't miss a thing. She knows everything about the neighbours, clocks them in and out, you know the sort. Good-hearted, though. She was worried about the children, left on their own, which it seems they often were. Why they weren't in the house today when it happened we don't know yet.'

'What did happen?'

'The fire assessors will be in tomorrow but when the Prof examined the body he found a piece of what looks like clothes line trapped under it. Suggesting the line was soaked with an accelerant and used as a trail from the back door to the body, then set alight by a match dropped through the letter-box.'

'My God, a racist attack? Here?'

'Why should Lavenstock be more immune than anywhere else?' He shrugged. 'But racist? I don't think so. It's unlikely that many people knew the occupants were foreigners, or knew them at all, if it comes to that. It doesn't do to be too neighbourly in Bessemer Street. Keep your distance, the less known about your affairs the better. In any case, it seems the fire was started to cover up the fact that he was already dead. He was badly charred, but not enough to hide that he'd apparently been strangled.'

Murder, he thought, draining his whisky, thinking of the routine procedures, the backbone of every investigation, that were even now being set up. It happened here in Lavenstock as well as in the big cities, but wherever it happened, it was nobody's idea of fun, even when the outcome was cut and dried, with a

19

self-confessed perpetrator holding a smoking gun or a bloody knife. No, murder was always the ultimate outrage – the waste of a life, the mess, the futility, the total disruption of a hitherto sane and ordered world. On the other hand, sweeping up the detritus of young lives ruined by drugs was pretty grim, too. Neither was the hopeless race to catch up with the criminal fraternity – always, it seemed, one step ahead – any joke. Or even, on another level, the eternal admin. Chasing a murderer when it wasn't immediately apparent who the culprit was at least gave you a chance to use your grey matter.

'So what about the children?' Alex was asking. 'Do you think they could have been taken away before the fire was started?' A cold finger ran down her spine as other possibilities occurred . . . that they might have been witnesses to what had happened, that somewhere the children, as well as their father, might lie dead.

'Good question. We've got an all-out search on for them, of course, but nobody seems to have seen hide nor hair of them. Let's hope to God we find them –' He stopped. 'What am I saying? Hope's got nothing to do with it. We'd damn well *better* find them.'

The meal over, she came into the sitting-room after loading the dishwasher, tidying the kitchen, setting out the breakfast things. He wished she'd leave it, just occasionally. Dearly as he loved her, his once and only love, it was trying, sometimes, living up to her standards.

She curled in the chair opposite him. Pale, creamy skin, eyes so dark a blue as to be almost navy, a wing of thick dark hair falling over her eye as she scribbled something in a notebook while he watched her and stretched out on the big, squashy, comfortably sagging sofa from which he resolutely refused to be parted. He'd agreed some time ago to have it re-covered, and that was as far as he'd go. After all, he'd bought it in his bachelor days, it had seen him through marriage, the loss of his wife, being a lone parent – all before Alex.

He was so grateful she hadn't allowed her sister Lois to impose her trendy decorating ideas everywhere, he'd made no demur about the rest of the alterations which Alex had thought necessary when they'd taken over the house from their landlady. He had to admit that the decision to buy, about which he'd had distinct reservations, thinking it too big, for one thing, had turned out to be a good one. There was a room for his daughter, Julie, whenever she came down from Scotland where she had alighted like a migrant bird and seemed to have settled for the time being, and a spare room for visitors; the attic with its strong northern light provided room enough for Alex to paint in and for Mayo to tinker with those of his clocks which were not otherwise dispersed throughout the house, where he'd persuaded himself their sometimes unsynchronised chiming was not as intrusive as it had been in the flat. And there were a couple of other small rooms – children's rooms . . .

Alex said she'd come to terms by now with the fact that they'd never be filled, except with the string of small visitors who appeared from time to time, she'd adjusted to it. And he believed she meant it – just as he believed she meant it when she said she didn't want to spoil what to her was an ideal relationship between the two of them by getting married. Useless to point out to someone like Alex that perfection was an unattainable state. But Mayo had – though wild horses wouldn't have dragged the admission from him – a strong conservative streak in his nature. Getting married had always had high priority in his mind. He hadn't brought up the subject lately, however, since it had begun to feel like the question which demands the answer no.

What the devil was it that was absorbing her so much in that damned notebook? She'd been scribbling away purposefully every night that week, a frown between her brows. In between staring into space. As if aware of his eyes on her, she looked up, gave him a cool, amused glance, smiled back and shut the notebook with a snap. He waited, semi-expectantly. But it was natural to her not to express her thoughts freely. She wouldn't share them until they were set in order. Anyway, whatever it was that was absorbing her so much, something lately had brought back the spring into her step. He'd even heard her more than holding her own in an argument with her sister, Lois, which cheered him more than he could say.

Happy with this thought, he reached out for the weekly paper and swore roundly, albeit under his breath. He'd never met a woman yet who could refold a map or a newspaper properly, and Alex was no exception. Worse than most, in fact. The *Advertiser* looked as though it had been used for wrapping fish and chips. How could someone as fastidious as she was *do* this thing? It irritated the hell out of him. And then he grinned – it was what he wanted, wasn't it? The flip side, the flaw which served to modify all those other attributes of perfection?

'What are you looking so cheerful about?'

'Private thoughts. Inadmissible.' He kept the smile as he looked at her.

She raised her eyebrows but didn't press him. 'Who's on the case?' she asked, reaching over her chair arm for the pot on the table beside her. 'More coffee?'

'No thanks, I want to sleep tonight. Abigail is, for the moment.'

'Not Martin Kite?'

'Not if I can help it.'

'And what does that mean?'

'Infighting, I suspect, though maybe that's putting it a bit strong. Whatever, it's definitely something, to pinch a line, up with which I will not put.'

'Between him and Abigail? Oh, it'll work itself out. Martin needs time to adjust.'

'Not to mention a kick up the backside.'

No doubt about it, Mayo was glad to have Martin Kite back in CID with him, after the spell in uniform following his promotion to inspector. He and Kite had partnered each other well, when he'd been a chief inspector and Kite a mere sergeant, a good partner though you had to sit permanently on his tail to keep him on the ground. Too gung-ho by half, sometimes. Then Kite's more ambitious wife, Sheila, had nagged him into taking his inspector's exams – a good thing, for Mayo doubted whether he'd ever have made the effort, left to himself. After his temporary departure from CID into uniform, Mayo had had to become used to working with a woman. It wasn't something that came easily to him, but he wasn't inclined to let go of Abigail Moon, his copper-haired, thorough-going and competent inspector, now that he had, Kite or no Kite. Previously, when both were still sergeants, Abigail and Kite had never had any trouble working together, but he now sensed tension between them which hadn't been there before. Kite was being stroppy for no obvious reason and Abigail, always ambitious, was showing definite signs of restlessness, both of which had high priority on the list of things he could do without.

'Want some music?' he asked, putting the niggle aside into a compartment marked 'tomorrow'. Moses, living dangerously, or perhaps cashing in on his previous success, made tentative attempts to join him on the sofa, but was toed out of the way in no uncertain fashion, back to the hearthrug where he sat, biding his time. Before Alex could answer, the telephone rang.

'Yes, Abigail.' Mayo listened carefully for several minutes to what she had to say, then put the phone back.

'They've found the children,' he told Alex. A wide grin broke over his face. 'And they're safe.'

2

The stink of the fire was even worse the morning after, in the rain. Rain which was, said the weathermen, not set to spoil the unending series of glorious days. The smell hung like a sour miasma, a horrid combination of wet ashes and chemical foam. Funny how a blazing bonfire in autumn smelled tangy and sweet, while demolition fires, or the smell of a burned-out house, were simply revolting. In this case, with a more sickening dimension added by the taint of murder.

The three of them – Mayo and Abigail Moon, with Sergeant Carmody towering above both – stood on the path bisecting the plot behind the house, a narrow piece of earth about thirty yards by ten, and stared at the blackened and desolate shell of what had once been a house, a home. Burned out, windowless, roofless, it looked pitifully inadequate to encompass even what had been such a small living space: two up, two down and a scullery stuck on at the back, with the addition, at some time, of a bathroom built on over the scullery.

The bit of land behind the house – a downright lie to call it a garden – consisted of long grass vying with dandelions, nettles and brambles, a broken-down fence at the back, privet hedges either side. A brick path led to what had once been a privy in the corner, the remains of a rabbit hutch and a child's indestructible yellow plastic lorry, long ago abandoned and nearly hidden under a huge patch of neglected michaelmas daisies, dingy and etiolated.

'Manually strangled, according to the Prof, so the killer didn't come equipped. That wasn't what he used his knife for, anyway. Maybe it was just a pocket knife,' said Abigail, speaking her thoughts aloud and pointing to the clothes post at the end of the plot to make clear what she meant.

From the post, and from a hook in the back wall of the house, between which the clothes line had evidently been permanently extended, dangled two cut ends of rope, what remained after cutting off the length which had been used to act as a wick to start the conflagration. A few brightly coloured plastic clothes pegs were still attached to one end. More pegs littered the path, and a wooden prop lay in the grass.

'Maybe he couldn't be sure about the knife when it came down to it,' Carmody said, Liverpool lugubriousness well to the fore, as usual. 'Takes some knowledge to know just where to put one in.'

Mayo grunted. He didn't think the killer had arrived with the intention of using a knife on his victim, either. Death from a lunge with a knife to the heart is more often a matter of chance than popular belief allows it – the chances of the knife glancing against a rib, or being hampered by clothing or the victim's movements, aren't easy to take into account. The pattern emerging so far suggested a quarrel blowing up, a set-to ending in the victim being throttled, and what followed being panic means intended to cover up the crime. That being so, although the local quota of known fire-raisers was even now being rounded up and questioned, he didn't expect anything to come of it. 'Anything come from the doorstepping?' he asked Carmody.

A squad of officers, armed with a list of questions, had been canvassing the area, house by house. Others, situated at the street corners and outside the Royal Oak, had questioned passers-by. 'Not a sausage, so far.' Carmody didn't sound hopeful that things would change.

'Cheer up!' Abigail added, tongue in cheek. 'There's always a chance somebody will suddenly remember seeing a strange car or someone carrying a petrol can – or even dipping the rope into his tank. Petrol, that's what Forensics reckon the accelerant was.'

'Remember? Not round here, they won't! I reckon he parked next door.' Carmody jerked his head towards the pub car-park. 'Empty that time of day, most like, when they're not busy. Most folks wouldn't bother going round to the car-park. There's usually plenty room in Victoria Road during the day, anyway.'

'That's right. Convenient for starting the fire here, at the back of the house, no one to see him.' Mayo pointed at the tatty back fence. 'And he'd only have to breathe on that to get through from the car-park. A length of clothes line slipped under that scullery door would pose no problem, either. You could drive a coach and horses under it.'

Carmody glanced at the blistered paint on the back door. 'Wasn't locked, nor forced, so the killer had it made. Unless he was let in, or had a key.'

'When's the fire investigator due?' Mayo asked.

'Any time.' Abigail, looking at her watch, spoke from under the shelter of a big red and blue golf umbrella advertising Martini Rosso. She wore a yellow waterproof raincoat, and with her bright hair, lit up the gloomy scene. Both men felt more cheerful, just looking at her. In fact, she glowed. Mayo reminded himself she was on a personal high at the moment, her significant other having returned to the fold. In Mayo's opinion he was another, like Kite at the moment, who needed a kick up the pants, wanting to have his cake and eat it. His opinion of journalists, even such likeable sorts as Ben Appleyard, was not high. Women constantly surprised him by their tolerance.

'I'll stay and have a word,' she went on. 'The fire officer's meeting Blake from Forensics here, and the SOCOs. It was too dark to finish collecting their evidence samples last night. When they have, we can go in. And then, unless anyone volunteers to stand in for me, I'm for the PM,' she said, pulling a face.

Gutted though the place might appear to be, there'd be trace elements, there was always something left. The killer, hoping to obliterate evidence of his crime when he torched the house, had underestimated, like countless others before him, the difficulty of completely destroying a human body, the possibility of evidence remaining even after exposure to burning. The pressure between this body and the floor meant that the tell-tale piece of clothes line trapped between them had remained intact and established a pattern of burning from the scullery door to the body. This was evident immediately the Professor – Timpson-Ludgate, the pathologist – had made his examination, but still, everything would be photographed, videoed, plotted, sifted through, in the search for more evidence. And a filthy job it would be, too.

'We need a translator to talk to those children,' Mayo said. 'Find out what happened, what they know, why they weren't in the house.'

Abigail looked worried. 'The little girl can speak some English but she's too overcome with everything that's happened to say much. Everyone at the station's tried. Jenny Platt's enquiring at the Polish ex-servicemen's club to see if they know of anyone who can help.'

Mayo said sharply, 'I hope nobody's told them about their father?'

'They keep asking where he is and we've done everything we can to put them off. But they've had to be told about the fire, why they can't go back. We really can't do any more without someone who can speak Polish.'

They stared again at the blackened shell where a man had perished, thinking their own thoughts.

'Poor little sods,' said Carmody. There was another measurable silence.

'Well, I can't hang around here all day,' Mayo said at last, unfairly, since it was he who'd called the meeting, the way he always did at the beginning of any investigation. He made it a rule to speak personally to as many witnesses as possible before leaving the investigation to the rest of his team.

As he turned to go, sounds were heard from behind the overgrown privet hedge, the one separating this property from its neighbour in the terrace, followed by the head of an old man, wearing a greasy flat cap that had moulded itself to the contours of his head. A cigarette with a long ash dangled from the corner of his mouth. ''Ere,' he demanded, ''ow long you lot going be messing around, disturbing me pigeons, eh? Eh?'

This was the old bloke, Carmody remembered, who'd given PC Dawson so much grief, refusing to move out of his house because he kept racing pigeons in his back bedroom, God help us. He'd have gone up in smoke himself rather than leave them.

As luck would have it, the fire had been put out and the danger to the surrounding houses and their inhabitants deemed negligible before it had been necessary to try and move him out by force.

'No problem now, sir,' Carmody said. 'We shan't be bothering you any more. Have much to do with your new neighbours, did you?'

'Nah,' the old man said, without removing his fag, 'they was foreigners, wasn't they?'

It seemed as though he wasn't about to enlarge on this self-evident explanation. Then he added, 'But quiet, I'll say that. Except for yesterday afternoon, just afore the fire started. I thought it was the kids as had turned up the telly, like. I'd got me broom handle, ready to bang on the wall, but it stopped, sudden . . .' He paused, rheumy old eyes staring at them speculatively. The ash on his cigarette trembled but didn't fall. 'They're saying as how there was a bloke inside . . . Gawd, what a bloody end, roasted alive! The kids not in there as well, poor little buggers?'

'No, they're OK,' Abigail reassured him. 'What time was this, when you heard the noise?'

'Half-three, spot on. I mek meself a cuppa every afternoon about then and go up and have a look at me birds. Sensitive, they are, racing pigeons. But I didn't see nobody come to the house, I told your lot. I don't go poking me nose out through me front curtains, not like some I could mention.' He poked the neb of his cap up to scratch his head. 'I did see a car, blue I think it was, just afore I put me kettle on, now I come to think on it.'

Always one, Carmody thought. Somebody who 'suddenly remembered' something they hadn't thought fit to tell the police about before, usually for reasons too obscure to mention. 'What make of car was it?'

'Don't ask me – they're all the same to me, cars. Don't reckon much to 'em. Me legs is good enough for me, or the bus. Blue, darkish, that's all as I know.'

'Yeah, well,' Carmody said, his bloodhound face creasing into what passed for his smile. 'Thanks for your co-operation, Mr . . .?'

'Pargeter. Arthur Pargeter. Any time.'

*   *   *

Martin Kite wasn't enamoured with the job he'd been landed with. Dealing with the clergy was not his forte, but this case had all the indications of being extremely dodgy. All the makings of a major enquiry, and as such requiring someone of his rank to investigate, which was why he'd come along himself, instead of sending some lesser mortal. He wasn't admitting the worry that secretly nagged him, that he might not be up to his new job, but at least he could make sure he didn't make a cock-up of this, his first test case, so to speak. While Abigail Moon was up to the ears in that arson and murder case, he could maybe do himself a bit of good with this one.

Hang on in there, he told himself, she'll be off soon, flown on to higher things – and good luck to her. Friendly and gregarious by nature, he'd no personal animosity towards Abigail, and no desire to emulate her either, knowing he'd exhausted his own ambition, reached the level of his own incompetence, if you like. Perhaps it was knowing this that was causing his disgruntlement. But he didn't like the atmosphere that had grown up between him and Abigail. One largely of his own making, his wife kept telling him. Bollocks to that, he thought, but Sheila was usually right where he was concerned.

He'd met Canon Haldane before, when some silver plate had been stolen from the church altar, due to the canon's naïve insistence on the Lord's house being kept open at all times for anyone wishing to enter. Since then, like many another clergyman, he'd been reluctantly convinced that not everyone entered churches for legitimate purposes and persuaded to institute a rota of volunteers for a church-watching scheme. Holy Trinity was now always either manned, or locked.

A big, tall man in his seventies, with a lot of presence, the canon was a familiar figure around Lavenstock, striding energetically along with his long black cassock flapping around his ankles. Short, iron-grey hair with a strong curl to it, a lean, beaky, at first glance intimidating, face, now grey with shock, sorrow and fatigue – and not least, with the struggle to come to terms with yet another disappointment regarding the fallibility of human nature.

'The vicarage, sir,' Kite had been told. 'It's Canon Haldane's wife. Looks like somebody broke in yesterday and attacked her –'

'And they've only just reported it?'

'Kept at her bedside, at the hospital, they reckoned.'

'Is she badly hurt?'

'Not too good. She was clobbered on the head, seemingly. She's in the General, intensive care.'

'Canon Haldane, eh?' He was reputed to be a fiery preacher, one who didn't suffer fools gladly, but he was well liked, for all that. And Mrs Haldane. She sometimes opened fêtes and prize-givings, the like, her photo was sometimes in the *Advertiser*. A lovely lady, according to Sheila, who'd met her. If there was one thing Kite couldn't stand, it was toerags who attacked helpless old women, especially since his Auntie May had been mugged and robbed of her pension. It'd make up for a lot if he could nail the bastard who'd done this to Mrs Haldane.

So here he was now, and here was the Reverend, looking as if the stuffing had been knocked out of him, uncharacteristically helpless, just back from another visit to the hospital, standing in the middle of the elegant vicarage sitting-room that looked out on to Folgate Street and the big grey church opposite. A room that *would* have been elegant, that is, had it not been ransacked. Yet there was something odd about that very thing. Kite had seen plenty such rooms before, and he felt instinctively that this one hadn't been done over in a professional, systematic manner, by some villain who knew exactly what to go for. Nor deliberately trashed, in the spiteful way of an opportunist thief, frustrated to find nothing in the way of loose cash or easily-disposed-of videos, camcorders and such.

No . . . as it was, a couple of chairs were overturned, cushions thrown on the floor, some of the pictures had been pulled off the walls, but the frames and glass were intact; a collection of delicate porcelain figurines that looked valuable – Kite was vague about that sort of thing – still stood on the mantelpiece, though one had been knocked off and lay smashed on the hearth, and small items of silver were left as arranged on an occasional table. On another low table two thin white china coffee cups and saucers stood unused on a silver tray. Beside them a cafetière, full, a silver sugar bowl and cream jug. A plate of chocolate digestives.

It looked more likely that the perpetrator had been in a big hurry, or had ransacked the room to give the impression of a robbery after searching the small secretaire standing between the two long windows. For it was this which seemed to have been the main focus of the intruder's attention. The drawers had been pulled out, their contents tipped on to the floor. It was an impression confirmed when the vicar said that nothing of the room's contents, as far as he could see, had been taken.

'Nothing missing out of the desk?'

'I'm not sure I can really say for certain. It's my wife's desk, I don't know exactly what she keeps in it – correspondence, writing paper, bills and chequebook, that sort of thing, I imagine. Her bank statements, maybe. We have separate bank accounts.'

'We'll check through the lot, then, with your permission, sir. If there's anything we need to keep, we'll give you a receipt, of course.'

'Of course.' The vicar readily agreed, although Kite noticed he looked slightly taken aback that the request had been made at all.

'Her address book, things like that, we shall need to examine them,' Kite explained. 'Her diary. May give us a lead, you know, tell us who she was expecting.'

'Then you think it was someone – who *knew* her?'

'Oh, it's early days yet to say that, sir.'

But it was what Kite was thinking. It had all the hallmarks. Those two coffee cups, for one thing: you didn't set out two coffee cups unless you were expecting someone, and if that person was innocent, it was someone who hadn't yet materialised. If guilty, they'd forgotten to remove the cups. No forced entry, for another thing. She must have let her visitor in, ten to one someone who was familiar with the layout. The canon's study, an obvious place for a casual thief to start, was on the ground floor of the house, just inside the front door, with its own door propped open and its contents visible to all. No, whoever had done this thing, it had been someone known to Mrs Haldane – someone who'd also made that 999 call from here, which had probably saved her life. But it was always easier to believe in a random attack than to have to face the fact that anyone known to you personally could have been involved in the violation of privacy and person. In murder, if Cecily Haldane died.

'Did Mrs Haldane say anything to you about expecting a visitor?'

'No, but she often has friends in for coffee, tea, a chat. My wife is a very outgoing sort of person.'

'This happened yesterday?'

'I should have reported it immediately – but I was in no state to think clearly.'

All the same, thought Kite. His eyes were fixed on a small modern watercolour which had been hung where it was displayed to best advantage, one of those which hadn't been torn off the wall. Mayo – or Abigail Moon, or his own wife – could have told him why he had the feeling that he'd seen it, or one like it, before, but pictures didn't really register with him. He merely commented on its escape.

'Cecily bought it only the other day. She assured me I'd come to like it if I –' The canon stopped, swallowed, then began again. 'I'm afraid I have rather dull tastes . . . she tries to educate me to appreciate . . . a hopeless task, I fear . . .' Finally losing control of his voice altogether, he turned his back and gazed out into the street.

The rain of the morning had stopped, the sky was bright again, but water still gurgled along the gutters, blocked by fallen leaves. Cars occasionally swished by as they exited from the multi-storey car-park at the far end. The Whittington chimes on the church clock sounded the first quarter, their musical notes in some indefinable way underlining the sadness in the room. 'Find out why this was done to my wife,' said Edgar Haldane, turning back to Kite with some of his old fire. 'Find out and I shall be eternally grateful.'

'Even the Prof was surprised.'

Abigail ran her hand through her coppery hair and sipped her coffee, very relieved to have got *that* out of the way. *That* being her presence at the post-mortem, a necessary but highly unwelcome evil. A particularly gruesome one, this time.

'There's a turn-up for the book,' said Mayo. 'T.-L. getting it wrong?'

Timpson-Ludgate was opinionated, but he knew his job, one of the best, and this had been brought home to them during the last three months, when he'd been off sick, during which they'd had to put up with a series of replacements. It was good to have him back, full of his old bonhomie, and though he was half the man he had been, he was rapidly making headway towards regaining his lost three or four stones, back on twenty a day. Doctors never seemed to take their own advice.

'Well, this time he was. There were soot particles in the larynx and windpipe, proving he was still breathing when the fire started. And they've analysed the heart blood for carbon monoxide as a matter of routine, and had a positive result.'

'What about the thumb marks on his neck, then?'

'It looks as though somebody *tried* to kill him, probably thought they had. The fire was certainly started deliberately, a cover-up attempt, it looks like. He had a crack on the head where he'd fallen, which must have stunned him before he was overcome by the fumes – not helped by the alcohol in his bloodstream. There was an old three-piece suite filled with that sort of rubber latex foam that's lethal when it smoulders. He actually died from asphyxiation.'

'How much had he drunk?'

'Enough to have fuddled him, apparently.'

'Do we know anything more about him yet?'

'Only that he'd rented the house from Mrs Stanley, the landlady, through an ad in the paper. Paid a month in advance when he collected the key.'

'Nothing on him at the Polish end?'

'No. He seems to have been respectable enough – he was a lecturer in biology at Warsaw University, but the authorities there have assured us they're looking further into his background. They don't move fast over there.'

'Put a squib behind them, Abigail,' Mayo said forcefully. 'Don't forget, we've a couple of children on our hands. All right last night, were they, with Mrs Parkes?'

'Yes, but they can't stay there. That little house is bursting at the seams, what with three of her own and a baby. She's not happy at the thought of turning them over to the Social Services, though.'

'Hmm.' Mayo was so non-committal that it did the opposite of what he'd intended and revealed another of his prejudices. Clearly, he went along with Mrs Parkes's views, though he fell over himself as a rule to be objective, recognising that not all of them could be as reprehensible as a bad press made them out to be.

'She's downstairs with them now,' Abigail said.

The brother and sister had been found, of all places, in the women's toilets at the Lavenstock shopping centre by Mrs Djamilla Singh, one of the team of cleaners who moved in after the centre closed for the night. Since Mrs Singh spoke little more English than they did, she had taken them to the security office and, seeing they were terrified of the uniformed guards, had stayed with them until a plainclothes policewoman arrived to take them under her wing. A run-through of the security video showed that they had been wandering around the centre for most of the afternoon. At one time they'd bought Big Macs and milk shakes, and must have slipped into the toilets just before the centre closed for the day.

'What the devil were they doing there? Hiding? According to Mrs Parkes,' Mayo said, tapping the papers on his desk, 'they never went out without their father.'

'Good question. The girl closes up and loses any English she has when she's asked about that, poor kid. Her name's Krystyna,' Abigail answered, spelling it, adding with a smile, 'She was quick to correct me when I spelt it Christina. The little boy's called Karol, also with a K.'

As she spoke, the telephone rang. She picked it up and listened for a while. 'OK, I'll be down.' Replacing the receiver she said, 'It seems they've found a translator, let's hope she'll fare better than the combined forces of Milford Street nick have so far done.'

A small young woman in a long, skinny skirt and flat sandals apparently designed for a Viking general's daughter, was waiting by the front desk. Peering from under a mane of crimped dark hair, she introduced herself as Danuta Lepszy. 'Thank you for coming,' Abigail said, extending a hand, 'we do appreciate it.'

'No problem, I'll be glad to help if I can.'

As they walked along the corridor, she explained that although her parents were now living in Chicago she, like them, had been born in England and had spent all her life here. Her grandfather was Polish, and through him she'd learned to speak the language fluently. He would have been pleased to come along himself, she added, but he was in hospital undergoing a series of tests for a heart problem, and since it was vacation time at the university where she was doing Slav studies, she was happy to deputise. 'I'm at a bit of a loose end, actually, but I've been doing quite a bit of this translation thing lately, one way and another,' she admitted, smiling brilliantly, blinking like a Shetland pony from under her fringe. 'I have to stay in his flat because they won't let him come out of hospital if they think he's on his own.'

'Right, come on and I'll take you to the children. Go carefully with them, Miss Lepszy, they've gone through rather an ordeal.'

'Trust me. Promise I'll walk on tiptoe. And please – it's Danka, short for Danuta. Or better still, Dani as my friends call me.' Despite the hair and the bits of metal dispersed around her small, appealing features, she was very bright, little and vibrant and evidently not intending to let her size make any difference.

The children were waiting with Debbie Parkes in a small room where efforts had been made to lessen their alarm with toys and picture books from the stock held ready for the express purpose of keeping unscheduled children amused. Plastic beakers of orange juice from the canteen had been partly drunk, but the toys and books lay unregarded. The two children, pale and wide-eyed, sat closely either side of plump Debbie Parkes, who had a sleeping baby cradled in her arms. Occasionally, she patted their hands or threw them smiles meant to be reassuring, but they looked too lost and bewildered to respond to either. Karol was a sturdy eight-year-old with dark curly hair and dark eyes in a pale face which looked as though it could be mischievous in other circumstances. Krystyna was older by about four years, quite unlike her brother in looks, her hair long, straight and blonde, her eyes very blue above wide, Slavic cheekbones. Both at the moment were solemn and silent, very shy, understandably withdrawn.

Dani Lepszy went across and spoke to them, and when they heard their own language, both children burst into a torrent of speech, as if the waters of a dam had burst.

3

It was Dani who first came up with the idea, after the problem had been batted around between them all for some time. Somewhere to stay had to be found, and without delay, for Krystyna and Karol. Bewildered by the babble of foreign language being spoken all around them, the loss of the only place they knew as home in this alien land . . . above all, feeling they'd been abandoned by their father, they were two very frightened children. Somewhere would be found for them, of course it would, but Sally George, the child-counsellor from the Social Services, was worried about them being looked after by anybody with whom they couldn't communicate, she could imagine their panic at being separated from Dani, to whose easy, friendly manner they'd immediately responded. She pointed out that Polish-speaking carers weren't around every corner, and looked hopefully at the girl for ideas.

Quick as a flash, Dani responded. They could stay with her at her grandfather's place, in his spare room, no sweat – except the room wasn't furnished and there'd be a problem of blankets and pillows, that sort of stuff. At the moment she herself was dossing down on the sofa in the small two-bedroomed flat, until she went back to college. 'Couple of sleeping bags would do, they won't mind,' she said, as one who'd slept on the floors of student rooms the length and breadth of the country. 'And Grandpa won't be home until next week, OK?'

She gave a quick glance at Sally George, who wasn't, however, prepared to stick her neck out over that one. 'Look, I'm sorry, that's very kind of you, but I'm afraid . . . well, it's all very unorthodox . . .' she began, carefully not looking at the nose and eyebrow studs, not wanting to say it was Dani's youth and daffiness which was the bar.

It was then that the thought of those two empty bedrooms in his house on the hill occurred to Mayo. A moment's hesitation was followed by the annoying certainty that in the circumstances, that wouldn't do, either. The rooms were constantly used as short stay accommodation for other children: those who'd stayed overnight when their parents, for one reason or another, had to be away; WPC Mary Lawson's little boy who'd occupied one room for three weeks while his mother was in hospital; children who stayed on after being taken out for a birthday treat by Alex, their honorary aunt. . . . But this was a different proposition. He'd be skating on thin ice, professionally speaking, involving himself personally in these children's welfare. He kept silent.

'Hang on, look, I've an even better idea!' Dani said suddenly. 'I know someone who I bet would be only too glad to have them. She's a widow with a grown-up family who helps down at the Polish club where my Grandpa goes. Her name's Livingston, but her parents were Polish, and she speaks the language.'

'Wanda Livingston?' All doubts disappeared from Sally George's face. 'Oh yes, I know her, you can rely on her for anything. I know she'd help.'

Within half an hour, the arrangements had been completed, and Abigail's office was empty again.

Mayo went upstairs to his own office, drank a cup of coffee while he made inroads into his paperwork. Then, on an impulse, he rang Alex at Interior – simply because she was in his mind, because he knew she'd be glad to hear the question of the children had been settled, because he needed at that moment to hear her voice. Perhaps even because, with an irrationality normally quite foreign to him, he felt he'd let her down by not offering to accommodate the children himself: he didn't analyse too closely what it was, but it didn't matter. Some things – so they said – can't be explained, and though he doubted this, it was convenient to think so in this case.

It was Lois who picked the phone up and she sighed heavily as she passed it over to her sister. They were in the middle of working out a complicated estimate for the decoration and furnishing of a recent warehouse conversion into furnished flats, taking advantage of the fact that a sunny September afternoon didn't usually bring many customers into the shop in search of fabrics, wallpaper or ideas from the Aladdin's cave that was Interiors. The very abundance of fabrics, the packed shelves, the walls lined with pictures and the corners filled with interesting objets d'art necessarily made for a certain stuffiness. The shop

had more pull for the buying public in the spring, when redecor-
ating was in the air; then, the place was chock-a-block with
people seeking advice. Or in the winter, when the glow from its
warmly lit interior drew customers in like a magnet from the
cold streets, to finger silk and velvet and brocade, to try out an
armchair or to be shown the exciting possibilities of this swathe
of curtain material against that wallcovering . . . Interiors was
full of ideas to stimulate jaded imaginations – and to tempt
hands to pull chequebooks from pockets and handbags.

Alex sounded astonished, as well she might. Mayo never rang
her just to chat, not when either of them was working, and
certainly never when he was in the middle of a murder case.
He told her that a young Polish translator had been found,
who'd been able to obtain from the children a pattern of their
movements, and went on to explain where they'd been discovered . . .

As he went on talking, Lois tapped her little gold pencil on the
desk, impatient to get on. He could have timed the call better,
but that was Mayo, she thought, her usual irritation with him
surfacing. They rubbed along, but they weren't cut out to be
soul-mates, the two of them. Finally she stood up, glanced at her
reflection in the mirror over the desk at the back of the shop,
smoothed her sleek black head, noted that her dark red lips
needed attention and disappeared with a flash of dangling ear-
rings and a clash of bracelets. She contented herself with letting
the merest tchk of annoyance escape at the interruption to what
they'd been doing. The terms of the sisters' agreement with each
other over the shop depended on give and take, and in her more
honest moments Lois was aware that if that was weighed in the
balance the scales would come down heavily in Alex's favour.
But since the shop was technically still hers, her own idea, her
own ultimate responsibility, and Alex had merely put in time
(and occasionally, a restraining influence) she considered she had
the right to be regarded as the boss. Especially since Alex's
interest, lately, had seemed to be unaccountably waning.

Mayo was explaining how it was the children had been out of
the house when the fire was started, and that a home had been
found for them with a motherly, Polish-speaking person. Alex
was delighted to hear it, but after that, conversation lapsed.
'Well, I just thought you'd like to know.'

37

'That was nice of you – and nice of you to ring me,' Alex said, and her voice was just as calm and unemotional as it usually was, but there was no mistaking the smile in it when she said as she rang off, 'Bye now, and take care, Gil. Love you.'

She knew just why he'd rung.

When Lois returned with Lapsang Souchong and thin china cups – no biscuits, since she was on yet another of her fad diets, this time one which included neither fat nor sugar – Alex had just put the phone down and was gazing into space.

'What was all that about?'

'What? Oh, I'm sorry, he was telling me about those children – the ones whose father was murdered in that house that burned down. They've found someone to take care of them.'

Lois poured a cup of bergamot-scented, straw-coloured tea and passed it across. 'Oh, good.' She examined her nails.

Putting down her cup, Alex said, 'They've found this girl – Dani, I think they said her name was – who speaks Polish. It's all rather ticklish. I mean, the children can't be told about their father yet – apparently they believe he's still in London and the little girl keeps asking what he'll do when he comes back and finds them gone and the house burned down. Sooner or later, someone's going to have to tell them the truth. Rather them than me.' She looked down at the desk.

Lois opened her mouth to speak, and then shut it. This was her tough sister – expolicewoman, expert in kung fu, who'd been shot at and wounded and received the Police Medal for bravery. And who'd lost a baby – a tiny embryo, scarcely formed, only just beginning to take life in her body. And who, since then, had developed feelings and emotions that Lois, who had never had a maternal thought in her life, couldn't hope to understand.

She shrugged her thin shoulders. 'Well, everyone has their problems. Where were we?' she asked briskly, and wondered why she felt so bleak.

Immediately Mayo put the phone down after speaking to Alex, it rang. This time it was Timpson-Ludgate, the pathologist. 'Your inspector's told you what we found? That your body wasn't dead after all before the fire got to him?'

'Yes,' said Mayo, wondering why he was ringing. 'And that someone had apparently attempted to strangle him.'

'Very nearly successful, too, by the look of those bruises.' And then came the real reason for his call. 'By the way, what age did you say he was?'

'Forty-seven, according to the authorities.'

'Thought that's what you said. Then I'll tell you something, old son. The cadaver we have here isn't his. This one on the slab's a young chap, somewhere between twenty-five and thirty, no more.'

Wanda Livingston was an attractive and friendly woman, Polish by birth. She'd arrived here as a small child with her mother after the war, when her father, a Polish freedom fighter who had decided to settle permanently in England, was eventually able to send for them. Before the war, he had been a music student with every intention of using his gift as a pianist to make music his career, but this had been put paid to by an injury received during the fighting, when he had lost the little finger of his right hand. Burying his disappointment deep, thanking God he still had a life to live, he had settled for what he could get, a job here in England, helping in a small bakery run by two elderly brothers, a job he regarded as a temporary expediency. Twenty-five years later, he'd still been there, the owner now of the business, and making a very good living out of specialising in Polish bakery: rye breads flavoured with caraway and honey, sponge cake topped with plums, cheesecake, poppyseed cake and the like.

Wanda had grown up bilingual, speaking English with her school friends and Polish with her parents at home – especially with her mother, who never quite mastered the language intricacies of her adopted country. She scarcely thought of herself as Polish now, except when she was helping at the small pensioners' club attached to her church, where many of the members were Polish ex-servicemen and their wives. Dani's grandfather, Michalik Lepszy, was a favourite with her, a cheery talkative man who liked to reminisce about a Poland she would, in truth, have remembered hardly at all, had it not been for a holiday once, when she'd been taken with her parents to visit relatives.

Always an active woman, as her children grew up and left home Wanda had filled her spare time with all sorts of voluntary activities, more so after her husband, Douglas, had died following years of debilitating illness. But even so, she was lonely. She missed her three children, now variously spread across distant parts of the globe, and sometimes she didn't know what to do with herself without her husband to care for, without the loving companion of thirty-five years. She'd thought about getting a job, but due to the early arrival of her children and the care Doug had very soon needed, she hadn't worked after she was married and now it seemed she was too old, nor had she the faintest idea how to work a word-processor, let alone deal with mysteries such as e-mail, faxes and the Internet.

So when Sally George rang and told her about the plight of the two Polish children, she hadn't needed to be persuaded. 'Of course I'll take them in, for as long as necessary, though I hope for their sakes it won't be long. I've still got the children's old books and toys. I'll get the boys' room aired immediately.'

'Bless you, I knew I could rely on you!' Sally hesitated. 'Just one thing. I wonder if you'd be prepared for Dani Lepszy to keep coming in to see them? They've already bonded with her and she can help if they prove too much.'

'Oh, she's very welcome, but I can cope,' Wanda assured her, already thinking about the sort of meals children liked and planning to telephone people she knew to arrange for other children to come along and play with them after school.

After some initial awkwardness, this last had proved a success. Children are resilient, and language was no barrier to playing on the old swing or climbing the apple tree. Wanda was less happy as to just how much she should encourage them to talk about what had happened. She was no psychologist, but she knew how children could hide their feelings. She needn't have worried. Dani was a lifesaver. Both children obviously adored her already and Wanda soon followed her example of casual acceptance, just going with the flow, as Dani put it, ready to talk when the children wanted to, equally ready with sympathy and a cuddle when the situation proved too much for them, though only Karol would endure the cuddle. Like most small boys, he was warm and loving, whereas Krystyna, Wanda had soon discovered, stiffened and drew away from any overt signs of affection.

It bothered her that the child was so quiet and self-contained. Was their father ever going to come back? Krystyna asked, eyes wide and worried. How would he know where they were when he did? Would they be sent back to Poland without him? The questions came out, one by one, quietly, unexpectedly, in the middle of a story or a game or when she was apparently absorbed in some TV programme. Thank God the body in the house had turned out to be someone else and not him – though this was not to be common knowledge, the police had warned Wanda; he had simply disappeared, and perhaps he'd turn up again, perhaps not. Wanda was so angry with this man Siemek for subjecting his children to this sort of trauma she doubted whether she could be civil to him if ever he did decide to reappear.

'Inspector Moon? It's Debbie, Debbie Parkes, from Bessemer Street. I thought as I'd better let you know ... It's that foreign bloke, the kiddies' father. I've just seen him!'

'What?'

'Saw him with my own eyes, I did. He was just standing, staring at the house – what's left of it. Could've knocked me down with a feather. I thought he was dead?' Her voice rose on a questioning note. She sounded frightened.

'When was this?'

'No more'n five or ten minutes since. About half-eleven? I was just wondering if I should go out and tell him what had happened when he turned and walked off. The baby's teething and she was crying her eyes out, so I couldn't leave her and run after him.'

'Of course not. You did quite right. You're sure it was him?'

'If it wasn't it was his double. What's going on?'

'Debbie, can I trust you not to say anything until I've seen you? I'll be with you right away.'

Two days before that, Tadeusz Siemek had been in London.

'My God, I thought you were Jerzy,' Piotr Kaminski had

41

repeated, for perhaps the third or fourth time, after his visitor had made him coffee, proper coffee, and the home help had finally arrived, dusted round them, and departed. 'A shock like that – it's enough to kill an old man. My God, how like your father you are!'

'So I've been told. He died when I was just a few months old, so I wouldn't know. Only from what my mother has said.'

'Elizbieta, ah yes! I remember her, what a beauty!'

They spoke in Polish, and the musical cadences fell sweetly on Kaminski's ears, came naturally to his lips, though he rarely, if ever, spoke his native language now. He remembered Elizbieta well, the young woman Jerzy had left behind – though without too much heart searching, Kaminski had always felt. A beauty, yes, that much couldn't be denied, but with a sharp tongue and a well-developed sense of property, in which she included Jerzy. He'd been a fool to get her pregnant . . . though if she – or Jerzy, for that matter – had known about it before he left Poland, he would certainly have stayed, Kaminski was sure. The child had been a daughter and Jerzy had honoured his obligations when he'd returned to Krakow after the war, grateful, perhaps, that Elizbieta waited for him and married him even though his health was in ruins after his release from the POW camp and any fortune he might have inherited from his father gone to the winds. Why hadn't he come back to England? Kaminski had never understood it. In fact, when he'd learned Jerzy had after all survived, he had written, several times, couching the enquiries in his letters in careful terms, but Jerzy had never answered his questions satisfactorily.

'Tell me about my father, what you knew of him,' Jerzy's son had said.

Tadeusz Siemek, this second child of Jerzy and Elizbieta, was nearly twenty-five years older than Jerzy had been when he was shot down, but he'd stayed young-looking, and the likeness to his father was unbelievable, especially when first seen, with his back to the light. Kaminski could see some difference now, which was mainly about the eyes. Jerzy's had been brown, too, in the same narrow face, but unlike his son's eyes, which were dark and haunted, accentuated by his pale and melancholy countenance, Jerzy's had smiled at life, as he enjoyed what he could of it to the full – though they had often blazed at its injustices, too.

'He was an idealist. We all were, we students, hot-headed and full of subversive talk, but Jerzy – we all thought he would go on to do great things.' Instead – what a way to end a life: shot down over Germany, surviving the horrors of the POW camp – only to die of consumption . . .

'Yes, my mother has told me this,' Tadeusz said impatiently. Elizbieta had made it plain that she had disapproved alike of Jerzy's student activities and of his decision to depart for England. It had been his duty to stay in Poland and work alongside other patriots, join the underground army and fight against the reign of terror that was submerging Poland, to protect his family and not to have listened to impetuous friends like Piotr Kaminski . . . 'But of when he was in England, during the war, she knows nothing.'

'It was a long time ago. I'm an old man, my memory is not what it was,' said Kaminski vaguely, letting it appear he was rambling. 'Such a lot has happened since then, my life has changed . . . As you can see, I live simply. It's not much of a place here but it wasn't always so . . .' He fell silent.

'Take your time.'

Siemek turned and stood with his back to the room, looking out into the sunny street, watching a dog of uncertain parentage trot purposefully along, pausing only to cock its leg against Kaminski's gatepost before resuming its journey. He saw, but didn't see, the litter which had blown into the gardens – or been tossed there by loutish passers-by – and the dozens of For Sale signs planted in them. He recognised only the evidence of relative affluence: the small, two-storey houses with – for the most part – polished and lace-curtained windows, the satellite dishes outside nearly every one, the cars lining both sides of the road, the young mother who came along the street, pushing two plump, well-dressed children in a double buggy. He thought of his own children and his high-rise flat in a grey and tawdry suburb of Warsaw, a block that harked back to the communist era, its concrete crumbling, its total floor area not twice the size of this one room he now swung round to face.

'You would call yourself a religious man, Mr Kaminski?' he asked, with a wave of his hand that included the reproduction of

43

the Black Madonna of Czestachowa, the most deeply venerated object in Poland, and the crucifix on the wall adjacent to Kaminski's chair.

'I don't get to Mass as often as I would like – I'm dependent on others to get me there – but yes, I would like to think I am a good Catholic.'

'Then I would say it is your Christian duty to tell me all you know.'

Kaminski, too, looked at the icon, she who could work miracles, the picture of a face blackened by time and incense fumes, the original said to have been painted by St Luke on wood taken from a beam of the Holy Family's house in Nazareth. He sent up a small prayer for her help. He badly needed it. This man who had arrived like a thunderbolt on his doorstep was all poised to ask awkward questions, and Kaminski didn't want to provide the answers, though he didn't see how he was going to get out of doing so.

To give himself time, he poured two generous tots from the bottle of Polish vodka Tadeusz had brought him, which they drank neat, knocking it back in one go in the Polish manner.

'*Nazdrowie!*' Their glasses clinked.

He pushed a mineral water chaser across to the younger man, and replenished his own glass with it, declining a refill of the spirits for himself, determined to stick to the mineral water. It took very little to make him drunk nowadays and when he was, he talked too much.

4

Mayo was reminded that he had a home to go to by the Town Hall clock striking seven simultaneously with his rumbling stomach. The pile of paper didn't appear to have diminished appreciably, but what the heck? Routine stuff had been dispensed with, his diary for the next week reviewed. Delia, his secretary, would give a resigned sigh when she saw the amount he'd left her, and bring in the next load – more of the same. Administration, always his bugbear. Reviews, meetings, more meetings. Budgets, resources. They formed a large part of his remit, though he refused to allow them to dominate his working life, as they did with some in the upper echelons. But he wondered, not for the first time, though less often than he used to, why he'd accepted promotion when he'd much rather be working at the coal face.

At last, he turned with something like relief to the main preoccupations of the moment – the two major investigations now occupying the whole of CID, making the place buzz: the Polish affair, already seventy-two hours old and now a full unexplained death enquiry, and the assault on Canon Haldane's wife, which might well turn out to be another murder enquiry if Cecily Haldane took a turn for the worse. Having to juggle with several crises at once was nothing new, but two major enquiries called for a deployment of skills and resources that would have taxed a better man than he. Mayo reread through the case file Martin Kite had left with him: Mrs Haldane was still in intensive care, wired up to life support machines, still unable to speak. No clues had turned up as to who her assailant had been, no reason for her attack had emerged. A brain scan had revealed the possibility that the injury which had made her lose consciousness had been caused not by being hit on the head but by a fall against something hard. The SOCO team had found blood on the corner of a mahogany wine-cooler used as a jardinière, full of plants, and it was blood which tallied with hers. So it might not have been a deliberate murder attempt, but if it were proved that she'd been knocked down, there was certainly a case to be made out for manslaughter. No one, as yet, had come up with any reason, other than obfuscation, as to why the room should have been ransacked, the desk so thoroughly gone through.

The hospital would not commit themselves to any firm opinion on the chances of Cecily Haldane's recovery ... it seemed to be simply a case of wait and see. Galling as it was, the enquiry was going to have to take its course. It wasn't exactly the sort of investigation Mayo would have chosen for Kite to lead, but needs must, and it wouldn't do him any harm to have to deal with a case that demanded persistence and patience.

He turned to the other pressing matter, this business of the Pole, Tadeusz Siemek, and after thinking about it for a while, picked up his internal telephone, pressed buttons and was answered immediately.

'Abigail! You still here?'

Abigail suppressed the obvious answer. Damnation, she'd done it again, cutting it fine when Ben was expecting her. Then the scowl was replaced by a smile as she remembered that at the moment, at least, she had the whip hand there. Ben was in no position to call tunes. His behaviour over the last year hadn't exactly been exemplary, and when he'd returned from his latest assignment, Abigail had decided it was time for a bit of straight talking. She'd made it clear her job was just as important to her as his was to him. He could go swanning off all over the world and find his job waiting for him when he got back (as, incredibly, he had) but could not expect to find her simply waiting, too. She'd felt better after saying it, anyway, whether she'd meant it or not. It had left Ben, quick-witted and mentally agile, empathetic with the subjects he wrote about but sometimes curiously unthinking of those closest to him, speechless for the moment. But when he recovered, there'd been a subtle difference in his attitude. Respect, she hoped.

'A quick word to bring me up to speed on the murder investigation, OK?' Mayo was saying. 'Should've done it before, but it's been one of those days.'

When isn't it? she asked herself. 'I'll be up in a minute.' She legged it up the stairs, passing a waste-paper basket which stood outside the door of CID, waiting to be emptied by the cleaners. It was filled more with empty polystyrene coffee cups and takeaway containers than paper, and she wrinkled her nose at the smell, but it reminded her how long it was since she'd eaten. She wished she'd remembered to grab a sandwich, or even a few biscuits, with her last coffee. Supper, with or without Ben, looked like remaining as some distant promise on the far horizon.

'Where have we got to? Sit yourself down and refresh my memory,' Mayo began without preamble, as she shut the office door behind her.

Since when had Mayo's patient, retentive memory ever needed refreshing? He rarely forgot anything, it was a gift Abigail envied. But she knew where to go from there, having worked with him long enough to recognise it as an opening gambit. As his junior partner, she'd learned to read him pretty

46

well over the years. Almost like a wife/husband relationship it had been, without the sexual bit. Though perhaps not, entirely. Was that ever true of any man and woman who worked closely together? Perhaps a sexual tension of sorts was necessary, the essential difference between the way a man and a woman thought, generating a different response. At any rate, they bounced a lot of ideas off each other. She admired his professional abilities and his unflappable approach. He was someone you could be companionable with. Never on his high horse, though he could be a son of a bitch with those who didn't toe the line. But at least you always knew where you were with him.

She took the chair he indicated, in front of his desk; at her back was the floor container of recently brought in, specially selected mixed plants that was thought to add gravitas to the office of someone of his rank. They were large plants, but not tall enough to hide the grimy, pigeon-dropping-splattered Town Hall which faced the window. Moreover, they tended to grab the light. 'I don't know that there's anything new, since we last spoke: the body's been identified, as you know, through his fingerprints, there was enough of him left for that. He was severely disfigured by charring, so it's impossible anyone could have identified him visually.'

That dismal thought hung on the air as she leafed through the notes she'd brought with her. The dead man had had a record, so that he'd been easily traceable through the computerised national index of criminal fingerprints. Stefan – a.k.a Steve – Kaminski. Polish father, Finnish mother. Started off with shoplifting, TWOCs, progressing to aggravated burglary. A spell in Feltham Young Offenders Institute, then involvement in an organised gang-bust of a warehouse, which had put him away in Winson Green for eighteen months. Released under licence nine months ago, since when he'd apparently kept his nose clean. 'He was a nasty piece of work, according to all who knew and didn't love him. He'd been living with a woman over in Handsworth. I've sent Farrar with Carmody over there now to see her. She works as a croupier in a night-club, sleeps all day and wouldn't see anybody until six o'clock.'

Mayo grunted. Sending Carmody was all right, but Farrar, always an irritant, was at the moment a major headache. Frustrated at being passed over for promotion despite having gained

47

his sergeant's qualifications, and with marital problems into the bargain, he was being bloody-minded, non-cooperative and working to the book while he looked for somewhere he could grace with his undoubted talents, hopefully here in Lavenstock where, due to George Atkins's long-expected retirement, they were short of a sergeant in CID. Mayo supposed they could do worse. You didn't have to be liked to be a good policeman.

'So what's the Polish connection? Siemek, Kaminski, there must be one.'

'We haven't found it yet. Steve Kaminski has an old father – they haven't been close for years, but maybe we can learn something from him. The local nick have sent someone to break the news to him about Steve, but I thought it might be useful if I went down to talk to him tomorrow.'

'Got to make a start somewhere. Who are you taking with you?'

'Carmody, I thought,' she answered, even as she spoke seeing Mayo prepared to ditch his weekend off, his interest roused, his eyes brightening at the chance to do some solid, hands-on, old-fashioned detecting. Sitting with his feet under a desk all day brought him out in a rash. His own words. But she knew it wasn't only that: he'd no need to say how worried he was about these two investigations he had on his hands, the lack of progress, despite the mountains of paper generated, the man-hours expended. It was involvement on a personal level he needed.

'I'll go with you myself,' he decided, no surprise to her at all. 'United are playing at home, Carmody won't want to miss that.' As good a reason as any.

'Sure. Ted'll be dead chuffed.' Nor was Abigail displeased with the idea of Mayo accompanying her to London, rather than Carmody. Good old Ted, they were a good down-to-earth pair, but if Mayo had decided to put in his two-pennorth on this one, had decided his presence was important, she wouldn't grumble. Like Mayo, she already felt in her bones that this case wasn't going to be one of the easy ones, and a bit of high-powered support wouldn't come amiss. She dreaded the thought of the investigation becoming too long drawn out, whatever the result might turn out to be, if only for the sake of the children. 'Those poor kids,' she said softly, 'how are they going to take all this?'

'What – the fact that their father's a murderer and an arsonist, as well as having abandoned them? Badly. How would any child of their age feel?' He rolled his pen between his palms, looking at her over the top of his glasses. 'You believe that, do you?' She sighed. 'It defies logic, but what else are we to think?'

'That Siemek comes home, finds his children gone and Kaminski waiting for him, murders Kaminski for some as yet obscure reason and sets fire to the house, you mean?'

She didn't believe that, either. 'Then just bunks off, leaving his children God knows where? No, it doesn't make a lot of sense. Especially as Dani Lepszy has the impression from what the kids have told her that he's a good father.'

'And even if he *did* do all that, can you see him coming back and hanging around, looking at the scene of the crime?'

'If we don't accept it, we're looking for someone else who killed Kaminski. It'd be more comfortable all round to think so, but this Siemek *could* be a monster, for all we know. Anyway, if he's innocent, why disappear? He just melted into the background while Debbie Parkes was on the phone to me.'

This second disappearance was ominous. Did he believe his children had perished in the fire? If so, it was unlikely he'd been the one to set it. Either way, he must be suffering the torments of the damned.

'If he's still in Lavenstock, he won't get very far.' It was depressingly unlikely Siemek would be found here though, not now. He'd be miles away. But yes, Mayo thought, mulling over Abigail's last words, what sort of man was he, even to *bring* his children into such a situation, never mind leaving them to whatever Fate handed out? Quiet, well-behaved children, obviously panic-stricken underneath. He'd seen them only for a few minutes, but their eyes haunted him.

'They don't really understand what they're doing here in England,' Dani Lepszy had reported to Abigail. 'Their Dad just told them he had some business to do over here and they'd have a holiday after he'd finished with it.'

'What about their mother? Where's she?'

'Divorced. She upped and left them a couple of years ago, poor little toads.'

About the day of the fire, Krystyna had told Dani, 'Papa said he had important business in London. He would be home very late. We must be good and wait until he came home. He said to open the door to no one and we promised.'

'What were you going to do all day on your own?' Dani had asked.

They had games and books they'd brought with them, and their father had bought a small portable television set since coming here, which seemed to Abigail to have been a gesture of limited use. They'd watched cartoons, though that had evidently palled after a while. The other programmes they couldn't understand, though Karol liked the commercials. There was the house to tidy, also, said Krystyna, prim, conscientious, a worried little housewife, but Karol was soon bored with this and complaining that he'd read all his books, and was hungry. 'He's being very good at the moment, understandably subdued, but it seems,' said Dani with a grin, 'young Karol's normally a bit of a handful.'

'What was the arrangement for your meals?' she'd asked them.

'I can cook,' Krystyna replied proudly, but the effect of this was spoiled by her brother adding his own opinions on that.

'She tried to make pancakes and burnt them! We couldn't eat them and I was *hungry*! I wanted a Big Mac.'

Big Macs, Dani explained, had become the highlight of Karol's visit to England. The soft bun, the savoury meat, the ketchup, the french fries, everything that went with it. The pint-sized Coca Cola. Heaven in a styrofoam package.

It was the stove, Krystyna excused herself guiltily, which had caused her to burn the food. The gas tap was difficult to adjust properly. She had turned it up too much and the pancakes had burnt. They weren't *really* very bad but Karol wouldn't eat them and he wouldn't stop whingeing about being hungry. They had been told not to open the door to anyone, but it seemed their father hadn't impressed on them with sufficient urgency that they mustn't go out. In the end, she had taken some of the money Papa kept in one of the kitchen drawers for emergency, written a note for him, locked the front door carefully as he had always done, but left the back door open in case he couldn't get in, and taken Karol out in search of food. To a child, that must have seemed logical enough.

The shopping precinct was quite near, and they were already

familiar with it, their father having taken them there several times before. They knew there was a Waitrose store at one end, Debenhams at the other, in between a fairyland of lighted shops offering an unimagined range of goodies of all description. Karol went wild for half an hour, riding up and down the escalators and the glass-sided lifts, watching the water cascade into the central fountain. Until the delicious smells from cafés, coffee-and-sandwich stops – and best of all, from McDonald's – reminded him of why they'd come.

They'd stayed in McDonald's as long as they could. Karol, having got his own way once, or perhaps to convince Krystyna his hunger had been real, had insisted on eating *two* Big Macs and french fries, plus a large chocolate milk shake, and some apple pie and ice cream. Very shortly afterwards, as they wandered around gazing at the shop windows, forgetting the time, Nemesis had struck. As the lift made its rapid descent once more, he'd announced he was going to be sick.

Krystyna had hurried him into the nearest toilet. It had taken some time to clean him up afterwards, and before he began to feel well enough to venture out again. They had emerged to find the precinct deserted, the entrances closed and themselves locked in.

They were terrified of this now huge, empty, echoing space, and once more they hid in the toilets, a wise choice since Karol had begun to feel sick again. It was an hour later that Mrs Singh found them. Communication between them failing, she took them by the hands and led them into the security guard's office.

5

Returning from the hospital late that afternoon, Canon Haldane and his two daughters, still numb with the shock of what had happened to Cecily, wandered into the sitting-room, now restored to its former seemliness and order, and looking comfortingly normal. The only difference was that, instead of four porcelain figurines standing symmetrically on the marble mantelpiece, just three remained, giving it a rather lopsided look. Olivia had taken the broken pieces of what unfortunately had been the best of them to be repaired, a finely modelled shepherd and shepherdess simpering at each other under delicate, flowering, foliage. It could be mended, said the restorer, but it wouldn't be worth much when it had been.

Rather too uncomfortably reminiscent of the prognosis on poor Ma, thought Julia, half-listening as Olivia repeated this already twice-told tale, adding that she'd given the man instructions to get on with it, the value of the piece didn't lie in its monetary worth but in its sentimental associations. It had, after all, come from the old family home in Camberwell, been given to their mother by *her* mother, now, of course, dead, and one didn't want to throw away family heirlooms, however damaged.

'Come on, drink this, it'll make you feel better,' Julia said to her father, handing him a cup of tea and dropping a kiss on his head, concerned at the lines of tiredness and bewilderment etched on a face that was normally somewhat forbidding, or until he smiled his rare, singularly sweet smile. He allowed himself to sink into the deep softness of a cushioned, chestnut velvet armchair, originally bought to accommodate Jago's large frame, one which Edgar normally eschewed for a harder, more upright one. His suit was, as usual, slightly rumpled: it was only due to the vigilance of Cecily, who saw to it that he was kept respectable, that his shoes were ever polished, his hair cut. Left to himself, Edgar would have chosen to live a kind of monastic existence, much at variance with this elegant, comfortable house which Cecily had furnished with such love and care over the years – though really, he scarcely seemed to notice it. As long as Cecily was happy – and of course, his children – that was all that mattered to him.

It wasn't only their mother they had to worry about, Julia thought, though Edgar perhaps looked a little better today than he had. Perhaps. Prayer and faith had surely sustained him. Or was it that he hadn't so much prayed God to deliver his beloved wife, as that he'd looked Death in the face and stared him down, willing Cecily to live? Such unswerving resolution was typical of him.

Cecily's condition was still grave, and it was a shattering

experience for them all being forced to watch her as she lay immobile in the hospital bed. All her vitality drained away, a less than human figure, attached to all those machines and tubes and monitoring devices, with a sturdy policewoman, vainly trying to look unobtrusive, sitting by her bed in case she came round and said something. It seemed somehow wrong to admit what exhausting work it was visiting her. Julia had never before quite realised the extent of the burden and strain placed on the relatives of those unfortunate people only heard about previously, who lay for weeks, years sometimes, in a coma. The hospital had advised them, Cecily's husband and daughters, to talk to her continuously, assuring them that something might just get through.

Strangely enough, it hadn't been Olivia, the one who usually had all the talk, or even their father, who could bring themselves to carry on speaking without any response. Edgar, who was at all times a tower of unfailing strength to others in distress, was bereft of speech whenever he looked at Cecily, his emotions overcoming him. And Olivia – Olivia, of all people! – was embarrassed to be seen chattering into an apparent vacuum, she who talked the hind legs off a donkey to anyone who listened, and quite often to those who didn't. It had been left to Julia herself to take Cecily's hand and say whatever came into her mind: anything – jokes they'd all once shared, that suit she was thinking of buying . . . family occasions, events she'd heard of in Cecily's past, before she was married, though it came to her with a shock that there were precious few of those, only gaps that she didn't know how to fill. This afternoon, she'd picked up a much handled book of poems she'd found in Cecily's desk, and read one or two of them to her. And she'd thought, and then decided she'd imagined, that she'd felt the slightest tremor of the cold hand beneath hers. Still, she'd mentioned it to the sister, who said she might well have been right, they must keep on trying.

Nothing else, so far, had brought any response.

Olivia, pushing the wings of her heavy dark hair away from her face as she spoke, was talking about the attack again. Julia wished she wouldn't. Couldn't she see how it pained their father? She was reworking the details the police had given them after the forensic team had gone over the room, coupled with what the doctors had said, the probability that Cecily hadn't actually been attacked – the greater likelihood being that she had struggled with the intruder and fallen over, hitting her head on the wine-cooler.

Well, any difference in intention was academic, the end result had been the same, and blame was still attached. If you broached someone's private space, there was no telling what it might lead to. Her mind swerved violently away from the thought that the end result in this case might well be at the very least, man-slaughter.

The baffling thing was, of course, that the attack seemed motiveless, for nothing appeared to have been taken.

'Time for Evensong,' Edgar announced suddenly, refusing a second cup of Earl Grey. Nothing would prevent him saying this daily service, a rite he performed as regularly as the phases of the moon or the tides of the sea, any more than he would have thought of neglecting his parochial and diocesan duties, even at this time of crisis. His assistant, the Reverend Mavis Snell, had been willing to step in and shoulder whatever burdens she could, but so far he had managed to keep functioning more or less as normal. 'I don't suppose,' he added, 'it's any use asking you two to come along with me?'

'I've already been to church this morning.' Olivia, who prided herself on taking twice-weekly communion, was busy opening the pile of cards and letters which had already arrived, express-ing shock, and full of offers of help. The letters were not only to show sympathy with their vicar, though they certainly did this, but it had also surprised and touched all her family to find, however unobtrusive her involvement in parochial and civic affairs had been, how much Cecily had done, how much she was liked for herself.

Julia merely shook her head in answer to her father's question. His look rested speculatively on her for a moment, but he said nothing more and left the room. Presently, his voice called, 'Anyone seen my waterproof? I can't find it anywhere!'

'Been sent to the jumble sale, if Ma's had any sense,' Olivia muttered. Raising her voice, she called out, 'You won't need it, it's stopped raining.'

'I know, but it's my specs I need. They're in the pocket.'

'Here we go again,' said Olivia, rolling her eyes. The spectacles in question, like many another of the vicar's possessions, seemed to have a secret, hidden life of their own, regularly departing of their own volition to some hitherto undiscovered limbo and returning likewise.

There ensued a search which brought forth no results and, after an anxious glance at the time, Edgar Haldane departed, spectacle-less, hoping that Mavis Snell would be in church with the spare pair she kept hidden for such emergencies, strictly for use only until the others turned up. If not, it didn't really matter. He could say the ritual blindfold. The two women went back to the sitting-room for more tea and further letters as the front door closed behind him.

'Good Lord, here's a letter from Cousin Paul!' Olivia announced presently, extracting expensively thick, deep cream paper from its matching envelope.

'Well, well. What does he have to say?'

'The usual things. Very sorry to hear and so on,' Olivia said, skimming the two pages of large, confident handwriting in the rather precious-looking brown ink he always used. 'I wonder *how* he heard. Crikey, he wants to come over for a couple of days and visit Ma!'

They gazed blankly at each other. 'Why?' said Julia.

'You might well ask. He doesn't say.'

Paul Franklin, their much older relative, was the only son of Cecily's much-loved cousin, who had died three or four years ago, shortly after her husband. Since then, communication between Paul and the family would have been limited to an exchange of Christmas cards, had it not been for Cecily, who'd always shown him great kindness and had kept in touch regularly with him. As did Jago, with whom he sometimes did business, but then, Jago took everyone as they came. Paul had always been one of those relatives endured for the sake of another, in this case his mother. She, unlike him, had been loved by them all, especially by Julia, whose godmother she'd been and who was said to resemble her – small and fair, neat, sharp-faced, with bright, intelligent grey-green eyes. Whereas Olivia took after the Haldanes, who were tall, big-boned and high-coloured, translated, in Olivia's case, into glowing skin, thick, glossy dark hair and brown eyes – and unfortunately, a tendency to put on weight.

'Oh, hang on a minute! He says he's in the district on business, anyway. I suppose it's because of –' Olivia stopped abruptly.

'Because of what?'

'Oh, nothing,' she said maddeningly. 'The question is, who's going to put him up? I can't,' she added quickly. 'Haven't the room, now Natalie's home from college, plus the spare room's being redecorated just now. And he can't stay here. Unless –'

'No,' Julia said firmly, forestalling any suggestion that she should stay on in Lavenstock in order to look after Paul Franklin. She felt she had enough on her plate, being in the process of severing the last few threads which tied her to Wolverhampton, where she'd lived for the last eight years. Soon she would be back permanently, at her new job, here in Lavenstock, but meanwhile, she was making the daily trek between the two places, between here and the hideous flat where she'd ended up after she'd walked out, following that row with Mark. And having to snatch time to visit her mother in between. 'What's wrong with him staying in a hotel? Or why doesn't he go back home, for goodness' sake? It's hardly the end of the earth.'

'Don't tell Pa he's coming, then. He'll only offer to have him here, and he's got enough to do looking after himself . . . since he insists he'll be all right on his own, which I wish he wouldn't.'

'If that's what he wants,' Julia said. 'It can be a strain, you know, having other people around you all the time, when you're not feeling up to it, advising you what to do –'

'I'm not talking about other people, I'm talking about family. Neither of us would be in the way.'

Oh, wouldn't we? Julia thought, but forbore to say what Olivia wouldn't understand. He wants neither of us – you talking fifteen to the dozen and bossing him around, nor me, making him feel responsible, feeling he ought to be offering me advice and support, when all I want to do is forget Mark, put the last few years behind me.

'Julia, you know what he's like, he'll forget to eat –'

'Mavis Snell and Mrs Porter between them will see he's looked after.'

The silent Mrs Porter worked like a machine programmed to clean and do a certain amount of cooking, if pressed, which was not often, since she was a terrible cook, and then disappear into the background, only to be there, on the dot, the next morning. And Mavis Snell, brisk and cheerful, was ever willing to do whatever was necessary, but sensitive enough to know when she was wanted and when not. There were also the parishioners with their seemingly endless kindness, offering gifts of cakes and casseroles and invitations to supper. Julia sighed. 'All right, I'll stay here tonight if he really wants me to, but I doubt if he will.'

'You still haven't got things sorted with Mark, have you?' Olivia accused.

'Yes, I have, Liv. As a matter of fact, he's agreed to sell the house, and we're meeting on Sunday to discuss who has what.'

'I hope you know what you're doing, Julia.' Olivia seemed about to offer sisterly advice, but after a glance at Julia's face, all she said was, 'Watch that it's all legally tied up, and that you get your proper share.'

'We're both solicitors,' Julia replied, rather sharply. She wished Olivia would go.

Perhaps it was because she, too, had the need to be alone with her feelings, that Julia felt she understood a similar need in her father. It was a necessity which had come on her more and more, ever since her break with Mark Fry. They had both worked in the Wolverhampton law practice for seven years, and had lived together for twelve months longer than that. Gradually, the feeling had grown on her that they were pulling in different directions, their aims and ambitions were diametrically opposed. Perhaps that wouldn't have mattered, had their personal lives been in harmony, but they were not, and hadn't been for the last couple of years. A basic incompatibility had arisen, over her desire to marry and have children when he couldn't see the need. She was nearly forty and until now had clung on to the hope that he might change his mind, but he had not. And yet, the final decision to break with him had come not over that, but when she'd found – unbelievably trite, but nonetheless true – a letter from someone else in his pocket.

'Anyway,' Olivia said, brightening, 'Jago's due back late tonight. Though I expect he'll be knackered, poor love, it was a marathon undertaking by any standards.' She smiled fondly. It was second nature to her to be protective of Jago. Eleven years stood between them, Olivia the eldest and Jago the youngest, and she'd always mothered him. In her eyes, her precociously talented brother could do no wrong.

He was flying back from Houston, Texas, where, on behalf of the big international auction house he worked for, he had for some time been promoting the forthcoming auction of an important collection of works of art, flying back and forth across the Atlantic. When it was made clear to him that there was nothing he could do by staying at his mother's bedside after her attack, he'd flown again to Houston to turn the arrangements over to someone else and return as soon as he could.

Olivia stood up, retrieving her belongings which were, as usual, scattered all around the room. 'Well then, I'll get home.' She did a double take. 'Where's that picture come from?' she demanded accusingly. 'I've never seen it before. Wells Cathedral's always been there.'

'Apparently Ma bought it the other day. Perhaps she felt in need of a change. I must say I can sympathise, that Wells thing's no great loss.'

Olivia looked suspiciously at the watercolour. 'It's very *modern*.' She added in a disapproving voice, 'I'll bet she paid a pretty penny for it, too.'

Julia laughed. 'Honestly, Olivia! You are a Philistine, sometimes.'

Olivia looked at Julia. 'You, too?' she said, and burst into tears.

Julia was appalled. 'Oh God, I'm sorry, love, it was only a *joke.*'

'Then it's in very p-poor taste. Why d-does everyone always think the worst of me – all of you except Jago . . . he never looks down on me – not like the r-rest of you, even R-Robert!'

'Look down on you? Liv, that's simply not true!' It was Julia's turn for a double take. '*Robert?*'

'Oh yes, since he got that promotion and that new dolly-bird secretary. She's half my age – and half my size, I shouldn't wonder. With a degree and everything, too. And suddenly, I'm such a m-moron!'

Robert Faber a large, genial, Billy Bunter of a man who wore round glasses and bow ties and had an enormous laugh. The ideal family man, churchwarden, Rotarian . . . and one who thought the world of his wife and his son and daughter . . . *Robert*, having a bit on the side? Olivia was being ridiculous – wasn't she?

'Come on, Liv,' Julia said gently, attempting to put her arms around her comfortably built sister, which wasn't easy, especially as Olivia resisted, pulling away and throwing herself down abruptly on the nearest chair and dashing away the tears that swam in her big brown eyes. 'Have you –' she bit her tongue on 'confronted' – 'have you talked to him?'

'How can I, with all this about poor Ma hanging over us? Isn't that bad enough?'

Julia felt remorseful. Maybe she did underestimate Olivia, maybe there was some truth hidden in the accusation she'd made. Olivia was practical, competent and good-hearted, without much sense of humour, and often barged in where even angels feared to insert a toe, true, though with every good intention. She could be overbearing, and in defence, people did sometimes take the mickey – even Jago, despite what she'd said – though it was obviously time that stopped.

Pulling a crumpled tissue from her pocket and scrubbing her face, from which the vivid colouring had paled, but looking better for having unburdened herself, Olivia said at last, somewhat defiantly, 'Well, you might all think me a thickhead, but at least I'm *there* when you need me!'

'Nobody's ever questioned that.'

'Jago hasn't, anyway.' She looked sideways at Julia. She'd always had a tendency to dramatise and exaggerate, and although it was very possible she was prepared – perhaps wanted – to be persuaded into revealing more, Julia had no intention of indulging her. More than likely, it was something and nothing, though she couldn't be as sure of Jago as she was of Olivia. He could be unpredictable.

Olivia was persuaded to drink another cup of tea, while Julia endeavoured to assuage her fears about Robert, and in doing so came to believe that it really was a case of Olivia reading into the situation something that didn't exist. She had brightened considerably by the time she was ready to go.

'Don't take any notice of me, I expect it's all in the mind. I should go on a diet and enrol with the Open University.'

'You could do worse.'

'Maybe I will. Well, keep your pecker up,' Olivia said, as she and Julia said farewell and embraced. 'Ma's going to pull through, you know.'

'I know.'

'And don't let that Mark swindle you out of what's yours by rights. Remember, you have every –'

'I won't, Liv.' Julia smiled. Olivia was going to be OK.

Despite their differences they were very fond of one another.

Stefan Kaminski's life had been one of miserable little scams and dishonesties, of trouble and grief to his father and all who knew him, and had ended, predictably, in the same way. Everyone who'd ever had dealings with him, from his headmaster to his prison governors and his probation officer, had railed at the waste of undoubted talent and what could have been a worthwhile life. Nevertheless, he'd had a right to that life and one person, at least, mourned his passing – his father, who had loved him, despite everything.

Presumably, too, that applied to the woman he'd been shacked up with, though any evidence of this was not apparent. Yvonne Prior was a small, thin, quick-moving woman with short-cropped hair of an improbable orange colour Nature had never intended. But it looked newly washed, and she'd recently applied a thick layer of make-up. She wore tight white trousers and an equally tight, sleeveless top in emerald green which revealed a bare midriff and a tattoo on her upper arm with wording which Carmody thought it better not to be able to decipher without getting closer. Her long, navy blue fingernails were decorated with silver stars. She was about thirty and already looked as hard as a million-year-old fossil.

'What can you tell us about Steve?'

She examined an inky blue varnished thumbnail, crossed her legs and let a white stiletto heel swing from her foot. 'We was together seven years, don't ask me why,' she said at last, then paused for another thought. 'Well, I suppose he was good to me, not bad, any road, considering. Good fun, he was . . . if he was in the right mood. And generous. When he was flush. But God, he could be a right berk, always messing around with them dodgy jobs of his, know what I mean? I don't know why you bother with all that crap, I said, it's harder work than going straight! Stupid, it was, seeing as how clever he was. He could answer them quizzes on the telly quicker than most of the contestants.'

'Pity he didn't use his talents better, then,' said Farrar, who fancied he could, too.

'Oh, it's all right you sneering, but it's not that easy to get work when you've been inside, whatever they say!' she retorted, quick enough to reverse views that were backed up by the fuzz.

'Right, well,' intervened Carmody, before Farrar could put his foot further in it. 'What can you tell us about us this last job he was on – and I wouldn't say no to a cuppa, blossom, if you could spare us one.'

Her eyes gave Carmody a quick once-over. 'Always this cheeky, is he?' she asked of Farrar, but she smiled – almost. 'Well, I suppose I could do with one meself.' She disappeared into the kitchen.

'She'll be taking a shine to you if you don't watch it, Sarge!'

Farrar's quip was received with the baleful look Carmody thought it deserved, as water ran into a kettle, crockery clattered and the two detectives took the opportunity to have a good look round the room, even though it was obvious they weren't going to find anything of great interest. Like Yvonne Prior herself, the flat was garishly coloured and aggressively clean, with nothing lying around. No imagination as to the decor. Only a few framed snapshots on the sideboard.

'This Steve?' asked Carmody, as she came back with three mugs of tea, thick enough to stand a teaspoon in. He ladled sugar in and drank appreciatively and nodded towards one of the photos: two men and Yvonne, one with his arm around her. It had been taken in bright sunlight, with all of them clad in tropical prints, beside a bright turquoise swimming pool.

'Yeah, on holiday, just after he come out last time. Torremolinos. A holiday as was paid for by *me*, in case you're wondering.'

Steve K. was blond, a handsome hunk with the well-developed pectorals and biceps of the prison gym, and a flashy smile. Hard to relate him to the horror of that blackened corpse without flinching. The other man was older, round-faced, his hair smoothly brushed, an oily smile. Someone as tubby and knock-kneed as that shouldn't have been wearing shorts. 'One of his oppos?' Carmody asked.

She nodded shortly. 'Not one of mine, though. I wouldn't trust that soapy bastard with next door's cat.' An assessment with which Carmody, looking at the face in the snap, couldn't help but agree. 'Thank God I shan't never have to see him again now, that's one blessing come out of all this.'

'What's his name?'

'Ray Bliss. Bliss by name but not by nature.'

'Good mates, were they?'

'No use me saying they wasn't, is it? You'll soon find out they'd been inside together – Winson Green, last time Steve was in.' She pushed the sugar across to Farrar, who declined, and sipped her own tea, looking at Carmody with alert brown eyes. 'You want to find out who topped Steve, you talk to him.'

'Are you saying he did it?'

She laughed. 'Steve was strangled, wasn't he? Bliss – well, look at him! He couldn't knock the bloody skin off a rice pudding! Steve would've shook him off like a fly.' She added a few more choice phrases, none of them complimentary to Bliss and some of them new even to Carmody, who'd thought there was nothing he hadn't heard before. Blimey! thought Farrar.

'All right,' he said, 'we get the picture – but he'd know who could, eh? In on something together, were they, him and your Steve?'

She gave him a look and didn't answer for a while, seeming to be debating with herself. Then she said, addressing herself to Carmody, 'All right. I'll tell you what I think it might be to do with – though I'll warn you, I don't know much. Steve was close as a bloody oyster at the best of times and he never said schtum about this, only what he told me at the start. If you could believe *anything* he ever told you, that is. He could charm birds off've trees but he wouldn't't've known the truth if it'd jumped up and bit him.'

'I'll remember that. Go on then, what was it he told you?'

'Well, he'd been to see his Dad, Steve had. I suppose you know he's a Pole – come over here during the war and never went back. Can't say as how I blame him, from what you hear, neither.

62

*How*ever, he hasn't done bad for himself, he had a posh job as an airline pilot, so he's not short of a bit. Or so Steve said. I've never met him meself, but I reckon he must be a good sort 'cos although he didn't approve of Steve, he come up with a few pounds now and then, purely to help him out. Let him have two hundred, last time. That was just after Christmas and Steve was a bit strapped, know what I mean?'

Farrar did, at any rate. Being strapped for cash was a chronic condition with him, his wife Sandra's tastes being what they were. He nodded gloomily.

'Well, they had a drink together and the old boy got proper pissed, so's he couldn't stop talking, like you do. Seems he had things on his mind, see – about this old mate of his as had come over from Poland with him in the war. When he was shot down, some stuff belonging to him – to this other bloke, that is – had gone missing. Steve couldn't hardly believe his Dad was still bothering about it, after all them years, would you believe?'

Carmody took another look at Schwarzenegger on the sideboard. He would.

She paused to think over what she'd said, as if it didn't make much sense to her, either, finishing off her tea in several gulps. 'Well, that's what he said. And that's *all* he said.'

'He didn't tell you what sort of stuff it was his Dad couldn't find?'

She shook her marigold locks. 'Fuss over nothing, he reckoned, what did it matter, now? But it seems the old bloke'd heard from somebody, and it'd brought it all back.'

'Who had he heard from, then?'

'Oh, come on! Think he'd tell me that, even if he knew? You want to find out, Ray Bliss's your best bet.'

'You reckon?'

'Whether he'd tell you or not I couldn't say, but you could try. Him and Steve was in one another's pockets for months over it.'

'Where does he hang out?'

'He did live somewhere in Selly Oak at one time, but I think he'd left there. We're not exactly on visiting terms, him and me. You wouldn't find him there any road, by now – he'll be long gone.'

'No bright ideas where he might have taken himself off to?'

'Bleedin' Fairyland, for all I know – or care.' She shrugged indifferently and looked at her watch. 'But you get that bugger and you'll be my friends for life.'

The offer was, said Farrar's expression, something he could learn to live without.

'If we could just look over Steve's things, before we go.'

'What things?'

'His papers and that.' Driving licence, credit cards, a diary if they were lucky. Because, thought Farrar without saying it, what was left of Steve's wallet, though it had been recovered from the body, was in no state to reveal anything.

'Papers?' She laughed. 'Only papers Steve ever kept was in here.' She tapped the side of her head.

And she was right. Two or three telephone numbers emerged, scribbled on the back of a betting slip, but nothing else at all. Long shots, these numbers, every one, but they'd try them all the same.

'Did he say anything about going over to Lavenstock on Tuesday?'

She shook her head. As far as she knew, he was going racing with one of his mates, she didn't know where, though.

'Did he take his car?'

No. The white Toyota, if he cared to look, was still parked down there in the street where it had been ever since Sunday.

'I'm sorry, love, about Steve,' said Carmody before they left.

'Yeah, well. He was more bother than he was worth most of the time, but life wasn't never dull when he was around, I'll say that for him.' Perhaps there was just the faintest discernible crack in that flinty surface. She touched Carmody's sleeve with a navy-blue-nailed hand. 'Never mind, there's always other fish in the sea,' she said with a look from under her eyelids as she closed the door.

'What did I tell you?' Farrar was hardly able to contain himself. 'Play your cards right and you'll be OK there, Sarge,' he said, his grin widening.

'Get stuffed,' Carmody growled. He might have said more – but he thought it wiser to terminate the conversation before Farrar noticed that his hard-nosed sergeant's ears had turned scarlet.

6

After Olivia had gone, Julia poured herself a glass containing something more stimulating than Earl Grey and wandered around, unable to settle, sipping the crisp white burgundy, her sister's outburst echoing in her head, worrying her. That had been a very odd thing for Olivia to say about Jago. Perhaps she, Julia, had let it be dismissed too lightly. Perhaps she ought to have pursued it more. She felt uneasy, without exactly knowing why.

The sounds of traffic had died down from outside, and Folgate Street was peaceful again, after the homegoing commuter rush. The sun had gone behind the house, leaving the front in shadow. The church clock sweetly chimed the half-hour over the town, where the traffic was now a distant murmur. 'Doesn't it drive you mad, that clock, all the time?' visitors were apt to ask, listening to the Whittington chimes strike the quarters, half-hours, hours, measuring the days. But living in the shadow of the beautiful old grey church, you couldn't escape them – and you not only got used to them, you came to love the familiar, mellow sounds, as had Julia, who'd lived in the vicarage for almost all her life. Shoppers, too, occasionally heard the plangent chimes drifting over the town and the public school playing fields during some unexpected lull in the traffic, when the wind was in the right direction, and were reminded of more leisurely times, before industry had claimed the town for its own and life hadn't all been kick and rush. They signified a sense of continuity, that some things at least never change, thank God.

Situated directly opposite the church, in what had once been a quiet, undisturbed thoroughfare, and was even now one of the more peaceful parts of the busy town, the vicarage had three steps up, straight from the pavement at the front. A tall, Queen Anne house of rosy brick, with symmetrically arranged windows in its three storeys and a fine pediment over the front door, it had been Julia's home until she went up to university.

She picked up the book of poems she'd taken to the hospital

65

and walked through the wide connecting doors which could be thrown open to enlarge the sitting-room and to encompass a view of the garden at the back. In contrast to the front, the walled garden was filled with sunlight. It was Cecily's delight, though she was a gardener only when she felt like it, so she was fortunate to have help in the tending of it from an elderly parishioner who needed a little extra income and something to fill his time. It was a quiet, simple garden of manageable proportions, with a herbaceous border down one side, whose edges spilled over on to a mossy path flanking a strip of lawn in which was planted an ancient mulberry tree surrounded by a wooden seat. Set into the back wall, framed by a climbing yellow rose, was a wrought iron gate leading into the kitchen garden beyond.

Julia walked out on to the small flagged terrace and sat down facing the garden, which wore a distinct look of autumn, dressed in warm golds and reds. A haze in the air hinted at future frosts to wither the roses and put paid to the dahlias: to cut down the Bishop of Llandaff, as her father's perennial joke went. Meanwhile, the plant stood tall and majestic in its blaze of deep red. Mulberries, ripe and luscious, lay around the tree on the grass where they'd fallen. She ought to fetch a cloth, shake down the rest of the fruits, a hilarious ritual that they had always done when they were children. But an image of the fruit, red as dark blood on the cloth, made her shiver and avert her eyes. She sat down on the wall and breathed in the heady combination of fertile earth and mouldering leaves, overlaid by the bitter-sweet tang of the bronze border chrysanthemums, and after a while opened the book, a collection of English poetry . . .

She had read at random this afternoon, not choosing the poems, but reading merely for the sound of familiar words: Rupert Brooke, Auden, Stevie Smith . . . She tried to remember which one she'd been reading when Cecily's hand had stirred under hers, but she'd forgotten which one it was. Then, as she leafed through the pages, there it was.

They are not long, the weeping and the laughter,
Love and desire and hate:
I think they have no portion in us after
We pass the gate.

They are not long, the days of wine and roses:
Out of a misty dream
Our path emerges for a while, then closes
Within a dream.

The book had fallen open naturally at the page, as if it had been opened many times at that same poem. It wasn't one Julia recognised, apart from that phrase everyone knew – *the days of wine and roses* – but then, she never had much time or inclination to read poetry. What had it meant to Cecily? What long-gone events did it recall? *The days of wine and roses* . . . an idyllic youth, some treasured moment between her mother and father that had meant a great deal? Perhaps she should ask her father.

Julia closed the book, knowing how impossible this would be. It would be an invasion of privacy even to speculate on their private memories, she knew it would pain Edgar beyond belief.

He had always cherished her mother. *Cherished.* That was the only word to describe his tenderness towards her, a love that was all the more amazing in view of her father's reserved attitude towards his children, what had seemed to her to be a distancing of himself at times. Was that because, she had some-times wondered since she had grown up, he couldn't trust himself not to be too harsh with them? She had seen him angry, often – his wrath directed at injustices and cruelties and wrong-doings. But never with his children – nor had she ever had any reason to think he would be. They had all had what most people would have regarded as an idyllic childhood, with never a finger lifted against them, and she had adored her father, glowed when that treasured word of praise fell to her. No, it had been more than that which had subconsciously troubled her, a feeling of exclusion, a certain knowledge, hard for a child to bear, that you were not the most important being in the universe, that one above all mattered to Edgar Haldane, even if that person was your mother.

She began to pace along the mossy path, shivering and hug-ging herself, though it wasn't cold. But the sun had gone down and shadows were beginning to encroach into the garden, the colours of the flowers were intense in the moments before twi-light, limned against the growing dusk. She stared into a great

67

clump of tall Japanese anemones, into the unsullied purity of the white petalled flowers, the acid green boss surrounded by golden stamens, and wondered for the first time if her parents' perfect marriage hadn't spoiled them all, been a role model for perfection that was unlikely ever to be attained ... for herself, and perhaps Olivia, too.

Some awareness of being watched in the half dusk made her look up. Her heart jumped into her mouth, she felt the blood literally draining from her face and fingertips, she was filled with an atavistic fear, as if she had deliberately conjured up a malignant spirit.

He stood near the mulberry tree, a tense figure, dark as Lucifer in its shadow.

'You,' she whispered. 'What are you doing here?'

The M1, Saturday morning, found Abigail driving on the south-bound carriageway towards London, with a sobbing violin solo issuing from the stereo. Enduring classical music, whether you liked it or not, was a fact of life whenever you drove with Mayo. So much a part of him was his enjoyment of music that it never seemed to occur to him that anyone could object, and mostly Abigail didn't, but today the high violin notes were setting her teeth on edge. She tried to shut her ears and concentrate on her driving. Mayo, beside her, was ostensibly busy with some routine paperwork, but she knew his mind, like hers, was occupied at some deeper level with trying to make sense out of this apparently motiveless crime they were investigating.

Progress was less slow than during the week, though slow enough, and nothing to what it became when they'd turned off the motorway and their speed gradually became reduced to a leaden crawl. Abigail hoped Mayo was regretting the decision not to have come by train as they were sucked into the Saturday morning shopping crowds and polyglot, immigrant London. Halal butchers, Greek banks, Irish pubs, Cypriot greengrocers displaying sacks of potatoes, gigantic piles of oranges. People jostling for room on the pavements, jay walking ... she inched the car along, no accidents, but only by a miracle, nothing but sheer weight of traffic and crowded humanity slowing them up.

Too many people packed into too little space, Mayo grumbled, irked by their slow speed and putting aside his papers, too many cars on roads not designed for them, too few houses for those needing them. 'Who in their right mind would want to live down here? Mayor of London? Ken Livingstone's welcome to it!'

'Oh, I don't know,' Abigail said cussedly, a small retaliation for those violins, 'it's alive.' An unfortunate remark in view of their mission, but Mayo either didn't notice, or didn't bother to point it out.

She got in lane for Stoke Newington and a skin-headed youth in an ancient, battered Cortina cut them up at the traffic lights, missing them by a cigarette paper, giving them two fingers. She stood on the brakes, lurching them forward, and heard Mayo suck in his breath through his teeth. She made a bet with herself that he'd decide to drive home. A park, graceful crescents of once elegant, now run-down houses, an attractive church, a turning off the narrow High Street. Several more twists and turns. 'Whoa, here we are,' Mayo announced, pleased at any rate that she'd arrived at his map reference without any wrong turnings.

They rang the bell and stood back. Behind them free-spirited, fourteen-year-old skate boarders diced with death between oncoming traffic and the cars parked nose to tail either side of the road. They waited patiently for Piotr Kaminski to come to the door, having been warned that although he was expecting them, he could walk only with difficulty and might take some time to answer. Presently he arrived, leaning on a zimmer, and after they'd introduced themselves and he'd received their formal condolences with a grave dignity, preceded them slowly down the passageway into a largish front room. It was overfilled with furniture, most of it good, solid, dateless, and there was a wall of bookshelves, the other walls being hung with a crucifix and pictures, some of them holy. No obvious signs that Kaminski was in straitened circumstances, though the room was shabby and indifferently clean, as was the kitchen where Abigail went to make coffee according to instructions . . .

'I can offer you coffee but I'm afraid I have to ask you to make it yourself, young lady, if you want it. Moving around isn't easy for me, these days,' Kaminski had said immediately they were in

69

the room and he had lowered himself into a comfortably sagging armchair that had accommodated itself over the years to his shape. Next to it was a table crammed with books, newspapers, photographs, bottles of tablets, an overflowing ashtray and a remote control device for the television. 'Please don't drown it.' His smile had intent to charm.

Charmed in spite of herself, Abigail went into the kitchen, boiled the kettle and poured water on to coffee from a jar left ready, watched unblinkingly by a tabby the size of a young tiger, sitting on the outside window sill. She debated whether to let it in, then decided it was unlikely to be a family member, a hazard as it would be to Kaminski and his walking frame. She carried the tray, already assembled with milk, sugar and three small bone china cups and saucers, back to the front room, where she found the two men examining photographs. 'Mr Kaminski was just telling me that he fought with the Free Polish Air Force in the war,' Mayo explained, getting up to make room on a small table for the tray.

The old man handed her a framed, faded snapshot of about a dozen young men in flying gear, standing in front of cumbrous wartime flying machines. He didn't need to point out which of the men was himself. He stood several inches above the rest, a blond, handsome giant, who hadn't changed appreciably over the years. He was still a good-looking man, his hair, though white now, was abundant, his blue eyes clear. He hadn't lost what was obviously a natural attraction – nor what she was sure he would call 'an eye for the ladies', she noted, catching the appreciative glance that took in the bronze bell of her hair and travelled down to her legs. I'd have worn trousers if I'd known, she said to herself, though in her experience that could some-times be worse. She wondered how much the death of his son had affected him. There were shadows under those blue eyes, his mouth was drawn down in what might be more than physical suffering.

'Good coffee, where did you learn to make it, young lady? Inspector, I should say.'

'I just used plenty, as you said.'

'That's all it needs. It's not the science people believe it to be.' He spoke in an educated voice, with barely the trace of an accent, and smiled again.

'I know this is going to be painful, Mr Kaminski, and I'm sorry,' Mayo began, after they were settled with their coffee, 'but you know why we're here. I'd like you, if you would, to tell me what you can about your son, anything you know about his activities that may possibly have led up to his murder.'

Kaminski said nothing for a while, staring intently at one of the pictures on the wall. Mayo followed his gaze. An icon, wasn't it? A madonna with downcast eyes, a time-darkened face and a jewelled headdress. Down one cheek, a long scratch or scar. The Poles of course, he was reminded, were a strongly Catholic nation. The Pope was a Pole. Even Lec Walesa had been a Catholic, when he wasn't being Solidarity.

'You will already know of Stefan's record,' the old man said finally. Mayo nodded, and he went on, 'When things go wrong, in that way, for so long, one learns to expect the worst. I have prayed that nothing like this would ever happen, though I always feared it might.'

It was a sad, oblique answer that evaded the issue, and both Abigail and Mayo recognised it as such. Let it be, for now. Keep it for later. 'His mother was from Finland?' Mayo prompted.

'Where she is now, as far as I know. Our marriage, I am afraid, was a disaster, a second marriage for me, too late in life. I couldn't cope with raising a boy like Stefan when she left me. He was doing well at school, very artistic and intelligent, every-one expected him to go far, and then . . .' The old man spread his hands in a gesture of defeat, palms up. 'Well, by the time he reached his teenage years, he had got into bad company, his work began to fall off, he grew wild, out of control. Started getting into real trouble. I was too old, and maybe too dispirited to cope alone . . . what could I do?'

It was a question Mayo had heard asked a thousand times, and one which, as ever, he didn't attempt to answer, since the reply he was mostly tempted to give was almost certainly polit-ically incorrect. He changed tack and asked, 'What do you know of Tadeusz Siemek?'

'Siemek?' Kaminski took refuge again in the same palms up gesture, the one thing that even now, after a lifetime spent in England, might have dubbed him as a foreigner. The name, though, certainly hadn't come as a surprise to him nor, perhaps, the reason for the question. He was, Mayo suspected, a good deal more wily than he let himself appear.

'It was in his house, or a house he was renting, in Lavenstock, that your son's body was discovered.'

Kaminski didn't move, but his big frame seemed to have diminished in his sagging armchair. Eventually he reached out, without needing to look, for one of the photos on the table – the same one he'd shown them before. Abigail noticed a clean mark in the dust on the table where it had stood. He pointed to a tall, dark young man. 'That one is Jerzy Siemek, the friend I left Poland with when I came over here. See that face and you've seen Tadeusz Siemek.'

'His father?' Mayo asked, passing the photo to Abigail after examining it.

'Yes.'

'And you've seen Tadeusz recently?'

'He came to see me on Tuesday, Tuesday morning.'

Mayo and Abigail exchanged a swift glance. Morning. Leaving plenty of time to have returned to Lavenstock by late afternoon, when the fire had been started.

'Why is he over here in England, now?'

Kaminski sighed. 'It's a long story.'

'We're not short of time.'

The old man drank some of his coffee, reached out for his cigarettes. 'You don't mind?' he asked Abigail, as a matter of form. She did, and knew that Mayo minded more, but you couldn't say that to a man in his own house.

'We left Poland together in 1940. Our homeland had been invaded the year before, attacked on two sides – by the Germans and the Red Army. No one who wasn't living there at that time can have any comprehension what it was like. It was all over in a very short time, though worse was to come. But we didn't just lie down and submit. One day, the full story of the Home Army – the Polish Resistance – will be told ... we have a bloody history which has made us fighters, we Poles, having been a political football for centuries.'

He paused to light another cigarette, narrowed his eyes against the smoke and gazed unseeingly through the window. 'I am sorry. Memories are still bitter. More than a fifth of our nation was lost during that war, remember. And not all those

72

who perished in the concentration camps were Jews. There were gypsies, too, priests, and academics, potential dissidents of all kinds. We two, Jerzy and I, were young and idealistic, full of energy. Impossible for us to contemplate living under the heel of the Nazis, and rightly or wrongly, we chose to escape and fight them on another front, though there were many who thought we were leaving the sinking ship. The woman who later became Jerzy's wife was one of them. Perhaps they were right. We had plenty to eat, while in Poland people starved and lived in the constant shadow of death. Our lives were also in danger, but at least we lived in freedom after we'd made our way to England and joined the Free Polish Air Force here. And there is another heroic, incredible story, almost unbelievable, but true . . . the whole of the trained PAF escaping in the first days of the war by unbelievable feats of daring, overcoming all obstacles.' He fell silent, painful memories as alive today as they had been then. 'Well, there it was,' he said, rousing himself. 'Jerzy and I left, escaping over the mountains into Romania and eventually arriving here with only what we stood up in, and . . . only what we stood up in.'

He stopped, coughed and put out his cigarette. 'I talk too much. The past is indeed, as they say, another country.'

'No, no, please go on,' said Mayo, who would have revelled in hearing every detail of those incredible, heroic escapes and the reckless courage and determination with which those same men had eventually fought. Unimaginable for anyone who hadn't lived through it . . .

And of course, the old man, despite his words, needed no encouragement to carry on with his story, like old men everywhere, he couldn't pass up the chance to reminisce. His wartime years, for all the misery they contained, had been the best of his life. 'We flew Wellingtons. I became a pilot officer, later a squadron leader, Jerzy was a navigator/bomb-aimer. We had good times – it seems wrong to say it now, but we did. Until 1943, when his aircraft was shot down over Germany, and he was reported missing, believed killed . . .'

The waiting, the not knowing. How terrible, thought Abigail.

'I dare say it might have been better for him if he'd died with his kite. He turned up later in a prisoner of war camp, but he succumbed in the early fifties through the TB he'd contracted there. After the camp was liberated, he went back to Krakow and married Elizbieta Jarosz. Tadeusz was born in 1952. It was for his father's sake that he came to see me. And there you have the story.'

Not all of it, though, not by any means. There were still significant gaps in the narrative, not least how Steve Kaminski had come to be involved with Siemek. Mayo mentally put the conversation they'd just had back on replay, and heard it again, that stumble, that hesitation when Kaminski had spoken of his escape. He also recalled what Carmody had reported of his conversation with Yvonne Prior.

'What happened to Jerzy Siemek's effects?'

'His effects?'

'When he was shot down, he would have left personal belongings behind him.'

'Oh, yes, I see. Well, there wasn't much, a few family photos, his cigarette lighter, things like that . . . I put together what there was and handed them over to the adjutant. It was the usual thing for these to be returned to the next of kin, but for us . . .' Again he shrugged. 'It was of course impossible to send them to Poland. I don't know what happened to them. Perhaps they are mouldering away somewhere, still, waiting to be claimed.'

'That's all there was? Not even a diary?'

'A diary? Jerzy?' He laughed shortly. 'No, he wasn't the type to keep a diary! Too – compromising? His effects might well have ended up, sometime, for all we knew, in Elizbieta's possession, and . . . well, as you know, women find it difficult to understand these things.'

'He was a womaniser, is that what you mean?' Abigail asked bluntly.

'He was attractive to women, yes, but I wouldn't go so far as to call him a womaniser.'

'One woman, then? One woman in particular?'

Kaminski shrugged, but his eyes flickered. He hadn't liked the question, Mayo saw. The old man, he thought, had so far been frank enough, and he wondered why he was now prevaricating. 'Did he leave a will?' he asked suddenly.

'A *will*?'

'Weren't servicemen advised to make a will?'

'If they had anything to leave, perhaps, I don't know.' He laughed shortly. 'That didn't apply to us.'

'Are you sure about that, Mr Kaminski? We have information that Jerzy Siemek might have had something very valuable indeed to leave, something he brought with him out of Poland.'

'You have? I don't know where you got this story, but it is highly unlikely. I shouldn't take too much notice, he was always a joker. For one thing, his family were not wealthy. And I repeat – I will swear on the Blessed Virgin, in fact – that there was nothing of that sort in his personal effects when I went through them. I hope you are not suggesting I kept this mythical object?'

Mayo chose not to answer this. 'We believe it likely he *was* involved with a woman, and I think you must have known her. Do you remember her name?'

After a moment's pause, as if for thought, Kaminski admitted, 'There was a woman, called Vanessa. But she had left the station before Jerzy was shot down – she was a Waaf and, like us, she had to go where she was sent, you understand.'

'Vanessa what? What was her last name?'

'I forget.' He was not very convincing.

Abigail held up the coffee pot and, at the old man's nod, poured more. He drank it gratefully. She guessed he hadn't talked so much for years, and though it didn't seem to be tiring him, his accent, negligible on first meeting him, had become noticeable.

'So, what about the connection between your son and Jerzy Siemek's son?' Mayo asked, coming back to the point.

There was a long silence, during which the old man's expression grew even more guarded. 'I cannot tell you that.'

'Mr Kaminski. Tadeusz Siemek has disappeared, abandoned his children. He may have murdered your son. We have to find him.'

'You don't understand. I can't tell you because I don't know. The last time I saw Stefan was several months ago.'

'But the last time you saw Siemek was four days ago.'

'We did not mention Stefan,' he said, and Mayo knew he was lying again.

'All right then. Suppose you tell us what happened when you saw your son that last time.'

'Nothing unusual happened. The visit was not a very great success. He surprised me by arriving unannounced. It was good to see him, but I knew he wanted money. He brought a bottle of vodka with him,' he added dryly, his mouth turning down at the corners. 'I am not a rich man, but I'm not totally without means. I'm waiting for a hip replacement and that day the pain was bad. I don't drink much nowadays, but the first drink made me feel easier, the second more so ... I ended up half drunk, talking more than I should, an old man's boring reminiscences – just as I have now.'

'You're saying you were indiscreet in some way?' That would bother a man like Kaminski, Mayo guessed. He didn't really give out information easily; consciously or not, he preferred to have it dragged from him, a phenomenon Mayo wasn't unfamiliar with.

'What have I to be indiscreet about? To tell you the truth, I can't remember what I *did* say.' The strain of the interview was beginning to tell, and he looked tired and drawn, as if in pain. 'I'm sorry I haven't been much help to you.'

Mayo picked up the dismissal and decided to go along with it. He was aware that they'd lost the old man anyway, that he'd closed up, perhaps knowing he'd once more said more than he'd meant to say. 'You've been very helpful, Mr Kaminski, thank you for your time. If you think of anything else, please let us know. We may be in touch again.' Would be, for certain, Mayo promised himself as he stood up – when they found out what he hadn't been telling them. 'One more thing before we go – where were you stationed?' he asked.

'You mean when Jerzy bought it – when he was shot down? An airfield called Lindholme, in East Yorkshire, we were there for two years. Flat as a pancake but a good place ... I think it's a prison, now.'

They found a crowded pub for refreshments before they drove home. The sandwiches included prawn Marie Rose, pastrami on rye, BLTs and chicken tikka masala. Abigail savoured the expression on Mayo's face as he scanned the menu – 'Tikka masala,

76

Good God! In a sandwich! And all I wanted was a simple ham roll with plenty of mustard.'

Abigail settled for a bag of crisps, Mayo for a pork pie, then wished he hadn't. Living in Lavenstock, where pork pies didn't come any better, he was apt to judge them all by those standards. He pushed it away half eaten, took a sip of beer, grimaced. 'I shouldn't last ten minutes down here.'

He fell silent for some time after that. 'Three things,' he said at last. 'One, Kaminski's lying about that object Jerzy Siemek brought with him, whatever it was. Two, Stefan knew about it, and Tadeusz Siemek as well, it's probably why he came to England. Three, despite his denials, either Kaminski senior appropriated this object, or it was given to "Vanessa".'

'That's at least four things.'

Mayo gave her a look over the top of his beer glass. 'And five, why the hell should Tadeusz Siemek need to rent a house in *Lavenstock?*'

7

The first thing Paul Franklin had noticed when he came into the vicarage sitting-room on Sunday afternoon was that one of the four pieces of Chelsea porcelain was missing.

'It was broken in the attack,' Julia told him. 'Olivia's taken it to be mended.'

He tut-tutted, looking even more pretentious than usual in a suit of subtle, dark plum, with a shirt and a plain tie of exactly the same colour, heavy silver cuff-links, plus a large silver ring set with an amethyst on his beautifully manicured hands. He was very dark, the sort of man who had to shave twice a day, and the outfit gave him the appearance of a rather sinister Mafioso.

'We're talking Chelsea gold anchor here, Julia! I could have given you the name of an excellent restorer,' he said reprovingly. As though any person not chosen by Paul Franklin couldn't possibly be any good.

But then, his passion was porcelain, as his father's had been.

Walter Franklin, though not a man of means – he had been a teacher of English in a small grammar school – had managed, by dint of assiduously searching in junk and antique shops, attending sales, by denying himself certain pleasures in order to acquire a more important piece, to amass a not inconsiderable collection by the time he died.

It wasn't surprising that Paul had inherited this taste. As a teacher, it had been instinctive in Walter to want to pass on his knowledge, and he hadn't been averse to letting even the children hold precious pieces in their hands.

'Walter, don't!' Cecily had protested. 'We don't want any accidents!'

'Dad –!' came from Paul.

'It's all right, they won't drop anything, Cecily. You never did, Paul. There's only one way to learn about porcelain, and that's to handle it. Let them get the feel for it, teach them what to look for and it's knowledge they'll never lose.'

But of course, inevitably, Julia – seven or eight at the time – *had* somehow dropped a teacup, feeling it slip out of her fingers as though it had a life of its own. It slid to the hard-tiled floor and fractured into dozens of pieces, beyond repair.

'Never mind, chicken,' Walter said calmly. 'It happens to the best of us, once in a while. It had a hairline crack in it, anyway, so it wasn't worth much.'

It wasn't he who was angry, but Paul, who went scarlet in the face and shouted, 'It was Rockingham, crack or not!'

'That's enough, Paul! It wasn't the child's fault, don't upset her.'

Julia was upset, but not inconsolable, since she knew, she just knew, it *hadn't* been her fault. She didn't tell anyone, because they'd think she was making excuses if she said she'd felt a distinct jab between her shoulder blades, causing her to jerk forward and the cup to slip. Who would believe her when she said Paul had poked her as he stood behind her, when he was so upset about the breakage? It wasn't the sort of trick grown-ups played. And Paul must have been well over twenty at that time.

When Walter died, he left his entire collection to his wife, and when she died, it was passed on to Paul, with the exception of a particularly fine set of Nantgarw dishes, and these Vee willed

78

to Julia, who'd always admired them. Paul had immediately offered to buy them from her.

'No, I'm sorry,' Julia said. 'Aunt Vee wanted me to have them, otherwise she wouldn't have left them to me.'

'But they're part of a collection – and I'm offering more than their market value!' he countered, offended, quite unable to comprehend her refusal.

'I'm sorry,' Julia repeated.

'Well, just try not to break any of them, then!' He'd managed to summon up a weak version of his undeniably attractive smile – very white-toothed in his dark face – as he said it, but his meaning couldn't be misunderstood.

How those two lovely people – Walter, a kindly, amusing man, and Vee, full of life and generosity – had managed to produce a son like Paul was a question that was a complete mystery to the Haldane family. Except, perhaps to Cecily, who was tolerant of everyone.

He had gone further than Walter, and become, not only a collector, but a dealer in rare porcelain and china, expert enough to write about it in glossy magazines, and to be invited occasionally to appear on some of the television programmes devoted to antiques, where he'd become very popular. Viewers – especially women – liked him, and the easy, yet authoritative manner he projected, always coupled with an engaging hint of self-denigration. Showing them he wasn't trying to bamboozle them into believing he knew more than he did.

'Well, how *is* Cecily?' he asked now.

'We don't know yet, the doctors won't commit themselves . . . it's not as though she'd had a stroke or anything, but still, she's lucky to have survived at all, at her age.'

'Indeed. It would take more than a tap on the head to kill Cecily.'

'Well, the police don't think that was what happened. They think she fell – was pushed, perhaps – and banged her head on the edge of that jardinière. So if –' Julia stumbled, then went on bravely, 'if the worst actually happens, her attacker may be facing only a charge of manslaughter, not murder.'

Paul turned slightly greenish at the recital of such details. He'd always been squeamish. But he recovered quickly. His eyes narrowed. 'What exactly was taken, in the burglary?'

'Nothing. Nothing obvious, that is. The police think he may have been looking for something in her desk. Just what, I can't imagine, but since none of us knows exactly what she kept in it, we can't tell.'

'Ah.' There was a pause. He shifted in his seat, looking for something to say. 'She was always my favourite aunt.'

'Was? For heavens' sake, she's not dead, yet!'

'Of course not, God forbid! Do you think, Julia, I should go to the hospital, or wait to see her until she comes home?'

'She won't know you, and they really don't want visitors, other than the immediate family. I tried to ring you to tell you this, but I couldn't even get your answerphone, it must be on the blink.'

She thought he looked relieved. 'My journey here needn't be wasted, all the same. I have some business to attend to – and maybe I shall go and see Jago. I hear he's staying at Rodney Brightman's flat.'

'You just missed him, he was here earlier. He got back late Friday night and he's a bit jet-lagged. You may find him at Rodney's flat, though he seems to be out a lot these days. He has a new girlfriend.' Julia suspected that was why he'd chosen to borrow the flat from Rodney, away on a six months' sabbatical, for the duration of his mother's illness, rather than stay at the vicarage. Must be, it wasn't a very convenient arrangement, shunting as he did between his place of work in London and Houston.

Paul didn't reply to that one, seeming busy with his thoughts. Better not enquire too closely what he wanted of Jago. Without any justification, Julia always suspected him of trying to inveigle her brother into something dodgy – and was afraid that Jago, without ever being aware of what he was doing, might easily fall for it. One of those mild, normally sweet-tempered persons who only lost his temper (though rather ferociously) on rare occasions, he never dreamed anyone he knew could be devious.

Whether Paul's motives were of the best or not, it was certain that he tried to pick Jago's brains whenever he could. For although he was successful enough in his own sphere, he liked to dabble in other branches of the antique trade, especially in picture dealing, regardless of the fact that he'd made one or two regrettable mistakes in that line in the past. Whilst Jago, who had never wished to sell a picture in his life, not for personal gain, rarely made mistakes in authenticating one. He had studied history of art at Cambridge and the Courtauld Institute and worked for a while at the V & A before joining Greshams auction house. His tousled, youthful undergrad appearance, baggy cords and sweaters, tie askew, his air of living on another planet, was deceptive. His disorganised personal life disguised a very successful professional one.

The pause lengthened.

The mantelpiece clock was beyond the scope of her vision, unless she twisted her head round. Julia tried to squint at her watch, without it being too obvious.

'Perhaps I *will* have another of those delicious scones. Home-made, are they?'

'Yes, but not by us. One of Pa's parishioners.' How, in all this, did he imagine anyone here having time to make scones?

'And perhaps another cup of tea, if it isn't too much trouble?'

It was, yes, it bloomin' well was. The teapot was empty, after his third cup, and she should have been on her way to Wolverhampton by now. And though the horrid prospect of what she had to face there – a meeting with Mark to decide how the belongings they'd acquired over the years would be split up when the house was eventually sold – made her stomach churn, it wasn't bad enough to make her welcome Paul's company. 'I'll make a fresh pot,' she said with a smile, trying not to bare her teeth. When she came back five minutes later, he was staring into the glass-fronted china cabinet opposite the sofa on which he was sitting. She looked closer, and saw what was absorbing him so much. His own reflection in the glass.

Well, he wasn't bad-looking, by any standards, despite that conscious awareness of his own attraction. Looking much younger than his years. Dark, broody eyes, hair cut *en brosse*. A closed, rather secret smile that added a certain *je ne sais quoi* to his sultry good looks. She wondered if he realised how that affected, plum-coloured outfit clashed with the coppery velvet of the big armchair in which he was sitting.

Finally, he went. He said, in parting: 'If anything – if anything er, um, *happens*, I'd like to be of any use I can sorting out her things.' His gaze went back to the china cabinet and its pretty contents. Perhaps it hadn't been only his own reflection he'd been admiring after all. He really was a cold-hearted so-and-so.

The telephone rang. Mark, cancelling tonight. Something had come up. Could she make Tuesday instead. 'All right,' she said crisply, giving no sign of the relief she felt at postponing the evil hour, if only for a short time.

Because of who she was, and because of the popularity of Canon Haldane and his wife in the town, Kite's case had already attracted more publicity than the Bessemer Street fire and the murder of Stefan Kaminski, who had, after all, been unknown in Lavenstock. But it was the latter case which had been given the higher priority. Not to the unalloyed delight of Inspector Kite, given a skeleton staff to work with, an apology for an incident room, and only a share in the HOLMES computer. However, he couldn't argue with the rationale behind this. Not only were his own enquiries dribbling towards a standstill, the Steve K. enquiry was, after all, murder, and far more complex, and the scale of its operations necessarily larger. Everything in the dedicated incident room demonstrated this indisputable fact – a large section of wall, covered with diagrams indicating lines of enquiry, photographs, sketches, names ... extra personnel drafted in, officers diverted from other duties, electronic machinery of all kinds making obstacle courses of the paths between computers and printers, telephones and fax machines. A video screen had been set up and a photocopier was working overtime. Kite slipped into the room and sat in on Mayo's six p.m. Monday briefing. It was up to every officer, he reckoned, to keep abreast with what went on.

'I won't bore you with the details of Stefan Kaminski's miserable little life, since I trust you've all read the notes you've been issued with,' Mayo began, hitched on to the corner of a desk as he addressed his assembled team. A casual approach that none of his listeners were so mistaken as to take for laxness. 'He was bad news, been on the downward slope ever since he was thirteen, and he's committed some despicable crimes along the way – but that doesn't mean to say he deserved what he got. Murder is murder in anybody's book, and I want no effort spared to find his killer and bring him to justice.'

Having delivered himself of his little homily, Mayo plunged on ... 'As to his personal profile ... he seems to have survived on a mixture of charm, dishonesty and downright thuggery. Not averse to threats and aggro. This time, it would appear he might have set his sights on something bigger, something he latched on to when his father, Piotr Kaminski, was drunk. According to Yvonne Prior, who as far as we can tell has no reason to lie, Kaminski believed that Jerzy Siemek had brought into this country something of considerable value when they escaped Poland together to join the Free Polish Air Force here in England, and that it's still around, waiting to be picked up. Kaminski senior has refused to admit this, and it may not actually be true, but the possibility's there. Yvonne Prior seems to think Steve K. had the idea there was a woman concerned in the case, and Piotr Kaminski admitted Jerzy Siemek had links with a woman he could only remember as "Vanessa".' He paused and looked around. 'Who was looking into that?'

'Me, sir.' This was Farrar, keen to demonstrate his involvement. He was an experienced and able detective constable, he'd make a good sergeant, though few of the lads would be overjoyed if that happened. Tough. Farrar was difficult, the cross they all had to bear, but he achieved results.

'Turned anything up on her, yet, then?'

'Well, not so far,' said Farrar, not liking to admit it. He had, in fact, been shunted from one person to another in the Ministry of Defence, all of them apparently seeing it as their mission in life to keep from the public the name of any person, living or dead, who had ever in the last two hundred years served in the British armed forces. Perhaps they'd signed the Official Secrets Act and had promised, on pain of having their fingernails pulled out one by one, not to reveal the nation's topmost secrets. Perhaps they were just not very civil servants. However, he'd been cheered to learn that records were computerised, he said, so he was hopeful that if he could come across just one amenable person ...

'Hmm.' Farrar's faith in computers was evidently more than Mayo's – or more precisely, in the human element that programmed them. Mayo added, 'It's possible she has connections with Lavenstock, and that was why Siemek rented a house here.'

'I already thought of that,' said Farrar keenly, and unwisely, and went on, quite unaware of the sidelong glances being exchanged between others more circumspect. The gaffer encouraged ideas, even from the lowliest, but even young Andy Gibson, the newest recruit, could see that upstaging him wasn't a good idea. 'So,' went on Farrar blithely, 'I ran a check through the electoral registers for Vanessas – those of a suitable age, at any rate. There weren't many. Apparently it wasn't a name that was popular between the wars, certainly not around here.'

'The Redgraves,' said a voice from the back.

Mayo took his glance from Farrar and directed it to whence the voice had issued. 'Deeley. Glad to see you're still with us.'

'Yessir, sorry sir. I was just thinking. Maybe they made it popular, with their Vanessa. Look at Jade and the Rolling Stones . . .' His voice trailed off. 'Well, what's so funny?' he demanded of his grinning audience.

'Thanks, Deeley,' came from Mayo, with commendable disregard for the grins, which quickly subsided. Deeley was worth it, if you persevered. He was even perceptive, at times. 'Carry on, Farrar.'

'Well, the few I did find turned out to be a no-no,' Farrar said lamely.

'All right. Anything yet on Ray Bliss? Tip?'

'Rayner Wallace Bliss, sir,' DC Tiplady read from his notes. 'Born 1960. Did time in Winson Green with Steve K., out six months ago. Solicitor's clerk once, till he dipped his hands into the petty cash, since then half a dozen convictions for petty fraud. Real con-artist.'

Enquiries regarding the recent activities of Bliss and Kaminski, either as a duo or separately, had proved unproductive. Both had a network of unsavoury contacts, few of whom were willing to talk to the police. Everyone spoken to denied having seen either recently, or had been deemed unreliable informants, but Bliss's name had cropped up in connection with Kaminski too many times to be ignored.

'We've checked the numbers on the back of that betting slip of Steve K.'s,' Carmody offered. 'Nobody knows – or admits to knowing – either Bliss or Steve K.'

'Somebody will, sometime. Meanwhile SOCOs, as you'll all see from the info update sheet, say someone definitely forced a way through that back fence. They've found a few fibres, and the petrol-soaked clothes line suggests a car being in the pub car-park. Nobody spotted one?'

'Nobody's come forward. Bliss runs a clapped-out Escort, red, Steve K.'s Toyota was white. The vehicle the neighbour saw was blue. No record of any car hire to either of them.'

'Keep at it,' Mayo said. 'It's important we find Bliss. As for this woman Jerzy Siemek was said to be connected with, this Vanessa, we may be barking up the wrong tree altogether, maybe she'd nothing to do with it. We're only going on what we picked up from old Kaminski, but I want it following up, all the same.'

Soon after that, he wound up the meeting, the team were allotted their various tasks for the following day, and shortly afterwards, events took another turn.

Abigail was still there, wading through the reports of the Bessemer Street house-to-house interviews when Jenny Platt, the pretty component of CID, she who could run rings around the rest when she so wished, poked her head round the door in some excitement. 'The Pole's just come in, downstairs!'

'What pole?' Blinking, still stuck in the morass of Pete Deeley's contorted prose, Abigail looked up, momentarily disorientated.

'The Polish bloke we've been looking for,' Jenny said, unable to hide her impatience. 'Seemek – Sheemek, I mean.'

'Where did they find him?' Abigail asked, pushing back her chair.

'They didn't. He just walked in, five minutes since.'

'Can you spare the time to sit in with me on this, Jenny?'

'With pleasure!' Jenny was only too glad to be given respite from the doldrums of the Haldane case, to which she'd been assigned.

He was standing clasping the back of a chair in one of the interview rooms, a tall, thin-faced man who might have stepped right out of the photo Kaminski had shown them, except that he was wearing a shabby, cheaply tailored suit which looked as though it had been slept in. Old man Kaminski had been right, the likeness to his dead father was uncanny. He was pale and unshaven and his eyes were deep-sunken. 'Where are my children?' he greeted her.

'They're safe, Mr Siemek – the name is Siemek, Tadeusz Siemek, isn't it?'

'Yes, yes. Where are they?'

'Rest assured, they're with someone who's looking after them well. She speaks Polish, and they're quite all right – in the circumstances.' His white-knuckled grip on the chairback relaxed ever so slightly. 'Why don't you sit down and we can get this thing sorted?'

He stared at her, eyes burning. Then slumped on to the chair, in response to her matter-of-factness, or perhaps defeated by the impossibility of doing anything else.

'Right. I'm Detective Inspector Abigail Moon, and this is Detective Constable Jenny Platt,' she said, identifying them both for his benefit, and for the tape Jenny had switched on. She gave the time and date and opened her notebook, not strictly necessary, for Jenny would be taking back-up notes, but it was a prop she was comfortable with, and a routine that was tried and tested: one to take notes, one to listen. Even trained memories were occasionally unreliable.

He licked his lips as if they were dry. 'Would you like some refreshment before we begin, Mr Siemek? Tea, or coffee?'

'Please, coffee. Thank you.'

Jenny stood up and asked, 'Sugar?'

He shook his head and as Jenny left the room, Abigail asked, 'While DC Platt is out, perhaps we can establish a few necessary details . . . what is your occupation?'

'I am a lecturer in biology at the university in Warsaw.' He was forty-seven years of age, Polish national, divorced. The purpose of his visit to England? A holiday. He had come here for a holiday, intending to stay for three weeks.

Jenny came back with the coffee and Siemek stared at the grey liquid in the cardboard beaker which evidently confirmed everything he'd ever heard about English coffee. He didn't attempt to drink.

'Now, let's begin at the beginning, Mr Siemek.'

He flung up his hands. 'The beginning! Forget the beginning! Now is what I wish to know about, to know what has happened to my children!'

'Please try and be calm, Mr Siemek.'

'Calm! You tell me to be calm?'

86

'Perhaps it would be better if you just answer some questions.'

'Am I a criminal, then, to answer questions?'

'I don't know, yet, Mr Siemek,' she said sharply. 'The sooner we start, the sooner we shall find out.'

He gave her a long stare and then, with a visible effort, took hold of himself. 'Very well, I will do my best to answer.'

Well, at least we can understand one another and that's a start, Abigail thought, drawing her pad towards her. He seemed to have a relatively good command of English, better when he was calmer, and his voice was deep and pleasant. 'To begin with, tell me what you were doing on Tuesday.'

'Tuesday?' he repeated blankly, as if she'd asked him to reel off the Ten Commandments backwards, or to explain the second law of thermodynamics in simple terms.

'Tuesday was when you left the children in the house, telling them you were going to London,' she prompted.

'London. Yes.' He studied the formica top of the table and appeared to have lost himself in his thoughts. Finally, he spoke again.

His English was studiedly correct as he repeated what was perhaps a well-rehearsed speech, that the main purpose in coming to England was to take a little holiday, perhaps to visit the place where his father had been stationed during the war, when he served with the Free Polish Air Force. 'And I also wished to visit one of his old comrades.'

'I see. This person's name, please?'

'Piotr Kaminski. It was he whom I went to London to visit.'

'Leaving your children alone, at home?' she asked, severely, in spite of herself. 'Couldn't they have gone with you?'

Her censure didn't escape him. Colour touched his prominent cheekbones. 'I had no choice, my business was not of the nature that I wished them to be there.'

'It wasn't just a friendly visit, then?'

'With Piotr Kaminski, yes, perhaps. But I had other things to do.'

'What sort of things?'

'I do not remember,' he said, staring at the wall. 'I lost my memory.'

Jenny's eyebrows, as she bent over her notebook, shot up. You heard everything in this place.

After a moment, he went on, 'I must explain that I had a little accident, perhaps not so little. They say I did not look where I was going.' He became agitated and had to search for words, and the way to express himself. 'I crossed the road too hastily and I am knocked down, yes? I am – what did they say at the hospital where they took me? – concussed. Later, I do not remember anything of what happened.'

'Please go on,' she said when he showed no signs of expanding on this.

'They insisted to keep me there. They gave me something which made me sleep, so I had no choice. In the morning I still could not remember. Only later, I began to think of my children. But they – the doctors – would not let me go until they were satisfied I could travel. So, at last, I left. I simply walked away.'

'You can give me the name of the hospital, of course? We shall need to check.'

'The name of the hospital? No, I do not know it. I can only say I was on my way to the station when I was knocked down. Euston station, where my train left for Birmingham.'

'There are a lot of hospitals in London.'

'I do not know which one,' he repeated. 'I did not ask. I was in too much of a hurry to get home to my Karol and Krystyna. I took a taxi at the hospital gates for Euston station.' He looked defensively from the disbelieving face of one woman to the other, as if sensing how thin his story was. 'You can find out? You have ways to discover that I am telling the truth? Or do you wish for me to show you my bruises?'

'That won't be necessary, we can check,' said Abigail, beginning to believe him. 'But it's going to take time. Meanwhile, please continue with your story.'

'What else is there to say?' he asked, spreading his hands, shrugging. 'I took the first train I could and then another train from Birmingham. I came to Lavenstock, to Bessemer Street, and there I – there was the house, burned to the ground.'

She let him go on in his own way then, without interruption, his pain and bewilderment apparently genuine, as he told how he'd staggered away from the burned-out house, gone in search of somewhere to sit down and think what to do. To buy a cup of coffee in a café after picking up the evening paper, reasoning that such a fire would certainly have been reported in the local press ... and sure enough, he quickly saw headlines and photographs that told the story all too clearly. Relief at learning that his children were at least alive. Horror at reading that the body of a man had been found in the house when the fire had been put out.

'You've no knowledge of how that body came to be there?'

The question seemed to need some depth of understanding he didn't have. He gazed blankly at her. 'You had just visited Piotr Kaminski,' Abigail prompted. 'Do you know his son, Stefan?'

The silence continued.

'Are you aware that it was Stefan Kaminski's body in your house?'

'Stefan?' Siemek turned, if possible, paler than ever as he crossed himself. 'Stefan? Not possible. What day was that – I am still a little confused?'

'It was Tuesday.'

'But he was not supposed to arrive until Wednesday!'

'You were expecting him, then?'

'We made the arrangement to meet here on Wednesday morning. But this is terrible, to be burned to death!'

'I must tell you, Mr Siemek, that Stefan Kaminski's death was not entirely due to the fire. We believe someone tried to murder him, and the house was deliberately set on fire to try to conceal the crime.'

'But this is not possible.'

'I'm afraid it is. And we can't let you go until we've questioned you in more detail, checked your statement.'

'You think I killed him!' he said flatly.

'Did you?'

He seemed not to hear. 'My God, my children – where were they when this happened?'

She explained where they'd been found, and the circumstances of their being there, where they were now.

He buried his head in his hands, then suddenly leaped to his feet. 'They must believe I have left them. I must see them!' He looked so wild she thought seriously, for a moment, that they might have to use physical restraint, but when she told him he could be allowed to speak to the children on the telephone, he calmed down and slumped back into his chair, shrugging hopelessly. Bureaucracy, the defeated shrug said, was the same anywhere in the world.

He made the most of the telephone call, making it last more than fifteen minutes while he spoke to both children in turn, evidently reassuring them and even making jokes. His face crinkled into smiles as he spoke to them, the sadness lifted, and though Abigail couldn't understand what was being said, she wondered if he could possibly be the monster she had envisaged he might be before she had met him.

'Where have you been sleeping since you came back here?' she asked when he'd finished.

'Sleeping? Under the stars,' he said expansively, indifferently. Which sounded fine and romantic, much better than sleeping rough, but that was certainly nearer the truth, considering the way he looked. A night in a warm bed in the cells, even a few canteen meals, must surely be very welcome after that.

In the intensive care ward in Lavenstock General Hospital lay Cecily Haldane, to all outward appearances and according to the tests of the medical staff alive, but only just. Not, however, according to her own innermost self . . .

Snatches of thought and feeling ran through her mind, sometimes inconclusive, unrelated, but sometimes very clear and lucid indeed to her.

I remember when Sylvia Plath wrote a poem about being in hospital. She described, more eloquently than I can ever hope to do, what they were doing to her, how she felt. She wrote about red tulips and bright needles, about losing herself, letting things slip.

There are shining needles here, too, but no flowers in this room that I can tell. No air. No breeze to blow the curtains. No loss of self. Indeed, I grasp at life, rather than wanting to let it slip. I float in and out of perfect lucidity, and try to stay there, though no one seems to be able to tell, and I'm not able to tell them.

It's not so much present sensations as memories which assail me as I lie here – perhaps because I am so much older now than Plath ever became – in that half world where I am present, yet not present. My body lies here, attached to machines which ostensibly are keeping me alive, when I know I don't need them. For my body yes, perhaps, but I am aware of everything that is going on, the people who come to see me. 'Cecily!' they say. 'Can you hear me? Listen, do you remember . . .?'

Camberwell, where I was born. Oh, such a different place now to the one I remember, though even then it had changed. That old, silly joke we had about it. How we carried it on!

Dearest Edgar. I am especially aware of him, who stumbles in the effort to speak to me. But I know without words what he is saying, I can feel, as always, the power of his love.

I hear what they say, I see their tears, I know what's being done for me, yet I am bound by invisible cords to this bed, like Gulliver in Lilliput. Restricted in my movements, as one is in a dream . . .

'Our path emerges for a while then closes, within a dream . . .'

When Julia read the poem to me – yesterday, a week ago, ten minutes since? – I tried desperately hard to show that I'd heard and understood, and I think she knew I had at last managed to respond. Maybe it's a beginning, but perhaps it's only something such as that particular poem, with so much power to affect me, which will help me to break through the barriers of communication.

He and I read Ernest Dowson together, that poem and others – or rather, I read the poems to him. Does he remember, still?

8

When the telephone rang, Krystyna was being taught how to make chocolate cake, absorbed in learning how to work the food processor, as much a novelty to her as a word processor was to Wanda. She was a grave, careful child and liked to be helpful about the house, which she assured Wanda she did all the time at home. 'Never mind that, you go outside and play on the swing, m'duck, get a bit of fresh air,' Wanda tried to encourage her.

Krystyna complied with the instructions obediently, but it was clear she preferred to be indoors, helping Wanda, or if not, then reading the old Polish books which had been Wanda's when she was a little girl. Poor lamb, responsibility had been thrust on her too early, Wanda thought pityingly.

Karol, on the other hand, was more easily distracted. Ever since Wanda had introduced him to the model train set-up in the attic which had belonged to her boys, he'd been in a seventh heaven. She was very proud of her boys' achievements in making it (with a little help from their Dad, of course) and had kept it for *their* children, when they eventually came along. Karol's face had been a joy to behold when she and Krystyna lifted off the protective polythene sheet and revealed the realistically constructed scenery, mostly made by John, and the trackwork and electrics which had been David's special care. She could scarcely drag him away for meals and walks to the shops, and wouldn't have been surprised if he'd been prepared to forgo the trip to Dudley Zoo she'd promised them.

But when the telephone rang and, after she'd spoken for several minutes to the person on the other end of the line, she was able to tell them it was their father, both children dropped what they were doing and raced for it, Karol shrieking with excitement. Krystyna, from the kitchen, got there first. White-faced with tension, her hands gripped the phone, and when she heard his voice she couldn't at first speak. Then the words and tears came rushing out. 'It wasn't my fault! I didn't set the house on fire! I did turn the gas off, I did, I did!'

Wanda had had no idea the poor child had been blaming herself for the fire, what torments she'd been going through.

But whatever it was that Siemek said to her, the sobs gradually subsided, her face cleared and after a few moments she handed the phone over to Karol for him to say hello, waiting anxiously until he'd finished and she could speak to Tadeusz again.

Now that he'd heard his father's voice, the miseries of the last few days melted away for Karol. He couldn't wait to tell his father all about the model train set-up, which he was prepared to describe in minute detail. Tadeusz listened patiently, and also heard about the new friends Karol had made, the swing in the garden . . .

Then it was Krystyna's turn again. Siemek let her talk, too, until finally both children ran out of news and he had to ring off – but not before he'd promised he would be with them very soon. He didn't say when.

'We must finish the chocolate cake,' Krystyna said, satisfied, putting her hand in Wanda's and smiling up at her.

Folgate Street was a steeply sloping one way street, narrow where it ran past the parish church before opening out and making a double curve which ran upwards round the back of the market towards the exit from the multi-storey car-park. This older part of the street was a charming backwater, especially quiet at this time of the afternoon except for one or two pedestrians and cars passing from time to time. It contained several old buildings, some of them timbered, some built at a later date, most of them now turned into antique shops or genteel tearooms and other rather high class establishments. Opposite the Queen Anne vicarage was the ancient church of Holy Trinity, and next to that was the old graveyard. Beyond the graveyard, parts of the old monastery walls still existed and now enclosed what had become the Folgate Street Garden.

Jenny Platt was a conscientious police officer and, earlier that day, having canvassed the street with her list of questions for those who hadn't been there to be questioned the first time round by the uniformed officers assigned to the task, and having received only negative answers, it occurred to her that it was just possible that some of the old people who regularly favoured a seat and a gossip with their friends in the pleasantly aromatic gardens might have been there when the attack had taken place.

There was a quick scramble as she opened the tall wrought iron gates but when she was through them, no one was there except for one small, elderly woman with a stylish cap of white hair and bright blue eyes, who was vaguely familiar to her, sitting composedly on a bench and holding a lidded basket on her knees, enjoying the sun.

She smiled at Jenny when the policewoman joined her on the bench. 'Lovely weather again, quite an Indian summer it's turning out to be, isn't it?'

Jenny agreed. 'Do you come here often?' she began.

'Oh yes, almost every day, it's such a lovely garden. We've every reason to be grateful to William Corbyn for it, haven't we?'

'Oh, er, yes.' Despite having been born and bred in Lavenstock, Jenny had no idea that this dull and uninteresting little garden, full of plants but no bright flowers, had been given to the people of her home town and stocked with rare botanic specimens which William Corbyn had brought from all corners of the world.

'You haven't read that plaque on the wall over there, have you?' her companion said, wagging an admonishing finger. 'And you don't remember me, either, do you, Jenny? I taught you French for a year.'

Jenny stared. 'Oh goodness, it's Mrs Pritchard!' Her teacher, remembered as an ancient martinet, actually seemed younger now that she'd lost her permanent air of disapproval and allowed her hair to be released from the Brillo pad grey perm to a sleekly cut white. 'I'm sorry, I must have seemed rude. I'm not surprised you remember *me*, though. I must have been one of the worst pupils you ever had.'

'Well, not quite!' Mrs Pritchard smiled. 'Though very nearly! Never mind, you were only thirteen, and we all have our weaknesses.'

The basket gave a small, convulsive movement and Mrs Pritchard looked embarrassed. Jenny Platt was a shrewd policewoman, a sharp young woman on the way up, and you didn't easily pull the wool over her eyes. She knew exactly what was in the basket, and had a good idea why. There was a dog in there, and her old teacher had been letting it run around the garden, something which was strictly forbidden here, though not necessarily adhered to. The basket jerked again, and a small yelp was heard.

With a covert glance at Jenny, the old lady lifted the lid to reveal a tiny, pop-eyed little animal curled inside, a chihuahua, the sort that gave Jenny the creeps, one of those that shivered all the time, more like a rat than a dog, it was. He gave a shrill little bark and bared his tiny sharp teeth at her.

'There, there, Pedro, it's all right!' The old lady patted him and explained, 'I like to bring him out for a little constitutional, but he has to be carried in his basket, his little legs won't take him far.'

'I don't suppose they will.' Jenny smiled.

'I must confess,' said Mrs Pritchard, glancing sideways at her and speaking rather quickly, 'I *do* let him out of the basket occasionally, when no one else is around. He's absolutely harmless, such a good boy, although he's so old, and of course I don't let him *do* anything. I have my own garden – wonderful hobby, gardening, isn't it? – but he does need a change sometimes and I can't let him out in the park, those big rough dogs take advantage of his size, you see. One knocked him right over and another trod on him, once, and he's never been the same since.'

Apart from the smell of old Pedro, another, sharper, pleasanter but even more pungent scent issued from the basket, the smell Jenny associated with the Vick Vapour Rub her mother used to rub on her chest as a child, when she had a catarrhal cough. The wintergreen smell of the artemesia, the lad's love, her Grandad used to grow in his garden. Mrs Pritchard, as well as disobeying the injunctions about the presence of animals in the garden, had been snitching cuttings.

'You're a policewoman now, aren't you, Jenny?' the old lady asked with sudden apprehension, uncannily picking up her thoughts.

Jenny smiled. She didn't think she was going to arrest Mrs Pritchard, but she looked meaningfully at the basket once more and couldn't resist breathing in deeply to let the old lady know that she knew what she'd been up to. She was in plain clothes and asked how Mrs Pritchard had known she was in the force.

'Oh, I heard. And you were always the sort who'd grow up to be something of the kind.' Meaning thick, thought Jenny resignedly. 'Responsible,' Mrs Pritchard went on, absently stroking Pedro, 'a liking for order and discipline. You'll do well.'

Jenny blushed at her uncharitable thoughts. 'Oh. Oh, well, thanks, but I haven't got very far as yet. I'm still a CID dogsbody.' Not for long, she hoped. She'd never intended to fly high, but she'd changed her mind since joining the CID and decided to go for it. She wasn't a fast-tracker, like Moon, but she had grit and determination and she reckoned she'd make a decent, if not top-notch, grade eventually. 'At the moment I'm gathering information about an incident that happened at the vicarage on Tuesday.' She took out the questionnaire and a pen from her bag.

'Oh, you mean the attack on Mrs Haldane!' Mrs Pritchard sounded concerned, but relieved to have the subject changed. 'That was quite shocking! Lovely woman – and dear Canon Haldane, *such* a good man . . . Is she . . .?'

'She's still in a coma, as far as I know, poor lady. She can't tell us anything about what happened, so we're asking anyone who might have been around on Tuesday and might have noticed anything.'

'I'm sorry, I'm never down here on Tuesdays, that's my mobile library day.' Mrs Pritchard brightened. 'But I'll tell you who may be able to help you – Mr Summerford. He used to be the manager at the bank, you know, before he retired. He comes here nearly every day. He should have been here already.' Her cheeks had become quite pink and Jenny scented romance.

'Perhaps you can give me his address and I'll go and see him.'

'I don't think that will be necessary, he's here now.'

'Morning, Gladys, morning Pedro,' said the spruce elderly gentleman who was approaching them briskly, smiling and tipping his tweed cap, his words almost drowned by the deep, musical sounds of the clock chiming the hour, by which he checked his watch. He joined them on the seat, hitching his well-pressed trousers at the knees to reveal natty argyle socks and polished brogues. He also had on a tailored sports jacket, a dog-tooth check shirt and a yellow wool tie. Despite what he doubtless regarded as leisure clothes, the retired Mr Summerford didn't look vastly different from the sartorially correct presence who'd presided over the NatWest premises for as long as Jenny could remember.

Mrs Pritchard explained the situation in a few crisp words and Jenny enquired if he had been anywhere in the region of Folgate Street on Tuesday. 'Oh yes, always here, Tuesdays ack-emma. Usually bring the paper, sometimes a sandwich if the weather's pleasant,' the old man answered, tapping the shopping bag he carried.

From all of which, after working out that he meant Tuesday morning a.m., and further deducing he had at some time been in the army, or perhaps the Boy Scouts, Jenny asked, 'Did you see, or notice, anything out of the ordinary?'

'Yes,' he said promptly, and her hopes rose. 'I heard the

vicarage door slam – well, crash would be a better word, it made *my* ears ring and I wasn't inside. I was just coming into the garden, it was eleven-oh-five exactly, and I saw this figure running away towards the market, or the car-park exit maybe, as I suggested in my note.'

Jenny was suddenly alert. 'Your note?' There'd been no mention at any briefing of any note having been received, there was no record of anyone spotted running from the vicarage, of that she was certain.

'When I heard about the attack on Mrs Haldane, I put two and two together, called at the police station and left my statement there. I guessed – rightly as it happens – they would be busy, so I'd written it down beforehand to save time.'

Oh God, someone's head would roll over this one, Jenny thought. Thankfully not hers. But she couldn't understand how the information hadn't been passed on. The people manning the desk were civilians, but extremely reliable, Mr Summerford well intentioned, if mistaken. 'Did you actually hand the note over?'

'I indicated I was leaving it on the counter with the woman on duty,' Summerford said. 'She was on the telephone at the time.'

And had probably never noticed. And the envelope had probably been knocked to the floor, and ... Well, whatever, the information had obviously never reached the incident room.

'You saw this figure – could you describe him?'

'Might even have been a *her* – although it was a nice sunny day, the person was wearing one of those anorak things with the hood pulled up over their head, and running like the clappers. That's why I noticed particularly.'

'Well, thank you, that's a help.' Jenny had passed on the information. She couldn't actually see that it *was* going to be an awful lot of help, except for fixing the time of the attack, but it was another little fact that might eventually find its place in the larger picture. Unless someone else could be found who'd seen a running figure, unsuitably clad for the day and – unlikely, but always possible – if this person had been running towards them and they'd remembered the face. Which would be nice, but she knew it was a forlorn hope.

*   *   *

97

The chocolate cake Wanda and Krystyna had been making was for supper that night. Dani had asked if she might bring a friend round to meet them all and Wanda had invited him to supper.

'He has an old bull-nosed Morris,' she told Karol. When he looked puzzled, she explained it was small, old, very special, a connoisseur's car now. 'And if we're good he'll take us all out for a picnic in it sometime.'

Wanda hadn't met this friend before. He arrived, not in the old Morris but on a dented bicycle, full of apologies. Oh. Ah, yes, well, it had been like this, you see . . . He'd had an accident that morning, and his car was in dock, an argument with a bollard, all his own fault, he admitted disarmingly, he'd been late and hadn't had his mind on his driving.

Wanda's first impression was of a tall, rangy young man with untidy hair and baggy clothes. A disorganised individual, slightly diffident, good-looking, with a hesitant but engaging smile. Awkward and, she suspected, rather shy. Her second impression was that he wasn't all that young, in fact he was probably at least a dozen years older than Dani, which made her slightly uneasy. That was a big difference, when you were Dani's age, and in lieu of parents or grandparents, Wanda felt herself responsible for the girl. Dani, though she was basically sensible, with her heart in the right place, was impulsive and inexperienced, hardly past the zany schoolgirl stage yet, and . . . but then, Wanda admonished herself, she didn't know this fellow at all, and he seemed decent enough. Perhaps age was irrelevant. Love came in all guises – and who'd said it was love, anyway? Dani had been careful not to imply anything serious. But it was written all over her face.

It was only when the children had finally gone to bed that Wanda learned why his mind hadn't been on his driving that morning. He was still a bit jet-lagged, he confessed, after flying back across the Atlantic, and he'd been coming from the hospital where he'd been to see his mother, who was lying there injured, in a coma.

Haldane! The name hadn't really meant anything to Wanda when Dani had introduced Jago, but now she made an immediate connection with the main story in last week's *Advertiser*. 'Oh, I'm so sorry, I hadn't realised she was your mother. I know her slightly, she used to help at the Polish club occasionally, too, you know.'

'Yes, that's where Jago and I first met,' Dani said. 'When Jago was picking his mother up and I was waiting for Grandpa. We didn't meet again though, until a few weeks ago, through Natalie.'

'Should I know who Natalie is?'

'One of my best friends – she's Jago's niece.'

'I heard she had a friend called Dani with a Polish surname, from which I deduced she was the same girl.'

Jago smiled at Dani and Wanda saw that Dani was more than a little dazzled. His *niece*, though! He couldn't be *that* old, Wanda thought, even as he followed up, disarmingly, with, 'There's eleven years between me and my elder sister, Olivia, Natalie's mother. I seem to have been a sort of afterthought.'

'How is your mother?' she asked.

'Not – er, not very good, I'm afraid.' His face turned suddenly haggard – yes, now he *really* looked older than Dani. He took a long draught from the glass of beer she'd poured him and set it down, not quite squarely, on the coaster, where it tipped over and cascaded all over his trousers and on to the rug, much to his consternation. 'Oh, blast it, sorry, sorry! Lord, I'm a clumsy oaf!'

He did seem more than a little accident prone, Wanda thought, hurrying for cloths to mop up, despite what sounded rather a high-powered position with Greshams, despite his dismissal of it as just another job. She could understand his fascination for Dani, his combination of good looks, unassuming manners, and what sounded like a glamorous career, but what was in the relationship for him? she worried, on her knees in front of the cupboard under the sink. There was something here she didn't understand. And did she really like this young man?

Abigail had gone through the rest of Siemek's story with him, which had entailed another hour of patient questioning. She now had the details of it sorted out, crisply tailored, pared down to the essentials, neatly typed and ready for Mayo to assimilate quickly, thus dispensing with the irritations of winding and rewinding and listening to the tape. It had been a bind to do, but she felt virtuous when she'd finished and she didn't consider it time wasted, since it had helped to put her own overall view of the situation into perspective and her thoughts into better order.

The only verifiable fact of his movements so far was that he had visited Piotr Kaminski at the time which coincided with Kaminski's own statement. Afterwards, in the late afternoon, he had been knocked down by a car and had ended up in the hospital whose name he didn't know. He'd been detained for thirty-six hours, after which he'd walked out and returned to Lavenstock, where he was seen by Debbie Parkes.

'Didn't it occur to you it might have been very dangerous to go against the doctor's advice?' Abigail had asked. 'You might have passed out again.'

Siemek had waved away such considerations. He'd been desperate to get home, worrying about the children, who were alone and must be wondering where on earth he might be. And then . . . his arrival at Bessemer Street and seeing the burned-out shell of the house. The shock had been total.

There was a short silence after this while Abigail collected her thoughts and debated the best way to proceed. 'Let's start with what brought you to Lavenstock,' she said eventually, 'and what made you rent that house.'

'It was what I was instructed to do.'

'*Instructed*? By whom?'

'The lawyer, the solicitor who is working on behalf of Kaminski.'

'Solicitor?' Her interest sharpened. 'It was through him you met Kaminski?'

'Stefan Kaminski and I have never met,' said Tadeusz Siemek. A pair of hazel eyes regarded him steadily across the table.

'It is the truth. He was going to come here to Lavenstock on Wednesday, the day after I went to London, for us to meet for the first time, and to talk. He evidently changed his mind and came earlier, but why this should be so, I cannot say.'

They had never met. Astonishing. It was odds on that Siemek could in fact be lying to save his skin, but Abigail thought she recognised the truth when she heard it. He looked utterly defeated, then suddenly he caved in. 'I can see I have no choice but to explain everything that has happened.'

100

Hallelujah! 'I'm listening,' she said.

He was silent for a long time, gathering his thoughts. Not an impulsive man, this Tadeusz Siemek. Finally, he began.

It had been in April when he'd received the first letter from a man signing himself J.J. Halley of Halley, Oglethorpe and Halley, solicitors, an astonishing communication which had started a correspondence lasting throughout the summer. Halley was, he wrote, acting on behalf of a man named Stefan Kaminski, the son of Piotr Kaminski, who had been Jerzy Siemek's closest friend. Kaminski was a name Tadeusz had heard often enough from his mother: Elizbieta, after more than fifty years, still blamed Piotr for what she regarded as the calamity of Jerzy's life, for persuading him to leave Poland in the first place. Not to mention for the calamity of her own life – left pregnant and unmarried, disgraced. Although Jerzy had, when the war had ended, done the right thing by her and married her when he returned to Krakow and found himself the father of a daughter he'd known nothing about. None of that had stopped Tadeusz from wanting to know what Stefan had to tell him.

There had been a good deal of sparring in the first letters, each taking the other's measure. It appeared that Stefan Kaminski had learned something of interest to them both from his father Piotr, which he felt they should discuss face to face. He would not divulge what this was in a letter, and suggested it would be in Tadeusz's best interests that they should meet in England. Tadeusz wrote back to say he would need something more specific than that before making such a journey, which resulted in stalemate for a while.

In any case, Tadeusz had been in something of a dilemma. His job, not to mention the want of funds, had prevented him going to England immediately. He had responsibilities to his students. More to the point, he had his children to think of. His wife, Janina, now lived far away on the Polish border with her Hungarian lover, and there was no question of Tadeusz leaving the children in the care of their grandmother. Elizbieta was now nearly eighty and was not in any case the best person to take care of them. She was the cross, the burden that he had had to bear for most of his life, a woman whose life had not come up to her expectations, embittered as she was by her experiences in the war and even afterwards, when she was married to Jerzy. His older sister had married and left home as soon as possible and there was little contact between them now. As he grew up, Tadeusz was made very aware that his parents' short marriage had not been an unmitigated success. Not only because Jerzy's spirit, as well as his body, had been broken by his long imprisonment, but also, Elizbieta insisted, because he was obsessed with guilt over sins of omission or commission, connected with his time in England, that time he would never share with Elizbieta, however much she nagged. What she felt to be an exclusion had made a shrew of her, soured her relations with everyone. Tadeusz blamed her in no small part for the failure of his own marriage.

The letters which continued to arrive from England haunted Tadeusz all summer. Then Stefan, evidently sensing that he was going to get nowhere without giving more information, revealed that when Jerzy Siemek had been shot down, Piotr Kaminski had gone through his effects and been disturbed not to be able to find what he confidently expected to find there . . .

'Which was?' Abigail asked, clearly seeing old Kaminski's face as he vehemently denied any knowledge of such a thing.

A painting, Siemek cautiously admitted, after a while. A valuable painting which Jerzy had smuggled out of the country when he left.

Perhaps it couldn't be found because his father had sold it, Tadeusz wrote back. Then what had happened to the money? It wasn't just any old painting, he learned, but one of exceptional value . . . it was thought, in fact, Siemek told Abigail with a sidelong glance, as though not expecting to be believed, to be an original Paul Klee, even then considered to be a master. 'You have no doubt heard of him?' he asked out of politeness, evidently not expecting moronic police personnel to have heard of Paul Klee.

Some of them had. 'The man who said his art was just taking a line for a walk?' Abigail smiled to herself as his eyebrows rose in respect, but then she had to admit that was pretty nearly all she'd ever heard about the artist, it was just a tag that had stuck.

'Ah. Then let me inform you. Paul Klee was a Swiss, an Expressionist painter. He was already famous before he died in 1940, but now his experimental abstracts fetch unprecedented sums. His art was free fantasy, he was more poetic than any other painter of his time,' he explained didactically, his professional role of teacher unconsciously taking over. 'He was, too, an impassioned theoretical writer, a great teacher, a professor at the famous German Bauhaus school of architecture and design, and as such had an enormous influence on the next generation of painters. One of his paintings was sold recently in Germany and it fetched an unbelievable sum.'

He paused. Of course, he added carefully, he had no reason to believe his grandfather knew anything at all about art, and this painting he'd given Jerzy to take to England could, therefore, have been a worthless copy for all he might have known.

But, thought Abigail, watching Siemek closely, you hoped . . . As anyone would.

'How did your grandfather come to have something like this? Was he a connoisseur? Or perhaps he bought it as an investment?'

'No, no, not at all. My grandfather did not have that kind of money. He was only a small-time manufacturer of leather goods. I was greatly puzzled how something so immensely valuable had come into his possession. I asked my mother if she knew anything about it.' Siemek smiled thinly as he recalled his mother's reaction.

'If Jozef Siemek had anything like that,' Elizbieta had declared, 'he came by it dishonestly! My father-in-law was the biggest rogue on two legs. But your father? Poof, Jerzy would have had nothing to do with such! He was too high principled even to buy a precious bottle of milk on the black market, after the war, even when he needed it for his health.'

'So,' said Siemek, 'I did a little investigating on my own account. There is an old aunt still living, willing to talk. The story I put together was that Jozef had almost certainly obtained the painting cheaply – amongst other things – from a rich Jew who wanted to dispose of his assets quickly and secretly in order to buy help to get his family out of the country before it was too late. The man had no wish to flee his home, but he was a Jew, he knew what was happening in Germany, what could happen in Poland. Already the Nazis were confiscating the paintings of Klee and others from galleries all over Germany, as being degen-

103

erate art – degraded, corrupt.' He paused. 'You are finding this difficult to believe, Inspector.'

'It's hard to believe many of the things that went on during the war, but we all know they happened.'

'As you say. The story is partly – supposition – on my part, you understand, but Jozef certainly amassed a sizeable little art collection, about which he knew absolutely nothing, except that they were worth money, and I doubt if he could have got hold of them in any other way. As you say, such happenings were not unheard of at the time. I think now, to the shame of our family, that Jozef obtained them for a fraction of their worth, as a reward for his silence, until the Jewish people got away. How he persuaded my father to take the painting to England, I do not know. I suspect he tricked, or misled him in some way. By the end of the war, Jerzy probably had his suspicions of how the painting had been obtained. The type of man I believe my father to have been, that would have affected him deeply. I think this was partly the cause of his *malaise*, his depression.'

It was some time before he continued, but Abigail waited, not wanting to interrupt the thread of the story, for him to go on. After a while, he did.

'I would say now that whatever misdeeds Jozef, my grandfather, committed, they did him no good at all. He was rounded up by the Germans and perished in Treblinka, his entire possessions were confiscated, whether they were ill-gotten or honestly achieved no longer mattered. My grandmother, Barbara, was killed, and their daughters raped. Another of my father's sisters died simply of starvation. His brother was shot while stealing bread.'

This recital of horrific facts was made almost dispassionately, as if such an appalling history was something so commonplace in Poland that there was no expectation of surprise, shock or horror at its recounting. And maybe it was. But the sadness behind the pain-filled eyes told Abigail that it had not been forgotten, never would be. She understood as never before, that in that beleaguered country, race memories and antagonisms must be part of the very fabric of their lives.

'Is it possible the painting had been destroyed? Surely your father would have tried to get it back, if not?'

'Perhaps he did, and was unsuccessful, I do not know. He was ill, after all, long before he died.'

'All right, you were to meet, then, you and Stefan Kaminski, and discuss how to reclaim this work of art, if it still exists?'

'If? Stefan was in no doubt that it does exist. But I did not trust him. His letters worried me. They showed him to be – a greedy man. After all, there could only be one reason for his interest in the painting. Money. I went to see his father, to talk to him and make my own judgement on the truth.'

'What did Piotr Kaminski tell you?'

Siemek shrugged. He hadn't touched his coffee, which must now be cold and even more undrinkable than before. Abigail sympathised. She knew that brew. She said gently, 'You've forgotten to drink your coffee,' and to Jenny, 'Take this away and see if you can rustle us up some hot tea, will you? Civilised tea. You'd like some tea, Mr Siemek?'

Jenny smiled as she stood up, understanding civilised didn't mean cardboard beakers.

'A glass of tea would be good, thank you. No milk, no sugar, if you please.'

It eventually came, not in a glass, alas, but in a pot, accompanied by thick canteen cups and a plate of biscuits. He drank thirstily when it was poured, even accepted a second cup, but refused the Rover Assorted. Abigail repeated her question. 'What did Piotr Kaminski say?'

'Piotr?' Siemek, it seemed, had learned nothing more than they had from that wily old man. What little he knew had come only from the son, Stefan.

'What made Stefan so convinced this painting is still in existence?'

'He swore to me he knew what had happened to it. But he did not tell me how he knew, or where it is.'

'You believed him?'

He shrugged. 'I could not see what he had to gain by lying.'

'It was given to a woman, wasn't it? A woman your father met when she was in the WAAF? He'd given it to her?'

'So,' Siemek said slowly, 'so, you know about her – this Vanessa?'

She nodded, seeing no reason to enlighten him as to how she'd come across this information.

'Well, that is what Piotr Kaminski thought at the time, or so he told Stefan, that my father had given it to the girl – but it was only a guess on his part.'

'Did he tell you her surname?'

'He said he had forgotten it.'

Abigail sighed as she looked back over her notes, then went back to the question he hadn't yet answered satisfactorily. What had he really been doing, that he'd had to leave his children behind? After some evasions he eventually admitted that he had been looking for a lawyer.

'Any lawyer, or one in particular?'

The one, he admitted after further deliberation, who had made contact with him in the first place. The J.J. Halley of Halley, Oglethorpe and Halley, from whom he had received that first letter. The one, he added, who'd also been employed to trace this woman, Vanessa.

'Did he find her?' Abigail asked sharply.

'That was what I wished to find out.'

'Did Stefan not tell you?'

'You think he would tell me that, in a letter? Also, as I have told you, I did not trust him, and I decided to see the lawyer for myself. But as you know –' he spread his hands, palms up – 'I had the accident and never reached his office.'

'What's the solicitor's address?'

It was Combe Street, he said carefully, spelling it out, a small street behind Praed Street. He fumbled in his wallet and brought out the initial letter he'd received from the firm, signed with the flamboyant signature of J.J. Halley.

If Steve K., a petty criminal with plenty of low-class contacts, had descended to paying money for above-board professional help then he must have been pretty desperate. This solicitor, even supposing he existed at all, must be a bit dodgy. More likely, it was one of his mates who owed him one. She examined the letter, but it told her nothing. In these days of desk-top publishing, nothing was easier to fake than a false letter head. Find Rayner Wallace Bliss, and we've found J.J. Halley, she told herself. Bliss, the one-time solicitor's clerk and con man, would have found no difficulty in passing himself off as a bona fide lawyer. Abigail kept her eyes on Siemek as he refolded the letter into its original creases and put it back in his wallet. He could have been pulling the wool over her eyes, he could have been telling her a pack of lies. After seeing Piotr Kaminski he *could* have got himself back to Lavenstock, murdered Steve Kaminski and set fire to the house, then returned to London to provide himself with an alibi. But if he was to be believed, he hadn't known Steve K. was going to be there in Lavenstock. And more than that – what about his children? What had he planned to do with them?

Her deliberations were interrupted by Siemek demanding whether he would be allowed to go now that he had given her all the information he had, though demand seemed too strong a word for the weary way he asked the question. His air of despondency communicated itself to her and left her feeling deflated. If he hadn't killed Steve K., which admittedly had always seemed a bit iffy, they were left without any other suspect for the murder, with the possible exception of Bliss, Steve's accomplice.

'I'm sorry, Mr Siemek, I know you came in voluntarily, but in the light of what has happened, I'm afraid we shall have to keep you in while we check your statements.'

9

Abigail had set Keith Farrar on to checking the London hospitals to confirm Siemek's story. Farrar clearly thought this was below his dignity. But he didn't complain – not to her, at least, as he might have done once. Perhaps he was beginning to see the advantages of circumspection. More likely, it was the personal problems he had on his mind that were preoccupying him. His marriage was going through a bad patch and he wasn't getting as much sympathy from Jenny Platt as he'd expected. Jenny, sensible girl, possibly the only real friend he had in the station, had seen in time where her understanding attitude was leading and had backed off pretty smartly. She was fed up with the recital of his marital problems, which she was beginning to see stemmed as much from Farrar himself as from Sandra.

'Get a grip on yourself, Keith,' she'd told him briefly when he'd grumbled that this routine task was just about up to Deeley's level, or that idle sod Barry Scott . . . 'You do *want* Moon to succeed, don't you?'

Always quick on the uptake, Farrar immediately saw what she meant. A successful outcome of the investigation would spread kudos all round – though chiefly for Abigail Moon, which Farrar was bound to support. After all, her being upped to chief inspector would mean a shuffle round, and he, Farrar, had been hanging about, waiting in the front line long enough.

'Just get on with it, mate, and shut up moaning,' Jenny advised sharply.

He could see he wasn't going to get much sympathy there and he'd retired, injured – especially at that 'mate'. Bloody women. He picked up the phone and got to work. After twenty minutes he had what he wanted. A man had been knocked down by a bicycle in Praed Street and had been taken into Accident and Emergency at St Mary's, Paddington, on Tuesday afternoon, suffering from heavy bruising and concussion. He'd been identified by the papers on his person as Tadeusz Siemek, a Polish visitor to this country. When he came round, he had no difficulties regarding his own identity, but remembered nothing of the accident that had brought him there. Thirty-six hours later, he'd discharged himself, according to the thoroughly disapproving, starchy-voiced person to whom Farrar had spoken, simply walked out without checking whether or not he was in a fit condition to do so. 'It's not how we do things over here, whatever they do *abroad!*' she told him sniffily, adding that she hoped nothing untoward had happened, because the hospital couldn't really be responsible if it had.

As for the rest of Siemek's story . . . No Halley, Oglethorpe and Halley could be located with an address anywhere in the vicinity of Praed Street, or anywhere else for that matter. No Combe Street, either. To nobody's surprise, they'd never existed.

Mayo said, 'Sorry to have to ask you this, but we'd like to run through your statement again with you, Mr Siemek.'

He did it as briefly as possible, keeping his questioning low-key and to the point. They were all weary. It had been a long day, and it wasn't finished yet. Abigail had done a thorough job in the first place, and he learned nothing more than he'd expected, nothing came across that was new to him. It was more a matter of watching the man intently, summing him up and comparing what he saw with the facts. He saw this not as a waste of time, but a rewarding process. One which, moreover, suspects were apt to find unnerving. Finally, he thanked Siemek and said, 'I don't think we need keep you any longer, for the moment at any rate. How long were you expecting to stay in this country?'

'We have seats booked on the plane for Warsaw on the sixth of next month.'

'The sixth, hmm? We'd better get stuck in then.' Siemek might not have understood the idiom, but Mayo's expression said clearly enough that he doubted if Siemek would be on that plane, and a look of despair passed across Siemek's own features. 'All right, Mr Siemek, no doubt you're anxious to see your children. We shall need to talk to you again, so I'd like to be kept informed of your whereabouts. Where are you thinking of staying?'

'That I do not know, yet.' Siemek shrugged as if it were of no importance whatever, scraped his chair back, and stood up, hardly able to wait to be off.

'I'd advise you to find accommodation in this town, or at least somewhere near. Keep us informed of where you are, your address, immediately you have one.' Their eyes met. Mayo said carefully, 'Tell me one thing before you leave – how are you hoping to substantiate your claim on that painting, supposing it's ever found?'

Siemek held Mayo's look steadily, before answering with dignity, 'My claim? I think you have misunderstood me, sir. I know the name of the Jewish family to whom it originally belonged. I intend, when it is found, to see it is returned to them as soon as possible. Do you think I would have agreed to this outrageous plan otherwise?'

When he had gone, Mayo sat drumming his fingers on the table. 'Keep an eye on him, Abigail. See he's watched.'

109

She threw him a quick, surprised glance.

'I mean watched for his own safety. Somebody's already been killed over this business. I don't want Siemek to be the next.'

Despite himself, he believed the Pole's story, even his claim that he intended to restore the painting to its original owners. It was a lofty intention at best – almost unbelievably high principled in a world generally lacking in principle and utterly dedicated, so it seemed, to the pursuit of money – at its worst, it smacked of naïvety. It was the sort of statement Mayo would normally look upon with a jaundiced eye, but Siemek had impressed him with his honesty. Dangerous to allow that, maybe, but it was backed up by what had come through from the Polish authorities, who had at least found no traces of him being involved in anything remotely criminal. And the man was far from being a fool, he was not gullible. He had quite rightly suspected Steve Kaminski's motives, and Kaminski's death had patently shaken him. He must know beyond doubt by now, if he hadn't previously suspected it, that he'd involved himself with a bunch of crooks, whose only interest in him was as a means of getting hold of the painting and disposing of it for their own gain, that his own life, and maybe the safety of his children, wouldn't mean a lot to them, with the lure of such high rewards being dangled before them.

He pushed his chair back and went to stand in front of his window, watching the urban pigeons settling for the night on the ledges of the Town Hall. He sometimes thought, when he wasn't cussing them for their anti-social habits, and the less than attractive prospect they made of the view from his window, that he could almost envy them their uncomplicated lives.

At the corner, where Milford Road met Queen's, Dolly, the flower woman, was packing up for the night, stacking her few unsold flowers on a barrow. Watching her, he said, 'Siemek's right, Abigail – though outrageous wouldn't be the word I'd use to describe this scam. Downright off the wall is more like it.' He turned back towards the room, 'The trouble is, I'm having problems with the very fact of this painting. A genuine Paul Klee?' He blew his lips out in disbelief. 'Let alone in believing anyone would keep it hidden away for fifty years – not unless they're the kind of connoisseur who gets his kicks from gloating in secret.'

'It needn't have been hidden. It's not everyone who'd know an original Klee if they saw it hanging on the wall.'

'How true, Abigail! I wouldn't, for one, and very few others, I suspect.' He'd done his homework, looked Klee up in Alex's art books and immediately conceived what she had declared to be a jaundiced view. But he couldn't for the life in him see either the meaning or the attraction of those crazy 'fantasies', or what seemed to him to be childish scrawls and geometric abstractions. Being of the Emperor's new clothes school of thought, a natural sceptic, what he did think was that they looked as though they might be very easily copied.

The officer he'd spoken to at the Art and Antiques Squad obviously thought this opinion of Klee was hardly worthy of comment. His patronising manner raised Mayo's hackles straight away. The appearance of a *genuine* – he stressed genuine – Paul Klee (the pompous prat corrected Mayo's pronunciation to Powl) on the market, would have set the art world on fire. One, that is, which had been authenticated, for which provenance had been supplied and documentation provided to prove its entire history. The chances of that were, to put it bluntly, less than negligible, though Klee's *oeuvre* had been enormous. (A big output, amended Mayo to himself). Everything relating to his work was exciting, but what sort of work was the work in question, anyway? Klee had been a prolific painter, designer and etcher, who experimented with different techniques and materials. Much influenced by Blake and Aubrey Beardsley, not to mention Goya, and he himself had been an inestimable influence on future generations of painters. Thinking of certain creations recently acquired by the Tate, Mayo could appreciate this. As for a hitherto unknown work, the art squad man went on ... He sucked in his breath, tut-tutted. But he'd promised to look into it: to find out if there'd been any rumours of anything being passed along illegally. The art world was small, the circulation of works of art closely followed by those who had an interest. He'd been certain that if anything had been sold through legitimate channels, at any time since the last war, its sale would be traceable. 'But don't bank on it.'

'You ever get yourself transferred to that lot and I'll disown you, Abigail,' Mayo said, repeating the conversation, and Abigail laughed. 'He tried to bamboozle me with a lot more guff, but you get the picture – pun intended. Unfortunately, that arty-farty lot up there don't have the same sense of urgency over things as we have. We can only wait until they come up with something – or nothing, as the case might be.'

'Mmm.' Abigail thought about it. 'If it's not stealing to order, selling a work of art like this one's supposed to be is a long way out of their league – Steve K. and Bliss. That's where they'd slip up, if anywhere.'

'Someone already slipped up by killing Kaminski. Big blunder. We'd never have known about the Klee if it hadn't been for that. And why *was* he killed? Hmm?'

'If it *was* in mistake for Siemek, we're looking for a stranger – somebody who'd never seen either Siemek or Kaminski.'

'Right – and that takes Bliss out of the frame.'

Yes, thought Abigail. Bliss would hardly have mistaken for Siemek a man he knew as well as he knew Steve K. A falling out among thieves was more than a possibility, it happened all the time, but the place, the house where Siemek was living with his children, made a planned murder – or even a sudden quarrel, and a chance to settle old scores, resulting in murder – seem unlikely. It was looking less and less like a deliberate plan to kill Kaminski, and more and more as if some person or persons as yet unknown had seized an unexpected opportunity.

'Besides, there's no obvious reason why Bliss should want to get rid of Siemek. Defeat the object, wouldn't it, that? They needed him – he was the one with a legitimate claim to the painting. Unless Steve Kaminski intended to remove it when he learned its whereabouts, the idea must have been for Tadeusz Siemek, as Jerzy's son, to bring pressure to bear for its return to him.'

'A tad too subtle for the likes of Steve K., wouldn't you say?'

'Which means –' She saw where he'd been leading her.

'– that somebody who had an interest in their not finding the painting got wind of what was going on. Unless Steve K. and his mate Bliss were very discreet in their enquiries, which I for one am not inclined to favour, they must have been leaving feetmark all over the place.'

'Well, now Steve K.'s dead, there's only Ray Bliss likely to know, and that's only on Yvonne Prior's say so.'

'And old Kaminski, for a pound, though I don't want to go back to him unless we have to. Odds on he's been giving us the run around, and I don't like that, but I don't see how we can *make* him talk if he's decided not to. He's a tricky old devil, and I wouldn't discount the possibility that he could be lying in his teeth. He *says* the painting wasn't in Jerzy Siemek's effects, but we've only his word for it.'

Abigail frowned. 'Same applies. If he'd sold it, there'd be a record. If not, why keep it? He didn't strike me as being a closet connoisseur.'

'As a souvenir of his friend? All right, no, just a thought. I don't see that possibility, either.'

'Let me go and see him again, see what else I can get out of him.'

Mayo considered for a minute. 'How? Using your feminine charms?'

'In the absence of thumbscrews, yes. Feminist principles only go so far.'

'I have to say this opens up a whole new dimension to your character.' Then he grinned. 'All right then, see what you can fix úp.'

The first thing Mayo did next morning was to buzz for Kite. While he waited, he looked through the Haldane file again, read Kite's reports and sighed. Although feeling a certain sympathy with his inspector's evident frustration with the investigation, he knew he was going to have to do something which wouldn't be popular with him.

Resources were stretched as far as the elastic would go between the two major enquiries, both teams having to manage with less personnel than they'd declared possible. It was unrealistic to expect two lots of facilities to be set up, so the Haldane team were squeezed into a smaller room off the busy main incident room, sharing the HOLMES computer facility. The civilians who were manning the telephones and computers had been instructed in which direction to shunt information and queries. Not a very satisfactory state of affairs, as Mayo had pointed out to the ACC, but Lavenstock's incident suite wasn't automatically geared up to deal with two major enquiries at once. Sheering had done his best: personnel had been drafted in from the neighbouring Hurstfield Division, and Kite had been happy enough to have their own Jenny working with him. Thankful not to have been lumbered with Barry Scott (not one of Milford Road's finest) and to number Tom Maclean, a seasoned veteran, amongst his team.

All the same, there wasn't a lot of job satisfaction in an enquiry which was rapidly reaching an impasse. And Mayo knew from experience how quickly Kite could lose interest when he wasn't able to see quick results. He rubbed a hand across his face and assumed a non-partisan expression as Kite came in.

When Wanda Livingston opened the door and saw the stranger standing in her porch, she knew two things immediately. One, that he was Tadeusz Siemek, though not because he resembled either of his children, simply because he was indisputably Polish. And two, that the rage she'd felt against him had disappeared somewhere along the line. Rarely had she seen a man so exhausted: physically, yes, but also as if all his mental resources, too, were depleted by what he'd been through. He looked as though he hadn't had a decent meal in weeks and she had an immediate impulse to take care of him, to give him soup and bread, cook him meat and serve him some of the apple pie she'd just baked, offer him a hot bath and a comfortable bed. But really, she couldn't have done better than she did, which was to answer his tentative first remarks in his native Polish.

His face lit up when she said, 'Yes, Mr Siemek, I know who you are, please come in. The children are waiting for you.'

As far as getting information feedback quickly from the labs went, forget it, Kite announced when he arrived in Mayo's office with nothing new to offer on the progress of the Haldane case.

Which was getting on his nerves, to tell the truth, but it was his baby, for better or worse he was committed to it and he had been throwing himself into the business with all his usual enthusiasm, not to say impatience. Unfortunately, all the impatience in the world couldn't hurry up the tests on the hairs and fibres gathered from the crime scene – most of which were sure to be

114

eliminated – or the blood sample found on the corner of the jardinière. OK, so he'd just have to grit his teeth and resign himself to waiting, hopeful that he might possibly have results before the end of the next millennium. It didn't stop him feeling there must be *something* he could ruddy well do to break what had become stalemate almost from the word go, despite the piles of paper it had generated. 'It's getting me down,' he admitted, with some exaggeration, but perhaps a fair amount of truth.

'That's a luxury none of us can afford,' Mayo said shortly, looking at him over his spectacles. 'What else?'

Cecily Haldane wasn't yet out of her coma – if, indeed, she ever would be, Kite replied, long-faced. 'It's a bloody awful state of affairs for the family, not so wonderful for us, either. SOCOs have come up with an alien fingerprint or two, but it's nothing to get worked up about.' He'd had a hunch none of them would match up with any records on the national criminal fingerprint index, and felt grimly justified when they hadn't. 'There's a few foreign fibres on Cecily Haldane's clothing, just about as much good, unless we get lucky and find something belonging to a suspect to compare them with. Trouble is – no suspect.'

'What about this bloke, this person, seen running away? This male or female?'

'Most likely he was bloodstained – it looks as though he might have grabbed the Reverend's waterproof, which has apparently gone missing. The vicar's more bothered about his specs, though, which he says were in the pocket. Mind you, he seems to be your typical absent-minded cleric, so it might turn up where he's forgotten he'd put it. Not much hope of tracing it if it doesn't – along with a few hundred other folks, he bought it in the Army & Navy sale. It's a pointless exercise looking for it.' In the canal, or the municipal tip it would be by now, or incinerated on some garden bonfire.

'And that's the grand total of what we have.'

It took a lot to depress Kite, he normally fizzed like a bottle of pop, but he really did sound a bit down. Even the boyish curls that made him such an asset because they gave him a deceptively baby-faced look seemed limp. Mayo could find it in him to sympathise. You could whittle away at some cases for months until a solution of sorts was arrived at, but only if you'd something to go at. Sometimes, with a job like this, nothing ever did

115

emerge. Taxpayers' money couldn't continue to be wasted. He said abruptly, 'Martin, I'm putting this one on the back burner for the present.'

'Winding the case up?' Kite did not look pleased. He opened his mouth to speak.

'You know better than that,' Mayo interrupted warningly. 'We'll keep it active as long as necessary, but you know how we're fixed at the moment. Usual dearth of resources, manpower. Don't look like that – it'll still be in your remit. You can keep a couple of bodies on it and we might yet get a result, especially if – perhaps I should say when – Mrs Haldane comes round and can give us more information.'

Pending, thought Kite. The worst of all sodding worlds, neither one thing nor the other. 'What you're telling me is, you're pulling me off it, that's it?' he asked stiffly.

Mayo lost patience. Bracing his hands against the desk, he leaned forward. 'No, that's not it! Why don't you bloody listen for a change, and then you might hear properly? I'm not pulling you off it entirely, but I can't afford to leave you sitting on your backside while I'm short of an extra DI in other directions.'

Mayo rarely shouted, and when he did you took cover, if you'd any sense, kept your head below the parapet, but Kite couldn't let this unfairness pass. The Haldane enquiry wasn't the only one he was dealing with, he'd plenty of other, if lesser, ones on the go, making up a heavy caseload. He began to say so: he and Mayo went back a long way, they'd worked good-humouredly in harness for years, developing a warm, mutually respecting friendship in the process. They'd always spoken freely, but he looked at Mayo's face, read the signs and decided not to push his luck this time.

'As I said, I'm not expecting you to abandon Mrs Haldane – I need you to row both cases in together, and if anything unexpected turns up, we'll review the situation,' Mayo said more quietly, leaning back. 'Oh, come on, Martin, get yourself together, you can do it with one hand tied behind your back, and you know it.'

Abigail arrived at Piotr Kaminski's house on Tuesday afternoon, this time via train and tube. She took her case file with her,

116

intending to study it on the journey down, but she found her thoughts drifting towards the see-saw of her personal life.

At the moment, things were good, as good as she had ever hoped they would be. She felt alive, in the way she did only when she was with Ben. His quick-witted, effervescent personality rubbed off on her; they laughed a lot, they talked – or rather, Ben did, he was a great talker – they argued, made up, and made love and she felt the world was a wonderful place.

But. How long would it continue? She was only too aware of the tightrope she walked in her relationship with Ben, back now in his post as editor of the local paper, and writing thrillers in his spare time. Before he'd taken what amounted to a sabbatical, in order to work on an assignment in Israel with a national newspaper, they'd had what seemed to both of them an ideal understanding. They'd managed the demands of their respective jobs in what they'd considered a civilised manner, each agreeing to respect the exigencies and unpredictabilities of the other's, and neither expecting the sort of favours that were usually traded between press and police.

It had worked well, or so she'd always thought, but when he'd left, personal considerations aside (which were considerable) she had in fact experienced a certain sense of relief at being free from the perpetual tension imposed by their two separate careers. She wasn't at all sure yet, when the honeymoon of his return was over, how they were going to reconcile the situation. She would never pass information on – to do him justice, Ben would not expect that of her, but he had to feel free to report events as he saw them. She could feel unspoken questions hovering about the Haldane and the Steve K. cases, both big local news, making her feel perpetually on edge.

She tried to whip her thoughts back into order and began to think about the coming interview, but she was by now sharing a carriage with a pin-stripe suit, the type impervious to black looks, who'd decided to use his own and the two vacant seats next to him as his office – complete with lap-top, briefcase, cell-phone. After the latter had rung for the fifth time, she got up and changed carriages, but by then they were nearly at Euston.

When she'd telephoned, asking to see him again, Kaminski had

117

told her he was due to go into hospital within a couple of days for the hip replacement for which he'd been waiting.

'I'm sorry to have to trouble you at such a time –' she began when he opened the door. It was immediately apparent from the dark circles under his eyes, the sagging lines on his face that his health had deteriorated considerably in the few days since she'd last seen him.

He waved aside her apologies, but it was clear he was apprehensive about the operation on his hip by the remarks he made after they were settled with the coffee she'd once more made. Perhaps he thought there was a chance he'd never make it out of the operating theatre . . . but maybe it wasn't so much fear of the operation which had aged him so much, as a delayed reaction to the shock of his son's murder . . . whatever the cause, he seemed much quieter, more depressed than he had been on the previous occasion. Her determined intentions took a sharp nosedive, and she approached the interview much more gently than she'd meant to.

'Mr Kaminski, as I told you on the telephone, I'm here to go over again with you the information you gave us last time we spoke.'

'If you think it will do any good, go ahead.' Shifting uneasily, he reached for his cigarettes, lit up and coughed.

'I wondered if you'd been having second thoughts about what you told us, if perhaps you can remember now what it was you told your son,' she said, giving him a let-out. She felt sorry for him. He did look very ill. Reminding herself of how he'd led them up the garden path, she steeled herself not to be too sorry for him.

'As I told you, I was too drunk to remember even the next day what I said that night – and time has passed since then.'

So he was determined to stick to his story, stubborn old cuss. 'Let's see if I can help. You'll be pleased to know we've found Tadeusz Siemek – or rather, he came in to see us of his own volition.' She outlined briefly what had happened to Siemek after he'd left this house, and saw by his reaction that this, at least, was news to him, and unwelcome at that.

But all he said was, 'The way he was when he left me, it does not surprise me that he was knocked down.'

'He's told us that you and he discussed the events that had led to him coming to England. I guess that must have been a painful subject for you both.'

The long silence which followed was punctuated by a child's wail in the street outside, a mother shouting, the slam of a car door. The car drew away and the sound of its engine faded. 'Yes,' Kaminski admitted heavily, at last. 'It was what he told me that made me realise the extent of my indiscretion – how, how – *crass* I'd been!' His fist thumped the table in frustration, its contents jumped and rattled. 'By the time one reaches my age, one should know oneself better. I am fully aware what drink does to me nowadays. And, God help me, I knew what my son was like. Yet I allowed myself to . . . If I hadn't drunk too much that night, let my tongue run away with me, Stefan would still be alive. I told him things I had kept locked in my heart for over fifty years . . . and what was worse, I didn't remember afterwards what I had talked about. It was only when Tadeusz came to see me that I knew the full extent of what I'd done. And even then it was not finished.'

Suddenly overcome, Kaminski shielded his eyes with his hand, resting his elbow on his chair arm. She let him be until, alarmed at the length of the silence, she felt compelled to rouse him and said gently, 'Mr Kaminski – it would make things easier all the way round if you told me the whole story, right from the beginning.'

'The beginning,' he repeated, then sighed in a resigned manner. 'Very well. Give me a moment.' He lit a cigarette and drew deeply on it. After a while, he said, 'I suppose it began with old Jozef giving Jerzy what he said was a valuable painting, a thing of squares and triangles, bright childish colours, naïve, it seemed to us – certainly not *art*! It was quite small, painted on some sort of burlap, about eighteen inches by twelve, I suppose. We neither of us knew anything about pictures and we laughed at it, but Jozef insisted it was worth a great deal of money, that the artist was famous, and that it would be safer in England. I don't think Jerzy believed him for one moment, but he agreed to humour him and take it with him . . . he and his father had never seen eye to eye over Jerzy's student activities but neither of them wanted to part bad friends. I saw the painting just that once and never set eyes on it again – as I told you, it was not among Jerzy's possessions when he was shot down. I suppose it crossed my mind then that he must have given it to Vanessa, but it didn't at the time seem of any importance, such a thing it was. I scarcely gave it another thought for over fifty years.'

'So how did the business come to be resurrected?'

'Through a telephone call, from the widow of one of my old flying oppos, Janusz Dejmek. He married an English girl, Faye, her name is. She was a Waaf, too, a friend of Vanessa's, and she had received a letter out of the blue from Vanessa asking if Faye knew Jerzy's address. It seems they had ceased to correspond, Jerzy and Vanessa, but she was anxious to contact him now, "to make amends", she said. Well, Faye and I had lost touch, too, since Janusz died, but she still has his old address books and was eventually able to trace me, thinking I, if anyone, would know Jerzy's whereabouts. She, like Vanessa, had no idea he was dead.' He rubbed a hand across his face. 'Is there more coffee in the pot?'

'It'll be cold by now. Shall I make more?'

He shook his head. 'As it comes. Thank you.'

Abigail was elated, knowing that here at last was the lead they'd been looking for, the key to finding Vanessa. She longed to stop him and take down the details, but she didn't want to break the thread of his story now that he'd started.

He gulped down the cool, bitter brew, which seemed to help him to continue.

'Well, I have grown older, if not wiser since those long-ago days, and I know more about Paul Klee than I did then. Enough, at any rate, to know that if that painting was genuine, it was indeed valuable. Could Vanessa have held on to it all these years, I asked myself, and now wished to return it? I had no idea of Elizbieta's present whereabouts, whether she was still alive, even. I gave Faye the last address I had for her, and told her Elizbieta and Jerzy had had a son, born after the war. And that was the last I heard of the matter until Tadeusz appeared on my doorstep. My heart almost stopped, my God, so like Jerzy he is!' He looked almost pleadingly at Abigail, then asked in a low voice, 'Is it possible that he was the one who murdered my son?'

'We don't know yet who did that. We have no proof that Siemek did. But he's told us the full story, as Stefan heard it from you. Everything that passed between himself and your son.'

120

Kaminski's face blanched at this further underlining of where his indiscretions had led. 'I suppose it was uppermost in my mind at the time. I'd received the call from Faye only a couple of days before, and I was much exercised in my mind as to whether I'd done the right thing, giving her Elizbieta's address. I felt very strongly that the return of the painting through another woman – if that's what Vanessa intended to do – could only arouse painful suspicions.'

'If Jerzy gave it to her, it's hers to do with as she wishes,' said Abigail, wondering why he thought that the present of a Paul Klee might not compensate for any jealous feeling that might surface, after so many years.

'We are all old now, what does the past matter?' Kaminski said, seeming to agree with her. But then he added, 'Let sleeping dogs lie has always been my motto.'

She thought perhaps that was as true a word as any he'd ever spoken to her. That Kaminski had always been adept at shutting his eyes to what he didn't want to see. But when she said, 'I must speak to this friend who rang you. She'll have Vanessa's address, her surname,' she saw by his reaction that it was more than that.

'I'm sorry, I did not think to ask for her telephone number. There was no reason to, I had never known her well. I gave what information I could, and that was it as far as I was concerned.'

Oh, but he was evasive, refusing to meet her steady look, shrugging when she asked him, 'Where does she live, this friend?'

'I really have no idea.'

'Well then, her name?' she asked, praying for patience. 'She married a Pole, you say.'

'Dejmek, it was. But she has married again – and no, I don't know her married name.'

She believed him then but, pain or no pain, age or no age, she still felt the strongest desire to shake him.

'You realise how important it is that we trace Vanessa?'

'I'm not sure that I really see why.'

And then she saw what she ought to have seen before. His reluctance to speak stemmed only from a desire to protect Vanessa, quite apart from a mistaken, but perhaps understandable, wish not to involve her in the unpleasantness of a murder enquiry. She was very sure that, all those years ago, on that wartime East Yorkshire airfield, Jerzy Siemek had not been the only one to have been in love with Vanessa.

Suddenly, he seemed to collapse in on himself. 'However, I can tell you Vanessa's last name, her maiden name, that is. She was Vanessa Charlton-Armstrong.'

When Abigail had left, Piotr Kaminski sat slumped in his chair, his old body feeling the weight of his years and of all that had happened to him in his long life, nothing of which had taught him what was unequivocally the right thing to do in any given circumstances.

Did anyone ever know that?

Of course not. But he was tormented by the feeling that he ought to have known in this case – that he should, in fact, have told that young policewoman the truth, and not only what had seemed expedient.

10

While Abigail was collecting her thoughts in the creaking, swaying Intercity train, attempting to eat a Virgin sandwich and trying not to scald herself or her neighbours with coffee in a wobbly cardboard container, Ted Carmody was in the canteen, contemplating the highly polished, rock hard veneer constituting the surface of an alleged moussaka. Wondering whether to take a knife or a saw to it, or go home and face Maureen's cooking, which was unlikely to be better and might conceivably be worse, he was saved from an immediate decision by his bleeper. He was wanted on the telephone.

'It's Yvonne here, Sergeant,' the caller announced herself, in a gin-and-cigarettes, come-on sort of voice. 'Yvonne Prior, remember me?'

'Steve's girlfriend. Of course, Miss Prior,' Carmody said, establishing parameters right away. 'What can I do for you?' Realising that could have been better put, he amended quickly, 'Got something interesting to tell me, have you?'

'Well, you did say to ring you if I come across anything else. And I found a letter, see. I was, you know, packing up Steve's clothes and that, and it fell out of a book he'd bought just before he – well, just last week. Guess who it was from?'

'Ray Bliss?'

'Oh, very sharp! They didn't make you a detective sergeant for nothing, did they? Well, it was more of a note than a letter, really. Three or four lines, that's all.'

'Mebbe you'd better read it to me.'

'Hang on a minute, then. Right, here we go. "Dear Steve" –'

'Date? Address?'

'No date, and just Culver Street.'

'Culver Street where? Oh, right, OK, just Culver Street. Carry on.'

' "Dear Steve, I shall be going to Newcastle tomorrow to see what I can find out about this Dr Charlton-Armstrong –" Double-barrelled, that is. "Back Saturday, see you usual place. Wish me luck. Ray." That's all.'

'Which Newcastle? Upon Tyne or under Lyme?'

'Oh, come *on*! You want bleedin' jam on it? Newcastle's all it says.' She paused. 'Not going to be a lot of good, then, is it?'

'Oh, I don't know, could be,' Carmody said cautiously. 'Didn't say *up* to Newcastle, did it?'

'No, just "to Newcastle",' she reiterated, none too patient by now. 'I read it out *just* as it's written down here.'

'Well, thanks very much, Miss Prior. Now I'm going to ask you to do me another favour, if you will. Put it in another envelope, plus the one it came in, and I'll send a courier over to pick it up right away, if it's convenient. Be there within the hour.'

'There isn't no envelope. The letter was just stuck in that book. Must've chucked the envelope away after he'd opened it.'

'Ah. Very likely he did. Well, never mind, eh?'

'Tell you what, though – mostly, it was Bliss rung him, but he did have other letters from him, with a Brum or Coventry postmark, Wolverhampton sometimes.'

'Did he now? You're very observant.'

She laughed. 'Nosey, don't you mean? Well, it paid to be, with Steve!'

123

'No, I mean you've done well, Miss Prior. Thanks for taking the trouble to let me know,' said Carmody, over-polite.

'Oh, it's no trouble. Always ready to help a copper.' She waited, but he said nothing. 'I'm having bad dreams, I am. Not nice, the way he died, was it?'

'Not nice at all, Miss Prior. Shouldn't happen to anybody.'

'Maybe you could drop in sometime when you're this way round, know what I mean?'

'Oh, yeah,' Carmody said. 'Only it's not often I am, like.'

The smile faded from her voice. 'Oh, well, forget it, *Sergeant Carmody*. Unless you change your mind.'

Carmody put the phone down. Bloody hell. He hadn't been propositioned like that since his beat days as a wet-behind-the-ears PC, rounding up scrubbers in his native Toxteth.

Before Abigail got back to Lavenstock, Carmody had looked up Culver Street in the local A to Zs, and discovered there was a Culver Road in Birmingham, not a long way from the sprawling Longbridge motor complex, and another on a Wolverhampton housing estate, but these were *Roads*, and Yvonne Prior had said Culver *Street*, so he'd plumped for the only street of that name he could locate in the West Midlands area, one situated near to Coventry city centre, not exactly in the shadow of the cathedral, but not much more than a spit and a jump away.

He took the new information to Mayo and found him just shrugging himself into his jacket, preparatory to leaving for home. 'Don't want to keep you, sir, but I thought you should know a.s.a.p.'

Mayo waved away the apology. 'Sit you down, Ted.'

'It's all right, sir, won't take a minute, this.' Carmody remained standing in the doorway and relayed what Yvonne Prior had told him.

'Is she reliable?'

'Yeah, I reckon. She's a right slapper, but she hates Bliss, she'd do anything to get him nailed, especially if it's for topping Steve. I thought I'd send Farrar over to Coventry tomorrow after he's been to Warwick.' The racing calendar had been consulted, and had told them there'd been racing at Warwick on the previous Tuesday, which was a likely place for Steve to have gone, and maybe something could be picked up there. 'We're stretched, the rest of the lads are up to their ears and it's just the sort of thing he likes. Maybe I'll send young Spelman with him. He needs to get his feet wet and I can't spare anybody else to supervise him just now.' Andy Spelman was the newest CID acquisition, transferred from the uniformed branch, just out of detective training school at Wakefield. 'And he's bright enough to hold his own with Smartarse,' Carmody added.

'And what about this Dr Whatshisname –'

'Charlton-Armstrong.'

'*What* name did you say?'

Both men looked towards the doorway. Abigail had come up the stairs, just in time to hear the name. 'Charlton-Armstrong, would you believe,' repeated Carmody, rolling his eyes.

'That's what I thought you said. Not a name you often hear twice in one day. You tell me where you heard it and then listen to what I've to say.' To Mayo she said, 'You're going to love this.'

'Not if I've to listen to it with you two decorating the doorposts. Come in and sit down and let's get it sorted in a proper manner. You first, Ted. Repeat what you've just said to me, and then we'll hear what you have to tell us, Abigail.'

Abigail listened, not able to help feeling a bit dischuffed to have her discovery pre-empted like that, but that was how it went. Win some, lose some, it was all for the same cause. Days could go by when you were just fumbling in the dark, then sometimes information would all flood in at once. To have landed two such positive leads on to the same source at once had to be a bonus.

Fifteen minutes later, it was all beginning to hang together, Kaminski's story meshing with Yvonne Prior's. It seemed as though they were on Vanessa's trail, at last. 'This letter he wrote was undated,' she said. 'He could have been up in Newcastle weeks ago, couldn't he?'

'Steve only bought the book it was in a couple of weeks ago.'

'Doesn't signify. He could have kept it. They must have set this up yonks ago.'

Carmody offered to get the letter over to Forensics first thing tomorrow morning for fingerprints and handwriting to be checked against Bliss's custody records. 'Pity we don't know which Newcastle.'

'Kaminiski didn't know which, either. Only that it was somewhere in the north of England.'

'Anywhere north of Watford, he means, then. Cannibal country,' Mayo said, with a Yorkshireman's resigned acceptance of the ignorance of southerners. 'So send out a request for information from both Newcastles and see what they can turn up for us.' He addressed both of them, 'Oh, and you'll be having Inspector Kite on the strength as well, as from tomorrow. It's about time we got this thing by the throat and shook something out of it.'

Mayo had reminded himself several times during the day that he and Alex were due to drop in that night on his old friend and colleague, the police medical officer, Henry Ison. It was an evening he was anticipating with a lot of pleasure. Not only did Henry share his passion for music, he was a member of a malt whisky society dedicated to the pursuit of the finest scotch, and as such he was sent bottles from Scotland from time to time upon which to pronounce his opinion. As a fellow whisky buff, Mayo was often asked to join him in a dram or two. It was an inviting prospect, after a long day.

Nevertheless, dusk was falling when at last he came out of the station. He filled his lungs with a deep breath of hazy autumnal air, not sorry that he'd been prompted to walk to work that morning and would have the opportunity of legging it out briskly for home. A couple of miles in the open, after the stuffy recirculated air he'd been breathing all day, cramped at his desk, sounded like a lifesaver. In any case, he reckoned the extra time taken in walking would be more than offset by the waste of half an hour circuiting the one way streets and driving round the ring road.

He was, as a matter of fact, almost tempted to make a detour by way of Holden Hill, over the canal bank and the disused brickworks and up the other side of the hill to the home at the top he shared with Alex – a brisk walk he'd have thought nothing of in former days. But another glance at his watch showed him he'd hardly allowed enough time as it was, and in any case, they'd be walking home tonight.

The brightness of the floodlit car-park made Milford Road seem darker than it really was, its street lights dim. The Town Hall had closed for business, Dolly and her flowers were gone and her little cabin was locked for the night. One or two cars swished by him on the one way street as he walked along into the town centre and Victoria Road, which marked the divide before the climb up the hill, but otherwise it was quiet. Until he came to the traffic lights at the corner and into a scene like a Lowry painting; suddenly he was in the middle of the throng of shoppers milling around Sheep Street towards the Cornmarket. He'd forgotten the several new eating places, ethnic and other-wise, which had brought life to a town centre previously dead after six o'clock.

Too early yet, though, to spot much trouble brewing. The pubs wouldn't be turning out for hours, the ten-year-old glue sniffers were probably still watching *Star Trek*, the pushers of serious dope were still lurking behind the woodwork before emerging later to peddle their doses of oblivion in the discos and clubs, and the young tearaways hadn't yet drunk enough lager to be out hell-bent on their vandalism and joy-riding. It was a long time since this sort of trouble had been Mayo's lot. He often regretted this, the loss of contact with that other life which was still part of his own life, but walking through the streets rein-forced the satisfying feeling of staking out his manor, keeping his finger on the pulse of the town he'd adopted as his own.

His route took him past Tesco's jam-packed car-park and skirted the covered market, and as he came out into Folgate Street near the grey bulk of Holy Trinity church, he was just in time to see a black-cassocked Canon Haldane emerge from the vicarage and walk away in front of him with his rapid stride. They appeared to be going in the same direction, taking a diversion which cut a good half-mile off Victoria Road before emerging along it further up, but Mayo had no desire to chat, if indeed the canon should remember him; they were only very briefly acquainted. He followed at a distance the tall figure with its flapping skirts as it cut through Cat Lane and down towards the shops, cafés and warehouse conversions situated along the wide walkway, once the towpath between river and canal. It was

127

well lit by some fancy Victorian-style fake gas lamps which had suddenly appeared, in keeping with the fancy warehouse conversions and the new chichi housing across the water – and their fancy prices. Still, it was a move appreciated by the Black Bull, and the café owners, who'd found their clientele dropping off after the murder of one of Mayo's men down there a couple of years ago.

He was no slouch when it came to covering distances, but he'd have had his work cut out if he'd been trying to keep up with the energetic canon, and when he saw him sitting on the wall of the Royal Oak car-park, he hesitated. He'd no wish to intrude, but neither had he any desire to be the Levite who passed by on the other side. Edgar Haldane was an old man, after all. But even as he hesitated, the canon sat up straight with folded arms, gave him a civil salutation; he was evidently quite all right, simply taking a breather after his brisk walk; when Mayo looked back before turning the corner, the Reverend was walking away up Bessemer Street, intent on whatever business had brought him here. If he was seeking someone in need of that particular brand of hands-on Christianity for which he was well known, Mayo reflected that he wouldn't have far to look in Bessemer Street – if they weren't already beyond it, that is.

You could find a great deal to admire in the wholehearted dedication that enabled any man to devote himself to pastoral duties while his personal life was undergoing such turmoil.

Edgar Haldane was another of the breed to whom walking brought release. Release, as opposed to peace, the infinite peace to be found in prayer, or within the precincts of his church – peace that he now seriously doubted he would ever find again. A sense of proportion might perhaps be a more appropriate phrase. He'd found neither since the day Cecily was attacked, though he'd set off walking that day, too, hoping, unsuccessfully, to control the impotent rage storming inside him. They'd sent him home from the hospital, telling him there was nothing he could do for her, politely indicating that he was in the way. And then he'd gone home. And found that fateful letter in her desk.

In any case, he disdained to use his car very much and walked wherever possible, his tall, striding figure, his strong-featured, forbidding face as much a part of Lavenstock as the Victorian clock tower that dominated the town centre, or the redbrick buildings of Lavenstock College. He insisted that walking kept him fitter than many a man twenty years his junior, and nothing else, he had found in a long life, enabled him to put his thoughts in such clear order. The rhythm of his strides, his footsteps echoing his thoughts in some mysterious way enabled him to see a pattern where all had been muddle before. Not tonight, though, on this still, brooding, melancholy evening, with leaves susurrating round his feet, a smoky dusk and a mist round the moon. Without conscious volition, he had found himself walking away from the old part of the town and its medieval, sometimes beautiful buildings, and was now in the area just off the traffic-burdened Victoria Road, near the Royal Oak, an area simply old and run-down as opposed to ancient and picturesque. Unloved and uncared for, the buildings here were of no architectural merit whatsoever, and though some of the streets had been smartened up by the council and by young people buying the small houses as starter homes, Bessemer Street was not one of them.

He turned the corner and the burned-out shell of the end house struck him with such particular force his knees almost buckled, and he was forced to sit down on the low wall surrounding the public house car-park. His thoughts were so painful he scarcely thought of how odd he must look, sitting there, but no one was around to see him, except a tall man on the other side of the road, who gave him a keen glance and strode on, apparently satisfied that all was well after the canon had summoned up enough will to give him goodnight.

The traffic continued to roar along Victoria Road, but Bessemer Street, with battered cars and vans parked end to end along its litter-strewn gutters, was for the moment empty of even its gaggle of streetwise under-tens, young ruffians who normally were allowed to hang around until all hours. No doubt fetching themselves their tea from the chip shop. Or if they were lucky, having baked beans or pizzas thrust at them in front of the television sets that could be seen flickering through uncurtained windows. Canon Haldane was not unfamiliar with the ways of disadvantaged families, not only did he visit them, he offered practical help. He had once, as a young curate, found one of his sick old lady parishioners upset because she wasn't able to wash her front doorstep, and had taken bucket and scrubbing brush and promptly done it for her. The story of the dog-collared and cassocked young man, up to his elbows in soapsuds, on his knees in a public street, had followed him for fifty years, an undeserved reputation for saintliness which had much distressed, indeed almost angered, him. He was no saint, he knew his own demons and temptations well enough.

He continued to sit on the wall, still in the grip of the extraordinary compulsion that had brought him here, as if he were some other person, causing him to act quite outside his own volition. He stared at the burned-out house, which looked much worse than the photograph in the *Advertiser* had shown it to be, and, momentarily bereft, said an agonised prayer for the soul of the man who had perished so dreadfully in the flames.

After a while he roused himself. Mayo may have guessed at the turmoil in the old man's mind as he passed, but he couldn't have begun to know its extent. His life had been turned upside down from the moment he had found his wife lying on the floor in a pool of blood and heard, at the same moment, the arrival of the ambulance. Since then he had found himself acting totally out of character, unable to summon up the reserves of mental strength which had supported him all his life. It wasn't the residents of Bessemer Street who were occupying his thoughts, as he rose with more difficulty than usual from his uncomfortable position on the low wall and strode away, but the worries about what was going to happen to his family which beset him at every turn.

His two daughters, for a start, neither of whom, he sensed, were content in their private lives. It distressed him that neither had asked for his help. Even Olivia, unimaginative but steady as the Rock of Gibraltar, about whom he had never before had a moment's worry, was patently unhappy. And Julia. The child who had always been so quick and so responsive to ideas, but who was now often prickly and defensive, and seemed to be doing her best to avoid him. He could not find it in himself to be glad that her relationship with Mark Fry had ended – that was what they called it, wasn't it? A relationship. He had hoped one day it would lead to marriage; Mark was, in his opinion, a fine young man and Julia a fool to have thrown everything up in what he imagined was a fit of pique, though he had no idea what had caused the rift. Neither daughter seemed inclined to confide in him, though he realised this had ever been the way of children with parents – and nor had they, he was sure, confided in Cecily, otherwise she would have told him. Cecily and he, there was nothing they kept secret, nothing they did not know about each other. Or so he had confidently believed.

Which brought him back, inevitably, to Jago. Brilliant, vague, erratic, disappointing. Spoiled by his mother and his sisters, of course, her youngest, the only boy. Or was it true, as Cecily had always asserted, that you never spoil by an abundance of love, that it was lack of love that caused most of the world's ills? Even as a man of God, to whom love of every kind was a familiar concept, Canon Haldane knew this to be a flawed argument, a distortion of the truth. And as for Jago – that was something he could not contemplate without a pain that was actually physical.

Oh, Cecily, Cecily, my dearest wife. Why did this have to happen to you? The truest and most honest person I have ever known. All of us become aware of the sins of omission as we grow older – but why, oh why, did you have to take this upon yourself?

In sheer self-defence Mayo had learned over the years to compartmentalise his life. By now he was normally able to switch off from anything but the most worrying cases when he was off duty. But encountering Edgar Haldane like that had unsettled him, and aspects of the case fidgeted at the back of his consciousness all evening, until finally, the pleasure of good food and company won out. The light supper Viv had promised turned out to be pumpkin soup and crusty brown bread, a delicious smoked fish terrine accompanied by a watercress and rocket salad, a scrumptious chocolate confection for those who could manage it. The wine was excellent, the coffee good. Three of Henry's ambrosial whiskies later he and Alex walked quietly back home, arms linked, fingers interlaced. Mayo was feeling

131

distinctly mellow, which may have prompted him to say, as they were walking up the hill, 'Well, come on. Out with it.'

She pretended not to understand him.

'You've been bursting with it all night, for weeks, in fact.' Tonight she'd been lit up with an inner excitement, and he could tell she was too hyped up to go home and sleep without getting whatever it was off her chest.

'OK, I met Canon Haldane's daughter today,' she began obliquely, but smiling. 'Julia. The one who's a solicitor with the Crown Prosecution Service.'

'I didn't know that, and I thought I knew them all down there.'

'She's only just joined them, from Wolverhampton. She – er – interviewed me this morning.'

Hey!

Half way up the steep hill was a seat, set with its back to the pavement and the road, where the elderly and pregnant mums were glad to sit before completing the next leg of the ascent to the top. Mayo hadn't expected to need it in the forseeable future, but there was always a first time for everything. He guided Alex towards the seat and they sat like a couple of teenagers on their first date, holding hands, looking out to where the lights spread way beyond the town below, ribbons of street lights stretching tentacles though the urban sprawl of the Black Country towards Birmingham. Somewhere below and to the right was Bessemer Street and the old, shut down steel works. In the far distance, Birmingham's city centre Rotunda punctuated the horizon, truncated to no more than a stump from here. A magical sight at night, a jewelled panorama hiding the scars left by the Industrial Revolution, some of which were still all too visible during the day. Mayo wasn't at that moment seeing any of it.

'What's this, then, interviewed?'

'Yes. I didn't want to tell you until I was certain this was what I really wanted to do. There've been too many false alarms in that direction, haven't there?'

Too true. He understood what she meant by 'that direction', and not for the first time, he damned the basic lack of confidence which no one would ever have guessed at from her cool self-possession, that had its origins God knows where in her past. Leaving the police had been a momentous decision to take, the service until then had been her whole life since she was eighteen, but disillusionment with her own ability to cope as much as with the service itself had set in and there had seemed no cure other than to quit.

Since then she'd toyed with several ideas – probation officer, teaching . . .

And finally come up with this. She explained what it was going to mean.

'You'll be some sort of clerk, then?'

Christ, he hadn't meant to sound patronising, but he must have done, judging from the asperity in her voice as she came back sharply. 'What's wrong with that? Though as a matter of fact, I shall be what's known as a case worker. I take it you don't approve?'

The CPS, for God's sake. The Crown Prosecution Service. Which sometimes seemed to have been designed expressly to throw out prosecutions handed over to them by the police after weeks, months of patient evidence gathering. No realistic prospect of conviction, not in the public interest. He thought she'd be jumping back into the frying pan. But he held his tongue. Saying so would be a declaration of lack of faith in her, and already they were teetering on the verge: one step and they'd be into a quarrel. Or they could stay where they were, enclosed in the warmth and closeness the evening had engendered.

He said steadily, 'What made you think of it?'

'Abigail. She suggested it.'

'Wouldn't you know!' He didn't ask why Abigail, why she hadn't talked it over with him. 'I expect she suggested you might go on to qualify as a solicitor as well?'

Alex released a breath, relieved that the situation, if only temporarily, had ironed itself out. 'Well, yes, she did, but I've no intention of ever doing that, at the moment.'

'Don't dismiss it too lightly. It's something you'd be good at.' In all honesty, he felt that, but wondered whether she'd be satisfied with her decision for long.

'All right. Never say never,' she agreed, which sounded very like Abigail herself, the voice of the friendship which had developed between the two women when they were working together and had continued after Alex left the police. Alex had been there once upon a time with a shoulder for Abigail to cry on during the ending of a difficult love affair. Abigail, who didn't often need moral support, had never forgotten. And now it was Alex who needed the support.

'I'd hoped I could count on your approval.'

'Did you need my approval?'

'More than you think, Superintendent.'

She was smiling again. A late bus ground up the hill behind them, its lighted windows showing one lone occupant. The wind of its passing stirred her hair. Her profile was clear and regular against the darkness.

'What about Lois?' he asked, avoiding the implications of that for the moment. 'What's she going to do without a partner?'

Working with Lois had never been seriously regarded by anyone as a permanent solution; it was a stopgap which had nicely bridged the gulf between the police and a substitute career and given Alex time to think what to do. Despite his question, Mayo thought that Lois, shrewd as well as stylish, who had built up a highly successful enterprise from scratch, had every reason to be grateful to Alex, if only for her elegantly restrained input into the business.

'Lois? I can't see her being too upset, in view of Pilgrim.'

Richard Pilgrim, Lois's new man, always referred to simply as 'Pilgrim', had come on the scene only recently. A trendy architect, he had already begun to assert his influence in various spheres of Lois's life, notably Interiors, where his interest and his suggestions had undoubtedly been beneficial. It was fairly obvious he would not be unwilling to involve himself more. Lois, who ate men for breakfast and spat out the bits, was likely to find she was the one who was being spat out. Mayo was already watching developments keenly.

'I'm glad I can tell you, now that it's all been arranged.' She turned her cool, smiling face to him.

'Alex, I love you, but I wish I'd known –'

She put a finger on his lips. 'Ssh. There's hardly been an opportunity.'

He knew it was the truth. Not during the last couple of weeks. And before that, and before that. He sighed. 'Let's go home.' It was at times like this he was aware how fragile their relationship could be. How bereft he would be if it ever shattered.

11

Leaving Wolverhampton town centre and driving through Chapel Ash, Julia was struck again by how much one's view of a place is coloured by association. She had been more unhappy here than anywhere else she had ever lived (and happier, too, though at the moment that was something she resolutely refused to think about). It was the misery of the last year that had made her come to dislike the place so much, a dislike so intense it amounted to a physical revulsion, though it was no worse, after all, than any other ancient borough which had been consumed by heavy industry. Tonight, her stomach had begun to tie itself into knots as she drove towards the town through the industrial wastelands in the heart of the Black Country, and hadn't untied itself by the time she drew up in front of the house in Melia Road which she and Mark had occupied for nearly five years.

She hadn't been back since the night she'd walked out – flown out, slammed the door, sworn never to return – and was reluctant even to put her key in the lock. She *shouldn't* have come back, she thought, eventually forcing herself to push open the door, there was nothing she wanted, and the prospect of a share-out of the possessions she and Mark had gathered together, which was the purpose of this visit, filled her with dismay.

Why had she agreed to it? The appearance of Mark in the vicarage garden the other evening had shaken her to the depths of her being, so that she hardly knew to what she'd eventually agreed.

'You? What are you doing here?' she'd croaked, her heart beating like a mad thing inside her ribcage.

'I heard about your mother. I thought – I thought you might need ...' His voice had trailed away, uncharacteristically uncertain.

It had unmanned her. Mark, uncertain! Mark, always confident, upbeat, a young man on the way up, sweeping Julia along with him, warming her with the blaze of his enthusiasm, her own ambitions catching fire. It had once seemed to her there

135

was nothing they couldn't do, together. It had never occurred to her that he might feel otherwise.

'Katie' the letter had been signed, and because she'd known immediately who it was, the shock had been even greater. A pupil in the firm where they both worked. Young, sexy, beautiful, talented. Available and unscrupulous. Ignorance on her part was no excuse. Katie Muldano had known the situation from the start, that Julia and Mark were an item. But then, so had Mark.

'Julia.'

She had been so absorbed she hadn't heard him enter the house and walk along the thickly carpeted hall. He stood in the doorway, a well-built, attractive man in a good grey business suit, his dark hair cut very short in an attempt to curb its unruliness, brown eyes quick and alert. A bump on his nose where it had been broken, playing rugger. He stepped forward quickly and took both her hands in his before she could pull them away. His grip was firm. He exercised to keep fit and she was very aware of the muscular body so near to her, every inch of which she knew.

He was tall, and she barely came up to his shoulder. He looked down at her, saw the determined chin, the straight dark brows and the endearing sprinkle of freckles across the bridge of her nose, which he knew she hated, and thought he'd never loved her so much. Never regretted more the stupid flirtation with Katie Muldano which he'd only gone along with because things were going damnably awry in his relationship at home, with Julia. Things which he'd seen, too late, could have been so easily resolved with a little give and take on both sides. Which neither of them had been able to summon up then, but perhaps . . . perhaps now?

'Julia –' he began.

'Let's get this over,' she said crisply. His face tightened.

'If that's what you want,' he said at last. 'But I'll make some coffee first.' He disappeared into the kitchen, leaving her sitting there like a visitor.

She looked round and wondered where they would start. They'd lavished so much thought on what was not much more than an Edwardian semi, knocking the front and back rooms into one, later adding a small, reproduction conservatory. Choosing rich-coloured fabrics and wallpapers for this room, spending money on comfortable chairs with thick down cushions. And then for the rest, hunting down and buying, as and when they could afford, other items of furniture on which they'd done patient DIY restoration jobs, taking immense trouble to find exactly the right piece for the right place. Every item she looked at held a memory. She felt choked at the thought of it all tagged and labelled, like auction lots.

When he came back she noticed he'd taken the opportunity to change into jeans and a sweater while the coffee dripped. The Viennese coffee she loved, flavoured with fig. There were also the delicious, nutty, almond-flavoured cakes she'd kill for on a plate. He's trying to get round me, she thought, and a pulse beat in her neck.

'You haven't changed, Julia.'

She was uncertain how to take that after her sharp responses, and his steady look gave nothing away. She felt uncomfortable in her new suit which she'd thought so smart, the skirt an inch above her knees, the jacket a few inches above that, though she knew its subtle blue-green colour suited her and its silky finish felt reassuringly luxurious. She couldn't imagine why she'd chosen to wear it tonight.

'I had the house agent round yesterday,' he said abruptly. 'He was impressed.' He named the asking price suggested.

'*What*? He's not the only one who's impressed!' Julia did a quick calculation on the profit, and thought she had to be mistaken. 'Staggered, in fact.'

'It's not so surprising. We put a lot into it, Julia.' Her face closed again and he turned away, drank some coffee. She trembled, wanted to cry, was ashamed that she had so little authority over herself. 'I should have asked before. How is Cecily?'

'Still on the danger list,' she answered bleakly. 'They're going to operate to remove a blood clot.'

He crossed to the small bureau in the corner and from the top drawer extracted a pad of something soft and light. 'What do you think of this?'

Once opened, she examined curiously the large sheets of oiled silk, somewhat the worse for wear, closely written in spiky foreign handwriting, sealed and signed in various places. 'Deeds? Where did they come from?'

137

'They belong to Cecily. She asked me to have a look at them a couple of weeks ago.'

'*You?* Why on earth didn't she ask me?'

'I guess she didn't want you to know about it.'

Julia stared uncomprehendingly at the documents in her hand. It made no sense.

While Julia was sorting out her mixed feelings, her father was opening the vicarage door. He stepped inside and stood still, almost physically taken aback by the sense of loss that overcame him. Cecily's absence was a tangible, hovering thing that seemed to brush his cheeks with its wings. He stood for a moment, swaying, then pulled himself together. He didn't feel at all well, then realised he couldn't remember when he'd last eaten. Even so, he couldn't be bothered to cook himself a meal, much less fiddle about thawing one of those well-intentioned, lovingly donated casseroles with which he'd been inundated. He decided a cup of cocoa would do. In the kitchen, he opened the biscuit tin with a picture of Anne Hathaway's cottage on the lid that Mrs Cashmore, stout (in every sense of the word) Mothers' Union member, had presented him with that morning, hoping as he lifted the lid for some of her renowned home-made Cherry Shorties. He wasn't disappointed. There were Chocolate Peppermint Delights and Koffee Kisses, too.

Feeling only marginally better after boosting his blood sugar by consuming two of each with his cocoa, Edgar sat at the kitchen table, at a loss what to do, and fearing to let himself think. Especially about that ever-present, terrible decision which might at any time be forced upon him: the ethical dilemma of whether or not to give his permission for his wife's life-support machine to be switched off. Burdened with the awful knowledge that the truth could only be told with her death.

For the first time in his adult life he found himself weeping. Hot, difficult tears forced themselves from under his eyelids. Unable to control them, he fell to his knees and offered his agony to his Maker. Afterwards, long afterwards, he staggered to his feet with the same unaccustomed difficulty he'd found when getting up from the wall outside the Royal Oak, hauling himself up by means of the kitchen chair. But if not at peace, he was at least calmer. He fumbled for his handkerchief and blew his nose.

Replacing the handkerchief, his hand encountered his reading glasses, those which had suddenly reappeared, been found tucked down the side of the big chestnut velvet armchair in the sitting-room, in which he never sat. Except for that one time, when he'd returned from the hospital with his daughters, tired and depressed. Before these had turned up, he'd had to buy another pair of off-the-peg reading glasses from Boots for Mavis Snell to hold in reserve in the place she fondly thought secret. She wouldn't tell him where that was, saying it would defeat the object – he might easily take them out to replace the misplaced pair and lose *both*. He'd never told her he knew perfectly well the hiding place was in the cupboard under the altar, behind the old bound copies of the parish magazine, going back to 1881, and had resolutely refused to make use of his knowledge, however inconvenient it was: tiresome, yes, but the gesture was kindly meant.

He held the original pair in his hand. A pair of spectacles. Such an innocent, inanimate artifact to have caused him so much distress and heart-searching.

Although he was sometimes absent-minded about his possessions, he knew perfectly well he hadn't worn his reading glasses after returning from the hospital and moreover, Mrs Porter's thoroughness wouldn't have missed finding them when she cleaned the room. And instantly had come the appalling realisation of who must have returned them. And who, therefore, had attacked Cecily. It wasn't possible, he told himself, knowing that anything concerning human nature was possible. But ah, surely not *attacked*! By accident, not ever by intention!

The daily paper lay on the kitchen table, unread. Suddenly, a headline jumped out at him. So, the nationals had got hold of it now! The man who'd died in the fire at Bessemer Street had been identified. His name was Stefan Kaminski, and he was thirty years old.

Kaminski? *Kaminski?* Not Tadeusz Siemek? He put out a hand to steady himself, feeling a terrible life-draining sensation as the adrenalin left his extremities.

*   *   *

Since Carmody's expectations of finding Bliss still living in Coventry – if he ever had been – were not of the highest, he wasn't disappointed when Keith Farrar rang back reporting that their quarry had indeed recently occupied a bedsitter over a corner off-licence in Culver Street, up to a week ago, when he'd left suddenly. He'd given no reasons for his abrupt departure, but that hadn't worried his landlord, since his rent had been paid up to the end of the month.

'Get a look at it, this pad, did you?' he asked Farrar.

'Not much of a place, but it's clean as a whistle, every way. The landlord's wife's a mite particular . . . bed stripped, bedding to the launderette, drawers emptied, the lot. She swears Bliss didn't leave anything behind him, and I believe her. We had a good look round, all the same, but there was nothing there.'

Carmody grunted. 'What did you find in Warwick?'

'Kaminski *was* there on Tuesday – and Bliss was with him. The barman knows both of them, and he remembers them having a slanging match in the bar, says Steve was fit to be tied.'

'Was he now?' Seen together, and having a row into the bargain.

'We could stay on here a while, Sarge, find out where Bliss did his drinking, see what we can pick up. He lets himself go a bit when he's tanked up it seems, old Bliss, according to the chap that owns the shop. He may've let something slip about where he was going when he left here.'

'You do that, lad,' Carmody said after some thought. Tracing him was a priority. Bliss – or Halley, if you like – was at the moment the only known point of contact with the dead man they'd been able to fix on. 'If it's only a week since he departed hence, somebody's memory might still be functioning.'

Two faxed memos were brought to Abigail's desk on Wednesday morning, just as Mayo popped his head round her office door on his way upstairs.

She handed one to him. 'It looks as though this one can be put on hold.' The one she held stated that the Newcastle under Lyme police had been unable to trace any Charlton-Armstrong ever having practised medicine in the area, which seemed good enough to take as final. 'Of course, he didn't have to be a medical doctor,' she added. 'Could be a doctor of science, or philosophy –'

'Let's exhaust the medical profession first, shall we?' He read the one she'd given him. 'In any case, we appear to have hit the jackpot with this one from Newcastle upon Tyne.'

The police there had come up trumps in responding to the request for information. A Dr Thomas Charlton-Armstrong had been an ENT consultant in Newcastle General Hospital for many years, and had lived in a small coastal village some twenty miles from Newcastle from 1920 until his death in 1959. He'd had one daughter, named Venetia, born in the same year that he and his wife moved into the area.

'Venetia?' Mayo repeated. 'Old man Kaminski must've got it wrong. Venetia, Vanessa . . . it's near enough, for a bloke not yet speaking English like a native.'

The snag was that Newcastle had been able to find no trace of Venetia Charlton-Armstrong still living in the area. Further enquiries had revealed that she had, in fact, married just before the war, and moved away.

'Get back to them and see if you can prevail on them to look up the registers. Shouldn't be any problem, tracing the marriage, if they were married up there, Charlton-Armstrong's a distinctive enough name.'

Done that, said Abigail, who had already spoken nicely to the friendly Newcastle DC who'd undertaken the enquiries and sent the fax, and he'd promised to do what she asked.

'Good. If they can find out the name of the man she married, and where he came from, that could be where they went to live. One of them may still be alive, or they may have had children who are.'

'DC McLellan, Newcastle, ma'am,' came the soft Geordie voice. 'I've searched the registers and I've a bit more information for you.'

'You have? Go ahead.'

She took down the added information which he'd found out for her.

'Where did the man she married come from?'

'Leamington Spa. Not too far away from you, is it?'

'A good deal nearer home than Newcastle upon Tyne. Well, thanks a lot, Constable, you've been a great help.'

'Glad to be of assistance, ma'am.' He coughed and added diffidently, 'Another thing you might be interested to know. It seems somebody else was trying to trace the same person a couple of months ago.'

'Were they? That's encouraging, looks as though we're on the right track then.'

Encouraging, certainly. Except that the search for Venetia, or Vanessa, Charlton-Armstrong ended in Leamington Spa.

Reading through the careful report which Andy Spelman, detailed to make the Leamington enquiries and eager to make a good impression, had made on his progress so far, Abigail saw that Venetia and her new bridegroom had moved to Leamington from Newcastle. They had lived there for the rest of their lives. Both, however, were now dead, and had been for several years.

Impasse.

But Vanessa couldn't have been dead for years! What about that phone call Piotr Kaminiski had received from the ex-Waaf, Faye Dejmek? According to her, Vanessa had been very much alive when she'd written to her friend, a few months ago – unless it was a spoof, and the former Mrs Dejmek was playing some complicated game of her own, a remote possibility Abigail didn't want to acknowledge at this stage.

Somehow the trail to Vanessa seemed to have taken a wrong turning. Abigail was resigned to enquiries in which you came up against a blank wall, but she was unduly disappointed and frustrated in this one, having come so far. If the idea was accepted that Vanessa was the key to the murder of Stefan Karminski, it had seemed to follow that, having found her, the mish-mash of facts and suppositions would miraculously sort themselves out.

Then Spelman came in with his latest findings. It looked as though Leamington was not after all a terminus, but merely a stopping place. There was a son, still living.

Next stop, Warwick.

*   *   *

142

The view from the bridge across the Avon, of the loveliest castle in England, took Abigail's breath away. A brief glimpse of Warwick's great grey pile was all her driving allowed as she approached from Leamington, its towers and turrets rising romantically from the river mist, but she felt her spirits rise, as they always did at the sight.

There was this feeling you got, about old towns and cities, and Warwick, one of her favourite spots, was no exception. She parked her car near St Mary's church at the top of the High Street, within the boundaries of the old city walls, where the busy life of the present day continued in buildings old when Shakespeare was a lad. Over five hundred years ago, Robert Beauchamp had built an exquisite Perpendicular chapel in St Mary's. In the next century, Richard Neville, Earl of Warwick, 'Kingmaker', had attempted to turn the tide of history. Robert Dudley, Earl of Leicester, Elizabeth the First's 'sweet Robin', had named as the Lord Leycester hospital the timbered almshouses which still perched picturesquely above the road near the West Gate. Since then, not a lot of historical interest to the nation had happened in Warwick. It was still a good place.

She headed down the hill, her objective being a small but, she'd been assured, exclusive antique shop specialising in antique porcelain. Small, but not modest, she thought as she ducked her head under the lintel of a low-beamed doorway questionably bearing a stylised facsimile of the Warwick arms, the bear and the ragged staff, and entered a low-ceilinged, beautifully appointed shop, where porcelain glowed behind lighted glass cases set against white plaster between black beams. Other antiques stood about, and several of what appeared to be very nice oil paintings hung on the walls, but porcelain and china were evidently the mainstay of the business. The very best porcelain, no doubt – nothing about the place suggested anything but cost. A showroom rather than anything so commonplace as a shop.

She'd come unannounced, and found the owner engaged in conversation with a young man who didn't give the impression of being a customer. It wasn't a case of judging his ability to buy anything from that sort of shop by the standard of his dress, or his manner, though both might have given her reason for doing so, but rather that she was certain she'd interrupted two people who knew each other well in the middle of a not very friendly exchange.

They stopped immediately she came through the door and the owner summoned a professional smile as he came forward. She remembered the face, as Jenny had told her she would as soon as she saw it, though she hadn't been able to recall it from his name alone. She didn't often have the time to watch television.

'Paul Franklin?'

She presented her warrant card, which the man read and then raised his eyebrows comically. 'Lavenstock Police? Oh Lord, what have I been doing, exceeding the speed limit in a built-up area?'

'I don't know, have you? That isn't what I've come about, anyway. I'd like you to spare a little of your time, Mr Franklin, if you will, but I don't mind waiting until you've finished.' She smiled at the young man who was standing by, still simmering, and obviously not happy with her arrival.

'Oh, that's all right, we've finished, haven't we, Jago?'

'If you say so,' the young man answered, but the look he threw at the owner and the sidelong glance he gave Abigail before he left didn't accord with his words.

'Come into the back,' Paul Franklin said pleasantly as the door was pulled to, 'and I'll give you some coffee. I've just made some.'

He turned the 'Open' sign on the door to 'Closed' then pulled aside a velvet curtain for her to precede him into a back room at the foot of a flight of uncarpeted stairs used as a dumping ground, judging by the numerous bits and pieces stacked at the sides, presumably waiting to be carried up. The small back room was very different from the front premises, lit with a harsh fluorescent tube in the ceiling and evidently used as an office. There were a couple of chairs, filing cabinets, a small PC on his desk, several pictures standing on the floor and leaning against the wall. She remained silent while he fussed with the coffee maker. 'Now,' he said, 'I suggest you drink your coffee and tell me why you're here.'

The coffee was good: dark, rich and smooth, not unlike Paul Franklin himself. He handed her a plate of thin almond biscuits and she watched the way he stirred sugar into his own cup, the graceful way his long, beautifully manicured hands held the silver spoon, the elegant placing of the cup precisely into the saucer. She noticed the breadth of shoulder under the well-tailored jacket, the silk shirt that stretched across his chest, the dark-chinned face. The smile as he watched her watching him. She thought sharply, this one's a pseud. She said, 'We're looking into a case of arson and murder in Lavenstock last Tuesday. You may have heard something of it.'

'Sounds gruesome but no, I haven't. Lavenstock, that's a fair way off. Should I have heard?'

She ignored both comment and question, but she had tucked away that semi-jocular remark of his about speeding, and recalled that he hadn't seen the need to deny knowledge of Lavenstock then. 'We think the motive for this attack may go back a long way.'

'Well, I'm still mystified, but if you think I can be of any use, fire away. Another *tuile amande*?'

'No thanks. I'd like to ask you about your mother.'

His eyebrows rose but he barely missed a beat. 'My mother?'

'She was Venetia Charlton-Armstrong before her marriage?'

'Vee,' he said, and nodded. 'She was always called Vee.'

'Vee?'

'Short for Venetia. Her name was Venetia, but she hated it, thought it pretentious. She was always known as Vee.'

'Was she ever in the WAAF?'

'Good Lord, no! She was a married woman when the war broke out, and soon had an invalid husband and a child to look after. My father was wounded early in the war – in the evacuation at Dunkirk, as a matter of fact. He took years to recover and train to become a schoolmaster.'

'Do you know a man called Tadeusz Siemek?'

'No, I can't say I do.'

'Or Stefan, otherwise Steve, Kaminski?'

'They sound very like Polish names. They are? Sorry, I've never met any Poles in my life. Who are they?'

'Steve Kaminski is the man who was murdered and left in the house that was set on fire in Lavenstock.'

'How very bizarre. But may I ask why you're questioning me?'

'Your mother's name came up in connection with the case.'

'My *mother*?' His astonishment sounded genuine.

145

'Does the name Rayner Bliss mean anything to you?' He shook his head. 'Or J.J. Halley?'

The dark eyes flickered. 'No, Inspector, they do not, and I do not know any of these people you're asking about – Lavenstock isn't my stamping ground. I do go there occasionally, by way of business, but that's all.' He was lying in his teeth, about nearly everything, she thought, whatever the reason, though she was certain now that Venetia Charlton-Armstrong was not, after all, Vanessa. He was too wily to lie about something which could so easily – and would – be checked.

'And don't I have a right to know just how my mother is connected with this? Not to mention myself, and how you came to find me?'

'I'm sorry, I'm not at liberty to tell you, and I wouldn't want to worry you in any case about something that may turn out to be of no importance.'

It wouldn't do him any harm to sweat a bit. All friendliness had gone. He looked as though he regretted the coffee, not to mention his bloody *tuiles amande*. 'I shall worry more if I don't know.'

'I'm sorry,' she repeated, swallowing her own disappointment. 'There's no more I can tell you at the moment.' Abigail thanked him for his time and left him looking as worried as she hoped he was feeling.

Cecily sensed she was alone, that the presence was no longer sitting by her bedside. She felt a swell of triumph as she found herself capable of deducing that either the policewoman could no longer be spared from her duties or she herself wasn't ever expected to be able to speak coherently again. This last might well be so: she heard the words forming sentences in her brain, but when she tried to speak them aloud, they misunderstood her. They were pleased with her, though, they said so. You're doing splendidly, dear. We'll soon have you up and doing the polka.

She wasn't sure she wanted to be back in the real world, if that was how they were going to speak to her.

Perhaps she didn't deserve to live. Perhaps she'd been meant to die. She should have told Edgar what she intended to do . . .

but she'd been a coward, couldn't bear for him to know that she had deceived him. For over forty-five years. And because of it, she'd brought this on herself. Always headstrong, but vibrant and loving life . . . a good sport, they'd called her. She felt a small stir of rebellion. I always thought, when my time came, I'd be ready to go, but dear God, I'm not ready to leave yet . . .

We have left undone those things which we ought to have done . . . done those things which we ought not to have done . . . And there is no health in us.

It grew dark in here so quickly. She slept so much. Sometimes she was very confused. If you can hear me, God, don't let me be one of those vegetables they keep alive for years with modern technology, just to demonstrate that it can be done. But let me live . . .

What will Edgar do without me? Poor Edgar. So strong, he appears, yet so vulnerable.

12

'What did the hospital have to say this morning?' Kite asked Jenny, setting down a scalding plastic beaker of tea to cool, mindful of his brief to keep at least a watching eye on the progress of the Haldane case, however slow that was. On a desk adjoining hers he dumped a polythene bag, newly returned from the lab, its contents – everything that had been in Mrs Haldane's desk – having now been processed for fingerprints.

Jenny lifted her eyes from the screen of the computer where she was working. 'Oh, it sounds a bit better. The medics seem to think there's no reason to give up hope yet, though her age, of course, must be against her. She's opened her eyes and tried to speak, which is a very good sign, but they say it's early days yet.' She pressed the save key and swung round to face him, her pretty young face concerned. 'Apart from wanting the poor lady to get better for her own sake, it'd be great if she came to herself and could tell us who did it, wouldn't it?'

'We should be so lucky, even if she comes round. Look at that

Pole, Siemek. He doesn't remember a thing about being knocked down.'

Jenny nodded. 'Retrograde amnesia,' she informed him knowledgeably, feeling a little more disposed towards believing Tadeusz Siemek's story, now that she knew he hadn't been finagling.

Kite raised his eyebrows. 'I can see all this hospital liaison's going to your head.'

'She may remember everything, of course, amnesia doesn't always follow.' Jenny equably ignored the sarcasm. 'I guess she won't be feeling too good for a long time, though.'

'Not as bad as the ratbag responsible if I ever get my hands on him!'

The ratbag in question had made a 999 call, true, but then he'd scarpered without giving any details, callously left her lying there, an old woman unconscious and bleeding, possibly dying, for all he could have known.

Kite still didn't have the feeling that some casual thief had just walked in (though the vicarage doors, like the church doors at one time, were often left unlocked), had slapped Mrs Haldane around, duffed the place up and got the hell out of it; nor that it was the work of a seasoned villain. Any of the professional operators he could think of wouldn't have departed, even in a blind panic, without pocketing some of those small valuables, of which there were plenty lying around. It was possible, but on the whole his original hypothesis still looked to hold good to him: that someone had come to see Cecily Haldane by arrangement, for some reason things had gone wrong, and a quarrel had ensued. An amateur, but cool enough to take time before ringing for the ambulance to make it look like an attempted burglary. A professional would surely have made a more efficient job of it and trashed the place more. Nor would he have failed to remove the second coffee cup.

That coffee cup bothered Kite. The coffee tray had been ready, carefully prepared, suggesting at least a pretence at civility and discussion, but apparently the business had got out of hand before a drop could be poured.

He pulled out a chair that was too low to accommodate his length, stretched his lanky legs, sipped his own coffee and stared thoughtfully at the contents list of Cecily Haldane's desk. It wasn't a long list. It wasn't a very big desk, come to that, an antique writing desk suitable for a lady – a davenport, the canon had called it, the sort designed in the days when ladies needed desks only to write invitation acceptances, billets doux, or menus for the cook. Indeed, Mrs Haldane didn't seem to have used it for much more than that. Presumably most of her papers, things like birth certificates and insurances, a will perhaps, were kept elsewhere, but Kite didn't fairly feel he could ask to see them at this stage.

He opened the plastic bag and spread out what was in it: an address book, a small appointments diary, a few letters waiting to be answered, a current account bankbook with a tidy sum in it, bank statements showing nothing unusual in the way of transactions. She'd kept a careful account of her personal expenditure. In a clip were receipts and credit card slips for items of clothing and small purchases of various kinds, a hefty one from Interiors, the decorating shop, for two pictures.

Recognition came as Kite studied that particular receipt. So that was why the picture on the sitting-room wall at the vicarage had looked familiar! It was one painted by Alex Jones, there was one of a not dissimilar style by her on the walls of his own sitting-room. His eyes bulged when he caught sight of the prices. Hell's teeth! No wonder Sheila had failed to mention what it had cost.

Distracting himself forcibly from thoughts of his rising blood pressure and what, if anything, his wife might find to say to justify that sort of spending (he wouldn't have minded – well, not much – if she'd spent that on an outfit, but a picture!), he went back to reviewing the desk's contents: two small books of poetry, well thumbed, kept handy, as if Mrs Haldane read them often. A scribble pad with notes jotted on it for shopping. And from a tiddly-sized drawer that could have held little else, had come photographs of each of her children at about eight years old; also a cheap, enamelled brooch in the form of a butterfly, a heavy ring in some silvery metal, and a broken string of glass beads. Not the sort of jewellery he would have expected the elegant Mrs Haldane to choose for herself, perhaps presents from the children when they were small, the sort of things his lads had once bought for Sheila. Now they bought her heavy metal CDs in the hope (justified) that they would very soon find their way upstairs to their own rooms.

And that was the sum contents of the desk. Not a lot to go on.

He thumbed through the diary again, finding nothing new. Cecily Haldane's handwriting was truly awful, an impatient, thick black script, half Italic, half a kind of personal shorthand, with letters elided, i's undotted and t's uncrossed, the sort of indecipherable squiggles doctors assume to mystify any patient foolish enough to try and read his own prescription. He studied the notes against each appointment, abbreviated sometimes to illegibility. Evidence of an impatient nature or because the diary was one of those useless feminine affairs, not big enough for more than a narrow space a couple of inches across, for each day?

Ham 10	(Ham? No, hair, 10 o'clock)
Rosm ~rp 3	(Rosemary, approximately 3 o'clock?)
Dentist 930	(OK, Dentist)
Cvn 7d~1 r●	(Coventry Cathedral with Edgar? A long shot, but possible)

And so on. There were also ticks and crosses and highlights on certain dates, and presumably these had meant something to her. On the day she'd been attacked there was simply an asterisk in red biro, nothing else. Pity she hadn't put even an initial against it. It seemed obvious to Kite that it marked the appointment with her attacker. 'Why the devil do women use these hieroglyphs in their diaries?' he demanded irritably. 'Men never do.'

'I know why I do,' Jenny said. 'Use your loaf.'

Kite rolled his eyes. '*If* we could be serious for half a second.'

'I find that very serious. But it wouldn't apply to Mrs Haldane, her age.'

Kite rocked back in his chair and gazed thoughtfully through the open door at the paraphernalia of what was being called the Steve K. enquiry, in the next room. In one way or another, he'd managed to keep tabs on most of what was going on there, even before his official assignment to the case, and this morning he'd attended the daily briefing and brought himself up to speed.

Nothing new had emerged. Farrar's enquiries in Coventry about Bliss had drawn another blank, apart from the fact that Bliss had been talking of selling his car, an old Escort, hinting he was shortly expecting to be in the market for the latest model Merc.

Not that there was anything surprising in this, they never learned, villains. Big spenders the instant they and money made contact. Scattering the proceeds of a job on new cars, women, dope, whatever put colour in their cheeks. Living it up like money was going out of fashion, never a thought of keeping a low profile until the heat was off. Never mind that was how they often got caught. Not Bliss, though, not yet. He'd gone to ground, and neither hide nor hair of him had been seen.

Kite's eyes rested on a diagram he'd watched Mayo construct, drawn on a blackboard they must now call a chalkboard, since black was not PC and it was green anyway. And wham! It hit him. He peered at the list of names again, then began to sift through the pile of Cecily Haldane's effects until he came to the scribbling pad. And knew, with that leap of intuition which was characteristic of him, that he'd come across the break they needed so badly.

For yes, the note thereon, in Cecily Haldane's diabolical hand-writing, suddenly made sense to him, in conjunction with those names he'd been staring at on the board. What he'd taken to be the beginning of a shopping list, starting with Honey, or maybe Money (as in draw from the bank), followed by Jersey (as in woolly, to be purchased, maybe) now read – of course! – Halley – and *Jerzy*! J.J. Halley, and Jerzy, pronounced Yerzy. Which was why the conjunction hadn't occurred to him before.

His impatience and boredom magically dissolved, he assessed the options, his certainties growing.

His car was a seventeen-year-old Rover, and it was unwise to expect too much of it, but Edgar Haldane rarely drove above forty – fifty if he was feeling adventurous, though that was pushing it. A habit not calculated to endear him to other, more impatient, road users. Today he was driving erratically, as well, unaware of the hooting around him, his heart heavy.

He'd been out since early this Thursday morning, driving

151

north, and was nearing his destination when he spotted the romantic ruin of Bolsover Castle on a distant scarp overlooking the motorway, dramatic against the skyline. The sight transported him back to those faraway days and the long walks over those rolling Derbyshire hills which lay to his left, under the wide skies, sometimes with Cecily, more often alone. On an impulse, he took the next exit and drove up towards them.

It was another blowy autumn day, rain on the air, but he had time. To stop and walk for a few miles, letting the fresh air blow through his head, clearing his mind. It was territory he knew well, from those long walks, tramping across the moors, a sandwich for lunch and a book in his pocket to read while eating it. Today, he felt that out there, in those wide spaces, he could prepare himself for the rest of what he had set out to do. That accomplished, he could return home, filled with a new courage, and face whatever was demanded of him.

Julia had arranged to meet Olivia by the Cornmarket and walk up to the hospital with her, mainly because she wanted an opportunity to speak to her sister alone. She'd left the office rather earlier than she'd had need to, and finding she'd plenty of time dawdled along, shop-window gazing, always a favourite occupation. Her eye was caught by a delicious pair of bottle-green suede shoes in Russell and Bromley's window. When she saw they were a hundred and eighty-five pounds, she quickly diverted her attention elsewhere. But her eyes kept straying back. A pair of new shoes cheered her up like nothing else, and God knows she needed cheering. And they were gorgeous, they'd flatter her small feet, make her legs look longer, not to mention going a treat with the subtle bluey-green of that new suit Mark had eyed so appreciatively. The sort of sexy shoes he used to like her to wear.

Mark? What were bottle-green suede shoes to him? Or to her? However much they might turn him on. She spun smartly away and walked quickly towards the Cornmarket, her briefcase inexplicably weighing her down all of a sudden.

She was glad to put it down as she waited for Olivia outside Interiors, gazing while she waited at the display of household goods and other covetable objects you didn't know you wanted until you saw them. She was going to have to start this furnishing lark all over again, as soon as she found a decent place to live, but somehow the thought of it wasn't exactly thrilling, not after the fun and satisfaction of furnishing the Melia Road house ... *Don't*, she told herself, just don't think about it.

This was where Alex Jones worked, wasn't it? Not the sort of place you'd automatically have associated with her. Julia had liked her, and the humorous approach she had to starting what virtually amounted to a new career, mid-life, never an easy thing to contemplate. Not expecting too much but, knowing she had a lot to offer, not going to be content with being overlooked, either. Julia had admired the courage, thought the liking was mutual, knew they could work harmoniously and, since she was still so new in the job herself, pretty much learn the ropes together as they went along. It was an idea that cheered her a little and made her feel that her life couldn't continue being so downbeat. As soon as their mother got better, and that, thank God, was now becoming a distinct possibility –

'Gosh!' came Olivia's voice breathlessly behind her. 'What a rush! Couldn't find anywhere to park, I should've gone straight to the hospital.'

'You wouldn't have found any spaces there though, would you?' Lavenstock General's lengthy refurbishment had finally been completed, resulting in much-needed new wards which had been built out on to the old car-park, with the result that parking facilities for visitors were extremely limited. It seemed churlish to complain.

'I suppose Pa's already there?' she asked as they walked up the hill.

'I suppose he must be. I popped into the church and Mavis Snell was looking for him, says she hasn't seen him all day.'

Julia dared to ask what the situation was with Robert.

'Oh, that!' Olivia said, the heat in her face not entirely due to the exertion of walking up the hill. She was panting, and told herself she really, really *would* go on that diet. As soon as Ma was better. She didn't, after all, need comfort food now that she'd had it all out with Robert and found that it had all been in her imagination, that business about that office dolly-bird. She'd been a bit down, that was all. 'Storm in a teacup, nothing more.'

'Well, good,' Julia said, somewhat dryly, wishing she could so easily throw off her own malaise. Storm in a teacup, indeed, what had all the drama been about, then? It all seemed so trivial until, unexpectedly, she found herself wondering if that was how her own falling out with Mark seemed to other people. If perhaps it *was* trivial and unnecessary, and if Mark wasn't right in wanting to start again . . .

They hadn't, after all, made much progress in sorting out their affairs when they'd met. After talking and talking about what seemed to Julia that inexplicable action of her mother's in presenting those papers to Mark, they'd abandoned, by mutual consent, the task of going through the house (that's mine, birthday present from my friend Jane . . . the bookcase is yours, bought with your bonus last year . . . that cutlery, a house-warming present, how to split that up?). It was late, and he'd suggested a meal. Not Gianelli's, *their* Italian restaurant, just around the corner. No. The pub would do. Over a questionable goulash, when there was no escape other than running for the door, he'd asked, outright and intently, if they couldn't give it one more try, and she'd replied tartly that he'd had his chance, once. For a moment, he'd sounded savage. 'For Chrissake, Julia, haven't you ever made one mistake in your life? Don't you know the meaning of forgiveness?'

She threw off these disruptive thoughts, forcing herself to remember the reason she was here, that she'd contrived this opportunity to speak to Olivia alone, determined to get to the bottom of those hints she'd been throwing about all over the place.

'What's all this business about you and Jago, then?'

She'd hardly got the words out of her mouth when they were joined by one of the Holy Trinity parishioners, a middle-aged man whose wife was also a patient in the hospital. He was obviously deeply worried about her, poor man, trying to be optimistic, and in such desperate need of someone to talk to that it was impossible not to try and reassure him. He stayed with them until they reached the point in the hospital where the arrows on the floor, a visual aid without which it was impossible for disorientated visitors to find their way, divided their paths at the entrance to the wing where Cecily was, and the opportunity for further conversation with Olivia was lost.

*   *   *

It was the sort of quantum leap of intuition for which Kite was famous, that didn't always work, though this time looked as though it might. And suddenly, a sense of urgency pervaded the entire station, an optimism that energised the whole enquiry. The pendulum had started to swing and things could move fast from here on.

'Yes,' said Mayo. 'Why didn't it occur to us before?' Useless question, rhetorical, expecting no answer, not getting one, either. There'd been nothing to connect the two cases after all, two apparently unrelated events happening on the same day. Still wasn't, in the way of hard evidence.

Should've suspected, though. Somehow. Same day, same town. As usual, Mayo blamed himself when this sort of obvious concurrence made itself manifest, as if by some process of osmosis he should have known.

He said, however, playing devil's advocate, as much for himself as anyone else, seeing a pattern and not altogether liking where it was going, 'We've no proof, it's all supposition. Without jumping the gun here, we need to establish more. What do we have, apart from a *possible* connection between Mrs Haldane and Jerzy Siemek – and *possibly* Halley, Bliss, whatever he's calling himself?'

'The name Charlton-Armstrong, which led us to Paul Franklin. Plus she has a son called Jago, who was in Paul Franklin's shop,' Abigail answered, frowning.

'So what's Paul Franklin's connection with the affair?'

'His mother was Venetia Charlton-Armstrong, now dead, who was never in the WAAF. But Vanessa was called Charlton-Armstrong, according to old Kaminski, came from the same place, so it's possible they were related. If Cecily was a Waaf, we're there,' said Kite.

'And supposing she is Vanessa, and *does* have the Klee, where does that leave us?'

Abigail was fingering the broken string of cheap beads, looking at the brooch, the heavy ring. Sentimental keepsakes perhaps, commonplace trifles having so much more value to their owner than their intrinsic worth. This was why people found burglaries so upsetting: a woman might lose her diamonds and pearls in a robbery, but mourn the loss of a child's locket a hundred times more. She slipped the ring on her finger. It slid about, much too big, a man's ring. The butterfly brooch was obviously not of any monetary value, and its pin had become a little rusty; but it was pretty, gilt, with wings enamelled in purple, edged with creamy yellow. Fashion had come round full circle, and this sort of thing was in vogue again.

Kite, concentrated, all his energies pointed in one direction, said, 'If Mrs Haldane is the woman we're looking for, it could all make up into a neat package – except, of course, for the little matter of Steve K. getting himself fried. The man to talk to is Canon Haldane.'

'Always assuming he knows anything,' Mayo objected. 'These wartime affairs – if that's what it was with the Polish flyer – all very romantic, but she'd very likely have kept it to herself afterwards, wouldn't have wanted it known. Married to a clergy-man, at that.'

'Of course Cecily's Vanessa, she has to be,' Abigail interrupted suddenly. The thing that had triggered her intuition became clear as she smoothed the cool metal of the brooch. 'Vanessa's a species of butterfly, isn't it?'

'Is it? If you say so,' Kite was looking at her doubtfully, Mayo too.

'Yes, it is, I had a school-book – my Mum might still have it, but anyway . . . My guess is that Jerzy called her Vanessa for some reason, a pet name maybe, and that's why he bought her this brooch – why she's kept it all these years.'

'A bit screwy, calling her after a *butterfly*, huh?'

'Maybe he just didn't like the name Cecily. Perhaps it means something not very nice in Polish . . . I don't know. But I'll bet I'm right.'

There was a thoughtful silence.

Later, after further discussion, Mayo decided that Canon Haldane's assistance would have to be sought, and Kite rang through to the vicarage. He asked for the canon and then listened in silence for some time. A few terse questions and then he rang off, saying he'd be round there shortly. He turned to the others.

'We may be in difficulty. It seems nobody's seen Mr Haldane since late last night.'

Olivia and Julia parted at the spot where Olivia had left her car. They kissed and hugged each other briefly as they said good-night, knowing they'd see each other the following day, too heartsick over the despondent vigil at their mother's bedside to talk much. Olivia sat behind the wheel of her Discovery and rather guiltily watched Julia walk away towards her office car-park, sorry that she'd been so abrupt with her earlier in the evening. After all, Julia had only been showing concern, as well she might after that idiotic way she, Olivia, had burst into tears over Robert. Had Mr Thomson not joined them just before they reached the hospital, she might have explained.

On the other hand, she might not. She was still edgy over last night's encounter with Robert – though no longer feeling jealous over that girl in the office. His outrage and astonishment when she'd confronted him with that, when all her uncertainties had come out, had been genuine enough to convince her that any suspicions had been unworthy, and only in her own mind.

'I'm surrounded by clever women at the office. I don't want any of them. It's you I want, Liv, as I always have,' he said at last, which in the end had made them both smile, and brought her an overwhelming sense of relief. So much so that she'd finally been able to broach the subject of Jago. Which had been a mistake.

'Time to let him grow up, Liv,' he'd said in his gentle way, but not smiling now, quite angry underneath. 'Time to take a good look at yourself, give yourself – and me – a chance.' There was quite a bit more in the same vein.

She drove through the dark tunnel of trees, seeing the lights of the village ahead. You don't really believe he meant all those things he said, do you? she asked herself. But of course, she did. People say, 'I didn't mean that,' when they speak in anger, but that's often the one time when the truth of what they're *really* feeling comes out. Robert must have been thinking those things about her and Jago for a long time.

Of course he was wrong. It wasn't like that at *all*. If only he'd let her finish what she'd started to tell him, one part of her thought. While another part was very glad indeed that he hadn't.

Kite's car was already drawn up by the kerb when Mayo arrived at Folgate Street, just as the church clock was chiming a musical six thirty. Deciding to give the inspector the benefit of a little more time to get the relevant facts established before walking in on the interview, he crossed to the church and tried the door. He found it unlocked and, when he entered, empty.

Yet, although he couldn't discern anyone in the dim interior, he thought someone must be around, somewhere: tall, fat candles were lit, the flames wavering and flickering on to the great, richly coloured wall painting forming the reredos behind the high altar, and sending leaping shadows into the corners of a vaulted ceiling. An ornately embroidered altar frontal glowed gold on green, and a ruby sanctuary lamp winked and reflected itself several times over in brass wall-tablets.

His footsteps rang on the stone-flagged floor, polished by thousands and thousands of feet across eight hundred years. He took a seat in a back pew. It wasn't a church he was familiar with, and he gazed around the great interior with interest, at the Norman arches forming an arcade along the north wall, lifting his eyes again to the wondrous ceiling, his senses assailed by the smell of ancient stone and plaster, wax candles and the bitter sweet tang of chrysanthemums which issued from the huge professional-looking arrangement of autumn flowers, foliage and berries at the foot of the lectern.

He was glad to sit quietly for a while, feeling keyed up, as always when a case was on the verge of opening out, when he was on the brink of knowing what had happened, what past events had caused the recent tragedies which had disrupted so many lives. The past is another country, Piotr Kaminski had said ... but it cannot be separated from the present. He thought about Canon Haldane, the keeper and custodian of this Christian place and all the souls who came under his care, and why he had disappeared. A righteous, well-loved man, beyond reproach. He thought of all the other equally honest, upright and law-abiding people who had over the centuries sat here nursing their own sins and secrets, their own problems. He found himself asking that he might fit all the pieces, already there, into their appropriate places in the overall pattern before another tragedy took place. The unlooked-for thought disturbed him and he let the silence of the building help his subconscious mind tell him why. Time passed, but he was vouchsafed no understanding.

At last, he noticed a movement in one of the front pews and saw that a woman who had been kneeling there unobserved by him had risen, genuflected towards the altar and was now approaching him.

Mayo was still old-fashioned enough to be surprised by a woman in a dog-collar, a nice-looking, fresh-faced woman of about thirty who spoke sensibly and calmly about the canon's apparent disappearance after they had introduced themselves.

'He's a dear, kind man, but too hard on himself,' Mavis Snell said. 'I saw him here in church, about nine last night. I noticed a light on as I was passing, thought it must be him and dropped in to ask how Mrs Haldane was. He told me that they seemed to think she was very slightly better.'

'Did he seem quite as usual?'

'No different from what he's been like ever since Mrs Haldane was assaulted ... which is to say, he certainly hasn't been himself at all, as you might expect. He seemed all right when I spoke to him, but perhaps I didn't pay enough attention, because I was in a hurry. I have two children,' she said, surprising him again, 'and one of them has measles. My husband's an airline pilot and had to be at Birmingham airport by ten.'

'And Mrs Haldane? What has she been like recently? Would you have known if she'd seemed worried?'

Mrs Snell hesitated. 'Frankly, no,' she said at last. 'She seemed her usual self, charming, you know, amusing, wry. But then, I wouldn't say I really *knew* her – she wasn't the sort to load her troubles on to other people.' She sighed. 'Which is usually regarded as an admirable trait, but it isn't always, is it? No one can help you if they don't know you need it. Though of course, if that was a random attack on her, that wouldn't apply.'

'So there wouldn't seem any reason why Mr Haldane should have gone off like this?'

'None at all, that I can see. But his memory's not too reliable these days. He may have suddenly remembered something he should have done, and forgotten to leave a note. But I'll admit I'm rather worried that he's driving. He's not used to it, you see – Mrs Haldane used to chauffeur him when he had to use his car.'

Kite was having difficulty with his questioning of Mrs Faber, the Haldanes' eldest daughter, who'd apparently come over hot-foot from Brome village where she lived, the moment she heard the news about her father. Kite knew her sort: bossy, well-intentioned women who ran the village fête and the Over 60s

159

and Meals on Wheels and – in this case, at any rate – went to pieces in a crisis. A plump woman with a lot of shiny dark hair and flashing brown eyes, and a voice that panic was causing to rise to an unnerving whinny. Very handsome, if you liked that sort of thing. She made him think of a nervous horse.

She was making a big production out of what might after all turn out be nothing much that Kite could see: the canon had spoken to his assistant, Mavis Snell, last night, and then taken his car and left the house early in the morning, without telling anyone where he was going. No big deal, said Kite to himself, the poor devil was surrounded by women, perhaps he just needed to get away for the day.

And yet . . . with hindsight, that useful concomitant to logical reasoning, looking back to their first meeting, when he had come to the vicarage and found it ransacked, he had begun to feel disquieted, recalling that on that occasion he had been sure that Canon Haldane had been hiding something – and not finding it easy to do. Kite guessed Mr Haldane was normally a truthful man, as one might expect a man of the cloth to be – but expectations weren't always lived up to. There were probably as many rogues in the church as out of it – more, if one believed certain sections of the Sunday press. Maybe things had just got too much for him.

Julia Haldane, who had been watching him, spoke for the first time. 'You must understand we're not making a fuss over nothing. He was supposed to take early service this morning and just didn't appear. That's so out of character, we've every reason to be worried.'

Unlike her sister, she spoke quietly, but her anxiety carried all the more weight for that. Dressed in a dark lawyerly business suit which emphasised her paleness, she was calm, though obviously worried. She seemed a sensible woman. 'What's more, he's taken his car,' she added, and went on in response to Kite's questioning look, 'He's nearly eighty, and never has been, I have to say, a very good driver.'

Kite had been taken into the sitting-room, now restored from the disorderly chaos of his last visit. It was only Mrs Faber who seemed on the verge of hysterics, though give her her due, she was now trying her best to control it, to pull herself together. When a ring came at the door, she was the one who went to answer it. She came back with a dark young man who crossed the room in two strides and took Julia Haldane in his arms.

'Oh, Mark!' Julia said with heartfelt feeling, her determined calmness abruptly deserting her, her eyes filling with tears. 'I'm so *glad* you could come!'

Scarcely had the newcomer, who Kite thought was looking as though his birthday had arrived six months early, been introduced as Mark Fry, another solicitor, than the bell rang once more and this time, it was Mayo. Kite was more than glad to see him amongst all this family solidarity.

Mayo could see immediately that there was a great deal of tension between them all, and he couldn't dismiss the feeling that it was perhaps generated by more than the fact of their father being missing. If so, he surmised that none of them would be prepared to talk easily.

Kite gave him a quick summary of the relevant facts, from which he deduced that Canon Haldane had insisted, despite his daughters' wishes to the contrary, on staying here alone since his wife had been in hospital: Olivia, the elder daughter, who lived with her family out at Brome, was busy blaming herself for allowing this; the other, Julia, a different kettle of fish, lived in Wolverhampton, although she was working with the CPS here in Lavenstock. Neither of them had spoken to their father, they said, since early last evening, when Julia had left him after accompanying him home from Cecily's bedside. Mayo watched Julia as she spoke, with an interest not wholly to do with the present situation, and liked what he saw: a small, neat woman with fair hair, grey-green eyes and level dark brows, not inclined to be panic-stricken. It pleased him to note that at least Alex would be working with someone intelligent and of her own cut. Though someone, he thought, who was less tough than she tried to appear.

He said, 'We've put out a call for your father's car. If he's seen, we shall be notified at once. I have to tell you, though, that there may be reasons you don't know about yet connected with his absence.'

That drew the attention of all three. 'Such as?' Olivia demanded.

'We now have reason to believe the attack on your mother may have been in some way linked to the death of a man named

Stefan Kaminski, who died in the fire in Bessemer Street last week, which you've doubtless read about.'

A slightly stunned silence followed this announcement.

'Perhaps you'd like to tell us why you've made this connection,' said Mark Fry, after a glance at Julia which in part seemed to ask permission to speak, but also transmitted some message that couldn't be spoken, some strong current of feeling.

Mayo said, 'I may be able to explain that better after I have the answer to a few questions, if you'd allow me? Good. Firstly, what was your mother's maiden name?'

'Charlton-Armstrong,' said Olivia, 'though I can't see –'

'And during the war, she served in the WAAF?'

'Yes,' Julia said.

'Did she ever speak of knowing a Polish airman by the name of Jerzy Siemek at that time?'

'No, though it's possible she did know someone like that, I suppose.' Julia exchanged another long, slow look with Mark. 'She was always interested in anything Polish – music, you know, and food. She sometimes helped at the Polish club, though as far as I know she's never been to Poland.' She paused.

As far as I know. But how far do I – any of us – know my mother?

Olivia, Julia saw, was looking even more wretched than before. 'A *Pole*?' she repeated. She fidgeted uneasily with a length of strung-together amber pieces which hung around her neck and lay along her bosom, and her lips trembled.

'Tell me, what is this family's connection with Paul Franklin?' Mayo asked abruptly.

'We're second cousins. Paul's mother, Vee, was our mother's first cousin – well, they were more like sisters, really, they were brought up together, and we always called her our aunt.'

'Brought up in Newcastle upon Tyne?'

'As a matter of fact, yes, after Mother's parents died she went up there from Camberwell, where she was born.'

'Camberwell? I see.' The superintendent paused and looked down at his notes, and Julia, noticing the almost imperceptible smile that tugged at the corners of his mouth, wondered why he should find that amusing.

'What is all this?' Mark decided to ask.

162

'Bear with me and I'll explain.' Mayo rested his grave eyes on Julia. No trace of amusement now.

And then came an extraordinary revelation: the possible existence of the Klee painting, Cecily's silence regarding it for over fifty years, and the reasons for the resurrected interest in its whereabouts. The superintendent spoke with authority, but objectively, yet she was aware that he was watching them all carefully. He finished by telling them of the fire, and the man with the Polish name who'd died in it.

'Well,' said Julia, after they'd heard him out, 'one thing I can tell you . . . my mother never mentioned anything *at all* of any of this, not to me.' She looked at Olivia, but got no response. 'A Paul Klee? Hidden all this time? Are you sure? You must admit, a thing like that takes some believing. What's wrong, Liv?'

Olivia's head was bent and a wing of dark hair fell across her face. She brushed it aside and looked up, a flush deepening her already vivid colouring. 'Oh, nothing.'

'Mrs Faber.'

'Really, it's nothing.' Her mouth set obstinately.

'Liv, don't be so maddening. It may be important.'

'Of course it isn't.' She shrugged. 'It was just . . . well, mentioning Poland, it made me think of Dani Lepszy, a friend of my daughter's, that's all.'

'And Jago's current girlfriend,' Julia said, and Mayo saw the look Olivia shot her.

'We know Miss Lepszy. She's been helping us with the Siemek children. It might be as well if we spoke to your brother, Mrs Faber. Where can we get in touch with him?'

She answered reluctantly, 'There's the phone number of the flat he's using here, but he works in London and I think he must have gone in today. I tried to get hold of him this morning to tell him about Father, but he wasn't there.'

'His London telephone number will do.' Kite made a note of it and stood up at Mayo's signal that they were ready to leave.

'Just a minute,' Julia said. 'Before you go, I think you ought to take a look at this.' She dived into the depths of the huge leather satchel which lay on the floor at her feet. After a moment she produced several sheets of oiled silk, folded into a pad. 'This is in Polish, too, but there's a translation clipped behind that

Mark's had done. My mother asked him to look into it a couple of weeks ago. I can't really think it's a coincidence. They're the deeds for what appears to be a substantial property, just outside Krakow.'

Mark was standing by the window, and glanced out even as Julia spoke. 'There's no need to telephone Jago. He's here now.'

And then Jago was in the room, a dishevelled figure in cords and open-necked shirt, a baggy sweater.

13

It seemed to Jago that the last two days had been the longest of his life. Starting with breakfast on Wednesday.

His coffee had grown cold. His croissant was leathery, due to being seriously overheated in the state of the art microwave which sat on the counter in Rodney Brightman's state of the art flat. Jago was suitably grateful to Rodney, presently on a six months' sabbatical, for the loan of the flat. He'd presumably gone to a good deal of trouble to create this minimalist, open plan interior, chrome and glass, black and white. But Jago contemplated both decor and breakfast without appetite. He tipped the croissant into the waste bin and the coffee down the sink, then decided to make more: a simple enough operation when it only meant instant coffee granules and boiling water, leaving the state of the art coffee machine strictly alone, though the result wasn't an experience to savour and enjoy. Just about his level, it was. He'd never seemed to get the hang of this domestic lark, somehow, even at the expense of making life more comfortable for himself. A philosophy that applied to all areas of his life except his professional one. It wasn't the first time this thought had occurred to him, but it was the first time it had really bothered him.

He'd made a right cock-up of things, this time. Worse than usual. He could have borne this without too much heart-searching, had it not been that now, oh God, now it had gone a mile too far. So far that he couldn't bear to consider the consequences. He groaned and buried his face in his hands, unnoticing as the second mug of coffee grew cold.

He wished little Dani were here. She could be guaranteed to lift his spirits, never before in his life at such a low ebb. But he rather thought he'd better duck out of that one and not see her again. He was sorry he'd used her so unthinkingly, deliberately sought her out and cultivated her, simply because she spoke Polish. He was even more sorry, desperately sorry, that he'd agreed to put so much as a toe into the whole appalling business. But it was far too late for regrets. If his mother died . . . his eyes burned with unshed tears, and he found himself praying, for the first time in many years. It came to him that his father would have rejoiced to see it.

The doorbell rang. He sloped down the stairs to answer and found Paul Franklin on the doorstep. A bleary-looking Paul who stumbled up the stairs behind Jago and dropped as if featherlegged into one of the low-slung leather armchairs, which gave out a rude noise.

'Coffee?' Jago asked, picking up the Nescafé. It only occurred to him when he had to repeat the question twice that Paul might be drunk – if not completely, then well on the way. Paul looked at the jar, shuddered and shook his head. Not *so* drunk then! But Paul being even a little bit squiffy was so unusual as to cause alarm bells to ring. He was always far too careful of himself and the impression he made on other people to let drink, or anything else, overrule his actions and emotions.

'What's wrong?'

'Everything. That woman you saw in the shop yesterday, she was a detective. They're on to us, Jago, my friend.'

This was what Jago had been fearing since then, though he hadn't expected that Paul, previously so cock-a-hoop about the whole affair, would collapse like a pricked balloon at the first sign of trouble. It was odd that he himself felt nothing except a weary kind of relief that now, sooner or later, all this would be over. He'd been aware almost from the beginning that he never should have agreed to be involved. But he'd convinced himself that Tadeusz Siemek had a moral right to the picture, and shut his eyes to every other consideration. And then it had all gone damnably, wretchedly wrong. He and Paul, not to mention Siemek, had let themselves be taken in by a pair of minor league crooks – no, thugs, he amended – prepared to attack an old woman and leave her for dead, though one of them, at least, had got his comeuppance. Jago had never dreamed the affair would get so wildly out of hand. It had caused a row yesterday, in Paul's shop, when he'd blamed Paul bitterly for ever having approached him – or as much of a row as Jago ever allowed: though it rarely surfaced, he had the Haldane temper and was sometimes afraid of himself.

'Find me someone who can speak and write Polish,' Paul had said, months ago. 'Promise you'll give your opinion on the painting when we get hold of it, and that's all I ask.' He had implied that there would be money in it for Jago, but Jago didn't want money. If the picture rightfully belonged to Siemek, then that was all right by him. He was far more excited by the prospect of the discovery of an actual, hitherto undiscovered Paul Klee.

Jago was basically honest and fair-minded, that is to say that's how he would have described himself if he'd ever given such matters any thought. But he was not inclined to philosophical concepts, he meandered through life, taking things as they came, asking no more than to be allowed to live and work amidst the world's art treasures. He was acknowledged as an expert in several fields, yet he'd once overheard it said that he'd reached the limits of his professional attainments. This hurt, but he knew what it was: he lacked the aggression necessary for internal politicking.

Except on the occasions when he'd rouse himself to defend an opinion: he was rarely wrong where his work was concerned. He sometimes thought that was the only thing which made him come really and truly alive. He'd never been able to paint or draw, himself. But always, as far back as he could remember, he'd had this ability to know and recognise what was true and genuine and good in the work of those who could. The natural, critical sensibilities he'd been born with had been refined and honed by his studies: *Look, look and look again,* he'd been told. *Notice and remember, see how it's been done, and why, what the artist is trying to say, what emotion he succeeds in arousing in the viewer.* He *had* looked, with his eyes and his heart and his mind, at the great art of the world, until seeing and knowing had become second nature. The idea of his mother possessing such a thing as

166

an original Expressionist painting had at first seemed incredible to him; in fact, he was ninety-nine per cent certain in his mind that it was impossible. But it was that one per cent of doubt, the itch to know the truth, which had finally overcome any scruples he might have had. He had been inclined, at first, simply to confront his mother, but he knew her well enough to realise that if she *did* own it, and had deemed it necessary to keep it secret for so long, she must have had some compelling reason. More than that, she was unlikely to give it up just for the asking. The story that had been relayed to him of how she'd allegedly come into possession of it was, after all, not all that incredible: he'd heard too many of the bizarre but nevertheless true accounts which circulated in the art world about lost masterpieces and undiscovered geniuses to dismiss it out of hand. The fact that his own mother was involved was the only bizarre thing about it, but the explanation Paul had given had seemed plausible enough for him to suspend disbelief. He hadn't bothered to think it through, otherwise he might have seen it for the fiasco it had turned out to be.

It had started, for Paul, the first time J.J. Halley had walked into his shop, short and plump, a flash Harry in a blazer and a loud tie, not looking at all like the art collector he professed to be, but Paul had learned not to judge, they came in all guises. Probably some garage owner, he'd decided, as Bliss's accent occasionally slipped from painfully middle-class into a more natural Cockney, but money was money, whether it was new or old. He had lingered in the shop, and invited Paul to join him for dinner at his hotel to discuss possible acquisitions of paintings. Antennae twitching, Paul had agreed. During the course of an excellent meal, the conversation had turned to Paul Klee, about whom Halley did indeed demonstrate a superficial knowledge – more, in truth, than Paul's own. Paul had admitted that modern art was something outside his ken, and Halley turned the conversation into more general channels.

It was only gradually that Paul became aware that the probing had become more personal, albeit in a roundabout route, by way of some reference to the last war, and he began to have an inkling that something rather more than he'd expected was afoot. Had Paul's mother ever been in the WAAF? Had she lived when she was younger in Newcastle upon Tyne? No, to the first question, but his aunt had been a Waaf, Paul had answered incautiously. His mother's cousin, to be precise, now Mrs Cecily Haldane, wife of a cleric in Lavenstock. They had both lived near Newcastle as children, lived together in fact, been brought up more as sisters than cousins, Cecily having been orphaned at an early age and taken into Vee's family.

And then Halley had mentioned his associate Steve Kaminski, and the tale he had heard from his father. Afterwards, Halley had come out with the proposition, seemingly preposterous at first, for this son of Jerzy Siemek's to be persuaded to come to England and convince Cecily that he was the rightful owner of the Klee. Once in his possession, it would be sold and the proceeds shared out. There was a flaw, perhaps several, in this somewhere but Paul had never pursued it. Nor did Jago, who was brought in and enlisted Dani's help in the translation of letters to some person in Poland whose name she wasn't given.

The plan hadn't gone quite as expected. The Pole was dragging his feet, Halley reported, unwilling to come to England without more assurances. Finally, however, he had agreed, and Halley had arranged temporary accommodation for him in Lavenstock. Nothing fancy, he'd said, they must all keep a low profile. He had written a letter in English for Siemek to copy and send to Cecily, introducing himself as Jerzy's son and asking for a meeting. From then on, the whole ill-conceived operation had gone awry, ending with Steve Kaminski dead, and Cecily's life hanging by a thread. How could it all have gone so woefully, spectacularly amiss?

'We've been had for a pair of fools, haven't we?' he'd said bitterly to Paul. 'Never mind that we haven't actually done anything. Nothing illegal, that is.'

Paul didn't reply. He slouched back in the chair, dressed as flamboyantly as usual, today in that mulberry affair which made Jago wince – it would have taken an earthquake for Paul to be careless about his dress. But perhaps there had been an earthquake of sorts, for he'd forgotten to shave, something no dark-chinned man can afford to do, and looked villainous. Paul omitting to shave – that really said something. He looked . . . well, rough was the only word for it. And he had been drinking, undoubtedly. He began to laugh, and once started he could hardly stop. Finally, he said, chokingly, 'Oh, nothing illegal! That's rich, that is!'

'What are you talking about?'

'She rang me and asked me to come and see her, the day of the fire,' he said.

'Who did?'

'Cecily, of course. *Your mother.* Something she wanted to tell me. I imagined she'd got wind that I was concerned with trying to get hold of the Klee, I couldn't think how, but I dropped everything and went. But it wasn't the damned picture, not then, at any rate . . . she said there was something she wanted to get off her chest, something she should have told me years ago . . . went on and on, letting the coffee go cold . . . all about the war, and her in the WAAF, and Jerzy Siemek . . . oh, God, what the hell am I going to do?'

'You're not making a lot of sense, Paul. Have some coffee.'

'Well, that's the gist of it, anyway. I couldn't make a lot of sense out of him.' His big frame sank into the soft embrace of the amber velvet armchair he'd made a beeline for. 'But it's a relief to have got it off my chest,' he admitted with a diffident grin, as if absolved. He raked his hand through the hair that flopped over one eye, turned from one sister to another, but Olivia was looking horror-struck, Julia too, though her level glance was tinged with censure.

'What you've said doesn't make it any clearer, either, Mr Haldane, not without telling us how it ended.' Mayo wasn't inclined to have much patience with thirty-three-year-old men who acted like boys. A weak mouth, he noticed, a petulant glance as he sought support from his sisters, their baby brother, in trouble for pinching the jam tarts. Help, please! Not my fault!

'If Ma dies . . .' Jago said, and suddenly his eyes had a hunted expression.

'She's not *going* to die, Jago, she's going to get better,' Olivia said, rallying, using the words that were a sort of mantra for them all. None of them had yet voiced the terrible thought that lurked at the back of their minds: that though her body might her mind could be impaired. She crossed the room, knelt on the floor by his chair, took his hand and pressed it to her cheek. Nice to see such tender, sisterly devotion. Until you noticed the way the brother lapped it up. 'She'll get better and she'll tell us who it was did that to her.'

Jago started. He seemed about to speak, then stood up and walked to the fireplace. He put his head in his hands, resting his elbows on the cool marble. After a minute he turned round. He was shaking. He looked a wreck.

'I know who did it,' he said flatly, 'it was Paul. He pushed her over and she hit her head and he telephoned for the ambulance and ran away.'

Olivia gave a stifled cry.

Julia said nothing, her mind leaping back above the horror of it, the initial disbelief, to an incident of a dropped tea cup, many years ago. Then she said, 'Why? I mean, she was so nice to him, more than he ever deserved. She always seemed to have a special affection for him.'

Jago threw a quick glance at the two policemen, then at his sisters. 'I'll tell you later,' he said. 'It's something private. Nothing to do with all this.'

'Nothing's private, Mr Haldane,' Mayo intervened sharply, 'in a situation like this. I think what you have to tell us may well have everything to do with what we've been talking about.'

Life, someone had once said, is the art of drawing sufficient conclusions from insufficient premises. The same might be said about detection, he thought, not then realising where the intuition that made him speak had come from. He knew that he was right, though, as well as he knew that what he had intuited presented the key to the whole mystery. But Jago, in this pitiable state, looked incapable of explaining.

Mayo took a calculated risk. 'I think what you're trying to say is that your mother and Jerzy Siemek had a love affair during the war, and the reason for the quarrel with Paul Franklin was that he had found out he was their son.'

There was only the clock ticking, and the logs stirring in the grate, where someone had lit a real fire, and the sound of Jago's dry sobs as he put his head into his hands.

'He didn't find out,' he said dully, after a while. 'She told him. She was expecting to meet Tadeusz Siemek, and before she did, she wanted Paul to know. That's what he told me.'

* * *

You're not making much sense, he'd told Paul, and suggested he have some coffee, after all. And Paul had sat up suddenly, and said between clenched teeth, 'Oh, for God's sake, stuff the coffee! And don't be such a bloody fool, Jago! Can't you see I'm trying to tell you there's every possibility I might have killed my own mother?'

Lurid visions of Paul sticking a knife into Vee crossed Jago's dazed mind. But Vee had died four years ago, of cancer . . . Just how much had Paul been drinking? 'Oh, come *on*,' he said, 'what are you saying?'

'Come on, nothing! This Jerzy Siemek that she met when she was in the WAAF . . . the Klee wasn't the only thing he gave her,' Paul said, with a coarseness that was all the more shocking since he normally despised the use of such vulgarities.

Jago knew then that he'd simply been refusing to believe what he was hearing, unwilling to relate it to himself. It had needed more credibility than he was capable of, but now the scales fell away and he saw that Paul was indeed telling the truth. He heard someone who didn't sound like himself ask coldly, 'How do you know this?'

'She sent for me and told me so herself. After that fool Tadeusz Siemek had jumped the gun and written to her before he should have done, without saying a word to any of us, letting her know he was in England and asking to see her. She was going to tell him everything, but she wanted to tell me first.'

Jago got up and walked to the window. He reached out and steadied himself with his palms against the frame. He looked down into the street, where Paul's sleek black Citroën was parked. He felt as though he had aged ten years in as many seconds. More time ticked by.

'It wasn't Steve Kaminski then, or Halley,' he said presently, feeling deathly cold, turning back to face Paul. 'It was you who knocked her down. I might just kill you for that.'

He saw Paul looking at him, and knew that for the first time in his life he was finding himself afraid of Jago, the last mortal being on earth he would ever have dreamed could cause him fear. 'It wasn't an *attack*, it was an accident. If what she'd said was true, that Klee was *mine* by rights, forget Tadeusz Siemek! Not only had Jerzy given it to her, but I was his eldest son!'

Jago waited, a look of contempt on his face.

'When I told her that, she just stood there, looking at me. More in sorrow than in anger. Like some blasted plaster saint on a pedestal. I tried to grab her, to make her *see*. She stepped back, and tripped, and hit her head on that jardinière. She was bleeding, so I dialled 999.' He looked away and his skin rasped as he drew his hands across his unshaven face. 'I – I'm sorry, Jago. I never intended to hurt her. I don't want her to die,' he finished abjectly.

Silence.

'We have to decide what to do –'

'No, not we, Paul, not any more. I've already decided what I must do.'

Paul had cringed as Jago, terrifying in his rage, approached the leather chair and yanked him upright. With a hand on his collar and another on the back of his trousers, Jago frogmarched him across the room, let go with one hand until he could turn the knob and open the door, propel him across the small landing and then with a mighty heave use both hands again to shove Paul down the stairs.

Quite calmly he had listened to the hoarse shouts, the sickening thwacks and crashes as Paul's body rolled and bumped down, hitting the sides and treads of the steep, narrow stairs. Then he went slowly back into the flat and shut the door on the silence below.

The container lorry was a sixteen-wheeler being driven on the northbound carriageway of the motorway by a big Dutchman with a round, cheerful red face. He'd done the same trip dozens of times before and knew the best places to stop for a meal. The approaching services, still a couple of miles away, wasn't one of them, and he decided a shot of coffee from his thermos flask would keep him going for a bit. He'd poured the coffee and was listening to the radio, singing along as he passed the services entrance. Seconds later, a car drove out of the exit, ignored the filter and wove across three lanes of traffic into the fast lane, before taking a wild swerve back.

The Dutchman was driving well within the permitted speed limit, but it takes time for a vehicle weighing up to thirty tons to pull up, even with the brakes slammed to the floor. The result was a pile-up, a miracle in that only five vehicles were involved, and an even bigger one that no one was hurt, except the Dutchman, who scalded his leg with the hot coffee. And the car driver of course, who was underneath the wheels of the lorry, squashed as flat as a black beetle under the sole of a jackboot.

14

Rayner Wallace Bliss was a man who felt he was born to enjoy the good things in life, by which he meant the things that money could buy: wine, women, good food, a nice motor, a flutter on the gee-gees, though not necessarily in that order. Plus somewhere comfortable to live, the occasional chance to appreciate a good antique or two and a work of art here and there . . . he liked it to be known that he'd had a university education, that he was no Philistine, despite his lowly origins. The trouble was, his life didn't always, or even very often, fall within these desirable parameters. He'd been forced to forgo his keenest pleasures at certain periods of his life, i.e. when he was detained at Her Majesty's pleasure and compelled to associate with those whose susceptibilities were so much less fine. He was thirty-nine and had lately begun to wonder whether the easy pickings obtained from a life of crime outweighed the risk of being caught. But he was in a Catch 22 situation: if he went straight, he had no money for the luxuries he craved, if he sought luxury in the only way he knew how, it was a dead cert, with his luck, that he'd get caught, sooner or later: therefore, no luxury, and no freedom, either.

However, such philosophical conundrums weren't in his mind at the moment. Just now, his major worry was survival . . . how, precisely, he was going to get out of this place which was locked up like Fort Knox, and him without a key. Sometime yesterday he'd eaten a dried-up slice of bread with the only remaining tin of some disgusting sort of soup, scrounged around but found not even a stale biscuit for his breakfast. There was tea and coffee but what use was that without the means to heat water? How long could you survive on water alone? He was very near panic stations.

The wind rattling the windows didn't mean that they weren't

secured fast. It was the wind that had wakened him fully, the wild autumn wind that had moaned down the chimney like a banshee throughout the night and kept him tossing and turning. The antique shop had been many things in its long history but it had originally been built as a house, and Paul Franklin had retained the huge inglenook fireplace and wide chimney, believing it added distinction to his showroom. It might do that, but Bliss could have done without it, weather like this. He'd hardly slept all night and had dozed on and off throughout today, finishing off the last of his paperbacks, drinking water, finally falling into a heavy sleep in the late afternoon.

He swore and moiled around in the damp tangle of sheets, trying to find a comfortable spot for his hip, plagued by knowing most of this situation was his own fault. How could he have let it happen? He'd thought the plan was bomb-proof.

It had seemed like a good idea at the time, which could be said of most of Rayner Bliss's ideas. He should have hightailed it out of the country when it all went pear-shaped, but several things had stopped him, chiefly the lack of money, but also an inbuilt resistance to the idea. Even if he'd had the means to get away, who knew when, if ever, he would have been able to come back? He didn't fancy the idea of living in permanent, uncivilised exile, even on the Costa Brava, like others – admittedly more successful – of his acquaintance, in similar positions. Didn't go much on oily Spanish food, for one thing, and too much sun played hell with one of his gingerish colouring. Ought to have done it, though, somehow. Maybe borrowed money from Paul, left him his car in lieu. Fat bloody chance! He'd been offered four hundred pounds (say four-ten then, mate, seeing there's a nearly new tyre on the front nearside) on the old Escort, which was the only sort of car he'd been able to afford when he came out of the Green, in part exchange for the new Merc he'd been hoping for when this scam came off. Four hundred sodding nicker! How long could he have lived on that? After paying his way across the Channel and a night's kip, he wouldn't have had enough left to buy himself a *croque monsieur*.

No, leaving the country hadn't been an option, and when Paul Franklin had suggested holing up in these cramped quarters above his shop – well, he'd had no choice, had he, Bliss knowing what he did, and up to his neck in the business? – Bliss had been glad to agree. Between them, he and Paul had contrived a makeshift bed among the packing cases and other detritus that had drifted up here; there was a loo on the landing – Paul would bring in his food, reading matter . . . what more could he want? A hell of a lot more.

He only meant to stay here until he could make other plans and the fuss had died down and the dust settled. And this time he'd keep to what he decided. That was how they'd come a cropper, he and Steve, not sticking to their original idea. That was what came of having too many people in on the job, but Paul had been necessary. Just himself and Steve would've been better – though Steve had always posed a risk. He was unreliable, unstable as a loose cannon – even that little tart, Yvonne, had realised that. It was why Bliss had persuaded Steve to say nothing to her: she'd have waded in and stopped Steve. Bliss grinned disagreeably. Now she'd have to make out on her own, he thought viciously, forgetting that was what Yvonne did most of the time, and better than either he or Steve. He hadn't forgotten the way she'd made it very plain what Bliss could do with his offer of company while Steve was still inside.

By now, he was rigid with rage against Paul Franklin or, as Steve would have said in his vulgar way, bloody pissed off with him. Where in God's name *was* he? Why hadn't he come back? What was his game? He hadn't shown his face since Tuesday night, the shop had been left closed. The last meal Paul had produced had been a pizza in the afternoon, and Bliss had only eaten half of it because of the anchovies, which he loathed. He'd kill – unfortunate word – for that discarded half at the moment, or even just the anchovies.

He was also gasping for a smoke but Paul had insisted on his handing over the pack in his pocket – plus his lighter. No smoking here. Too much at stake . . . we both know what happens with fires, don't we? he'd said, looking at Bliss in a nasty sort of way.

He fought his way out of the uncomfortably rucked cushions and blankets spread on packing cases which was serving as his bed, and went downstairs, blundering around in the semi-dark. The bloody man had turned off the electricity and locked the cellar door where the mains switch was – couldn't trust him, of course, no matter that he'd sworn not to put a light on and run the risk of someone coming to investigate. It was around 5 a.m. by his watch, and a certain amount of light filtered in through

175

the drawn blinds, through which he could see the pattern of the metal screens which were fixed across the window and door when the shop was shut. He encountered, excruciatingly, one of a pair of French bergère chairs. He kicked it and sat down in it to rub his shin. Deciding the chair was more comfortable than that so-called bed upstairs, he leaned back and put his feet up on its companion, forcing himself to try and think calmly what to do. He tried to ignore the claustrophobic feeling of being banged up again but he wasn't very successful.

Paul Franklin had to come back sometime. You didn't just abandon a lucrative business like his. Like most antique dealers, his hours were erratic, he had to close the shop in order to attend sales. But three days? And the question was *when* was he going to return? Common sense dictated that he wouldn't leave him here to starve ... he was in enough trouble without another body on his hands. Bliss wasn't sure whether he believed it.

He tried the door again, uselessly, the window. Fast. Barred. No chance, even if he'd had much experience of opening locked doors, which he hadn't, his talents lying in other directions. He thought of the noise, the alarms being set off, and closed his eyes in despair.

After a while, he went into Paul's office and peered out through the rain sluicing down the back window as though some new solution might miraculously occur to him. Only six yards away, in the garage at the end of the yard, was his Escort. But the back door was solid as a rock. The key, a heavy iron affair six inches long, was missing. The back window was barred tight. He was close to weeping.

He sat in Paul's chair, picked up the telephone handset. Still connected. He put it back in its cradle. Summoning help from any of his associates that way was a non-starter. They'd laugh themselves sick. Set the alarms off? Bring the fuzz out in force? Do us a favour!

The rain threw fistfuls of itself at the windows and the wind pasted wet, dead leaves against the panes.

Fear began to crawl like maggots under his skin.

How could anyone have foreseen that the cosmic cloud of danger and violence which had begun to swirl about, unseen, over all that early autumn's golden radiance, would still be hanging around when the weather was breaking up as a prelude to

winter? A malevolent cloud that would mark and damage for-
ever the perpetrators, as well as the victims: for violence – as
much as the inability to forget or forgive a wrong – is a darkness
that diminishes those who hold on to it. Perpetrators can never
go free, though they often believe they can, even if, sometimes,
they are unaware of what they have done, or started. Or if they
become victims themselves.

The beginning of all this, mused Mayo, lay with Cecily
Haldane, helpless victim as she now was. Cecily, whom he'd
never met, had come to exert a hold on his mind, or rather, her
predicament had. Whatever mistakes she'd made, she didn't
deserve what amounted to a living death. His face, considering
this, held that brooding look, familiar to subordinates; he spoke
his thoughts aloud, more for his own benefit than for his listeners. 'Whatever we think, the whole thing was set in motion
when she wrote to her friend, Faye Dejmek, with her query
about Jerzy Siemek. As a consequence of which, Tadeusz came to
England – and the rest followed.'

He and Kite had returned from the vicarage to Milford Road
and found Abigail still there, though just about to depart for
home. She had already rung Ben, who was waiting for her at her
place, told him she'd be home within the half-hour. Chancing
her luck like that, she might have known she was dooming
herself to be caught out, she told herself wryly, ringing again to
cancel the previous message, and hearing his patient exhalation
of breath. 'OK, all right, flower, understood.'

Did he really understand, any more than Sheila Kite waiting
for her husband, or even, at times, Alex? But her heart lifted at
that softly spoken 'flower', a favourite endearment of his. It was
all right with Ben, it really was. They'd work things out.

She listened with singular impatience while Mayo told her
what they'd learned, and heard his conclusions, her sense of
justice offended. 'You're surely not suggesting what's happened
was her fault?' she said.

'Not deliberately. Though what she did does look like foolish-
ness. Naïvety at best. Look at it this way: before meeting
Tadeusz, she sends for Paul, perhaps intending to introduce
them to each other as half brothers, perhaps to arrange a share
out of the proceeds from the picture – which, incidentally, I'm
beginning to think will never materialise. Surely she couldn't
have imagined what she had to tell Paul would come as a

177

pleasant surprise, that he'd fall on her neck and call her Mother? Far from it! Presumably he'd loved and respected his parents, it must have come as a shock after all these years to learn that he had been adopted, to find out who his mother really was. Yet, even so, all he can think of is what he might get out of the situation, to wit, the painting. He tells her so, perhaps threatens her, who can tell? And she falls – or is pushed – against that wine-cooler. He panics and runs off. And then?'

'Then?' Kite raised an eyebrow. 'Well, I can't buy the idea that he went straight to Bessemer Street, where he knew Tadeusz was staying, strangled Steve K., and set fire to the house in an attempt to cover up! Unless he'd suddenly developed homicidal tendencies. You can see how the situation arose with Cecily – if we believe what he told Jago Haldane, it wasn't a deliberate attack on her, just a threatening gesture, a push maybe that went too far.'

Mayo said, broodingly, 'That's as maybe, but you're right, Steve's death is another story altogether, isn't it? Whether it was a sudden loss of temper or not, someone meant to kill him, and thought they'd succeeded. There's no obvious reason why that person should have been Paul Franklin.'

'Maybe he mistook him for Tadeusz?' Abigail suggested.

'Possibly. He may have known where Siemek was staying, but we've no reason to think they'd ever met – though we can soon find out.'

'Then the question's still why? Why should he have wanted to kill Tadeusz?'

'Because he believes the Klee is wholly his by rights?'

Mayo lifted his head, rubbed a hand across his face. 'I don't know. It doesn't stack. Only one person can answer this, and that's Paul himself.'

'If he feels so inclined. I didn't get much out of him before. He's as slippery as a snake,' warned Abigail.

'Never having met Mr Franklin, I wouldn't know. It's time I did.'

'Do you believe Haldane?' Kite asked after a moment. 'That Franklin got up after being pushed down a flight of stairs, that Haldane watched him drive away?'

Mayo didn't answer for several moments, then he said carefully, 'We've no reason as yet to think he didn't, but we'll find

178

the answer to that tomorrow morning. Meanwhile, we all need to go home, get some sleep. He'll keep until then.'

Edgar Haldane had walked for much longer than he intended over the moors, and he was glad to sit in the front seat of his car to rest for a time. He fell almost instantly asleep and awoke after a couple of hours cold and stiff. He tutted as he looked at his watch. Foolish to have wasted so much time, it would be growing dark by the time he got to Baylewell. The town was forty-odd miles north of Lavenstock, a small industrial town where he'd begun his ministry, not far from Sheffield, and one which held many fond memories. Dusk was indeed falling by the time he reached his destination, unlooked-for traffic having delayed him even further.

It was still standing, the little church in what had once been one of the outlying districts, where he'd been curate-in-charge, and where he and Cecily had made their marriage vows. More surprisingly, it was still consecrated, still being used as a place of worship, though its priest apparently looked after what had once been three parishes. He went slowly up the well-remembered path and found the door locked. He sighed, and turned back, unsurprised at that, though there was no reason to think there would be anything worth stealing here at St Margaret's, any more than there ever had been. Simple brass candlesticks, a wooden crucifix and nothing in the way of money. Only the odd foreign coin or button deposited by mischievous choirboys in the box labelled 'for the upkeep of the church'. None of which were much incentive for petty thieving.

The noticeboard by the gate indicated the vicarage was to be found at number two, Rainsford Close, which must be the new housing development across the road. When he had worked here, he and a fellow curate had rattled around like a couple of marbles in the big flat above the parish hall in the centre of the town, next door to the parish church, with a daily housekeeper to see to their wants and a bicycle for him to reach St Margaret's. How things change!

He made his way across to the vicarage, and only then did it belatedly occur to him as he rang the bell of the small semi-detached, that he should have telephoned and arranged an appointment. The Reverend James Denby might be out, busy, or even away from home. But almost immediately, a light appeared in the hall and the door was opened by a ginger-haired, bearded young man in jeans and sweater. He wasn't wearing a dog-collar, but that didn't signify these days.

When Edgar gave his name and said that he had once ministered at St Margaret's, he was immediately welcomed inside with a muscular handshake, accompanied by a steady look from a pair of bright blue eyes, and then, before he'd even made his business known, offered tea.

'That would be very welcome, thank you.'

'Make yourself at home, I won't be a minute,' Denby said. 'I was just about to make myself some before I went out.' In case this might be misinterpreted, he grinned and added hastily, 'That won't be until half-seven, though.'

The room where Edgar waited was part study, part living-room, untidy, with a desk in one corner and a television set in another. A gas fire sent imitation flames up the chimney and Edgar stooped to spread his cold hands before the blaze. When he felt a little warmer, he disposed his tall frame into one of the chairs, a modern affair with a wooden frame and loose cushions covered in what appeared to be flour sacks. He hitched more comfortably back and was immediately and painfully propelled upright again when the base of his spine encountered a wooden bar going right across the back. He surmised, rightly as it happened, that comfort, or the appearance of things, meant as little to James Denby as it did to him, and wrongly that there was no Mrs Denby.

'My wife's taken the kids to visit her mother, so I'm leading a bachelor existence this week,' the young priest told him cheerfully, returning with two pottery mugs and a large teapot on a tray, plus a towering pile of hot buttered toast. 'Dig in and help yourself.'

Edgar found himself feeling hungry for the first time in days, and gratefully accepted a hefty slice, plus a mug of thick, sweet tea, not even noticing what a far cry this was from the delicate china cups and saucers with their accompanying silver spoons, the thin, crisp toast that Cecily would have offered.

Hunger satisfied with the one slice, he politely declined more and sipped his tea, watching as Denby demolished the rest with schoolboy enthusiasm, while managing to carry on conversation as well, most of which centred around Edgar's time here and the changes that had occurred. When two mugs of tea and the last

crumb of toast had disappeared, Denby wiped his mouth, brushed his ginger beard and folded his arms. 'Well now, may I ask
the reason you've made this journey here, Mr Haldane?'

He listened without interruption while Edgar spoke, his open
face becoming grave and concerned. When the recital had come
to an end, he sat thoughtfully without saying anything for
several minutes.

'Hearing confessions has never been much in my line, to be
honest. Not much call for it, in any case. Very few people
nowadays admit the existence of sin. Nothing whatever that
they may feel inclined to do is wrong, so what have they to
confess to?'

'More's the pity,' said Edgar. 'Society has condoned too much,
for too long. Though I've never been in the habit of making
regular confession, myself, except to God. But, forgive me,
I don't have the time to get into that sort of discussion. To be
brief, will you or won't you hear me?'

Denby looked at him steadily. 'I will, if you wish it, but . . .' He
paused and sucked in his breath. 'Why me? How did you know
that I'd be prepared to do this?'

'I wanted it to be a stranger who hears what I have to say.
More than anything, I had a fancy for it to be here, at St
Margaret's. However, it wasn't entirely accidental. I've always
kept in touch with each diocese where I've worked, even to
having the diocesan news sent to me. What I've read and heard
of you I have liked. From what I've seen of you, I believe you to
be an honourable man.'

The praise, or perhaps that old–fashioned word 'honourable',
caused a flush to rise in the younger man's cheeks.

'You realise the position you're putting me in?'

'Yes, but I don't think you will dodge the issue. I think I have,
perhaps by chance, perhaps by God's guidance, come to the
right man. And I promise you,' went on Edgar, 'that I will not
ask more of you than you can give. You will never be asked to
choose between breaking the seal of the confessional and doing
your public duty. I have here –' he fumbled in his pocket and
drew out an envelope – 'I have here the letters I spoke to you
about. It may not be necessary, but in the event of anything
happening to me . . .'

The startled young clergyman took the envelope which was

held out to him. 'You are not –' he began, deeply concerned by now, '– I hope . . .'

Edgar smiled, the smile which transfigured his stern face and had made people love him throughout his life. 'My dear Denby, I am a priest. I have no intention of ending my own life – and I also have a wife who may need my support in the time to come. But, it can't be denied that I'm also seventy-eight years old . . . until recently, I rarely thought of death in regard to myself, but we are none of us immortal.'

At length, Denby said, 'Well, then, if you really must . . .'

'The letters are for my son and the police. The absolution is for myself.'

They walked across to the church.

Afterwards, there was a long silence, then James Denby clasped his shoulder and when Edgar said that he would like to be alone for a while in the church, prepared to leave him. 'I must go, I'm afraid. This parish meeting. Here,' he said, 'here are my keys. Lock up and turn out the lights when you've finished and you can let yourself into the house. Don't stay too long in here or you're likely to get frostbite! We can only afford to heat the place when there are services due – and then only in winter, so that it's always cold.'

Edgar smiled faintly at the familiar story. He would only be a few minutes, he said, and then he'd be on his way.

Denby hesitated, obviously deeply troubled by what he had just heard, and threw a worried glance at the old man. 'Are you sure I can't offer you a bed? It's a long way to be going home this time of night and –'

'Thank you, but I must go home.'

'Very well. It's been a pleasure to meet you, sir.'

'And you, James.' The two men shook hands and Denby left, the door making its hollow clang behind him.

St Margaret's was a small, plain, late nineteenth-century church, built originally as a chapel of ease to the parish church some miles away. During the day, it was cool and restful, its plain, cream-washed walls reflecting light through the leaded windows and accentuating its quiet simplicity. But after dark it had always been cheerless, its lighting inadequate, and tonight the temperature was not far off freezing.

Edgar knelt in the front pew with his face buried in his hands, for so long that his feet and legs began to grow numb in the bitter cold of the empty building. He barely felt it. He was suffused with a sense of release, and peace at last. Cecily was very near and the feeling that all would be well with her was strong. He knelt like some medieval saint, upright, his hands together in prayer. And now the seeping cold which had started in his feet seemed to be reaching into the very core of him, its fingers touching his heart, turning him to stone. The lights became even dimmer, until gradually, little by little, the cold and the darkness, the beat of his blood, and every other sensation, ceased.

The news of Edgar Haldane's death was transmitted via an early telephone call on Friday morning from the vicarage to Kite, who'd asked to be immediately informed of any developments. Still swallowing his cornflakes, he was told that Jago Haldane had already set off to Baylewell, at the request of the vicar in whose church Edgar had died, Mark Fry driving him there so that Jago could drive Edgar's car back.

Kite relayed the news through to Mayo. 'Apparently, it was the place where he began his ministry, years ago. Why he went there's still something of a mystery. The vicar seemed to know something about it but he wanted to see Jago Haldane – who has to identify his father, anyway. There'll have to be an inquest – sudden unexplained death and all that – but the doctor who saw him says the cause of death was obviously natural. He was knocking eighty, so it's not surprising his heart just gave out. Not a bad way to go. It's what we all die of in the end, isn't it?'

'Just when we're safest,' Cecily thought . . .

Then how did it go? No use, the quotation had slipped away, as everything else did. She tried to grasp why it was so important. Something she'd thought, about letting things be, not upsetting the equilibrium . . . She closed her eyes, drifted away, then came back suddenly, her mind moving into one of those sharp, clear patches, as if the sunlight were illuminating it . . .

Don't rock the boat, that's what I always told myself, let it be, don't resurrect the past, no good will come of it. I was safe. Safe from old memories, painful emotions. Safe and protected and dull, until that day when I began to feel that stirring against the skin, that rebellion against being too old to do anything to make amends before it was too late . . .

'Just when we're safest –'

There, that was it, out loud, but they've pretended not to understand again. Not even the little nurse who washes and tidies me, who understands me better than anyone. They won't listen, they're embarrassed by my gobbledegook.

Why doesn't Edgar come?

Edgar. Oh, my dear. I ignored your advice after all. For years I coasted along, and then I felt this compulsion to rock the boat. And knew instantly that I was no longer in control. Somehow, somewhere, there was a warning . . . the Grand Perhaps.

'Just when we're safest, there's a sunset touch . . . Someone's death . . . the Grand Perhaps.' Yes, that's it – I have it at last – or part of it, something very like it. What a very modern *poet he was, Browning, not like some of his contemporaries, that namby–pamby Swinburne, all that alone and palely loitering stuff, or was that Keats?*

But how very cynical. And how very true, all the same . . .

Paul.

The sunlight disappeared, and darkness flooded in.

When she opened her eyes again, the ceiling light was on, harsh and cruel. Edgar still hadn't come.

15

Mayo had asked Abigail to accompany him to Warwick, where they were to interview the man himself, little suspecting what they were to find. Their objective was one of the elegant Georgian houses in Leamington, where Julia Haldane had told them Paul Franklin lived.

'Early start, but no dramatics,' Mayo said. In his book, dragging bods out of bed with no pyjama bottoms on was strictly for TV cops or situations that really demanded surprise tactics. 'He's toughed it out so far, he's not going to panic at this stage.'

'I noticed he doesn't open the shop until ten.'

It was actually a few minutes after nine when they arrived but there was no answer, although Abigail rang the bell under his name several times. He had the downstairs flat of two, converted from a spacious, white-painted house in a quiet, select crescent, with a small but well-maintained garden in the front. Heavy lined curtains could be seen drawn apart at the big sash window that faced the road, but plain nets obscured any clear view into the front room. 'Security conscious, anyway,' Mayo remarked. A burglar alarm was installed above the front door.

'I dare say he has plenty worth pinching, that's why,' Abigail replied as they went back towards the car. 'Wait till you see his shop.'

'I can imagine. This ain't such a bad little place, either, come to that.'

Handsome houses, all of them in this crescent, the sort of select area that spoke of money. Large, and built long before the time when every house had a car or three, some of them had coach houses which served now as garages, but there were still cars parked in the road, all of them underlining the prosperous nature of the neighbourhood. The antiques business must be doing very well, thank you, Mayo decided, or maybe it was those television programmes, Paul Franklin's celebrity appearances at antiques fairs and suchlike that helped to keep up what seemed to be a fairly affluent lifestyle by any standards.

'He must have gone in early, it can't be more than ten minutes into Warwick,' Abigail remarked as he fired the engine and pulled out into the traffic.

Warwick and Leamington, linked administratively and spoken together as indivisibly as fish'n'chips or salt'n'vinegar, did in fact run almost seamlessly one into the other. The old town, when they arrived, was already very crowded this Friday morning with shoppers and tourists, and there was no parking within half a mile of Franklin's premises. When at last, after having accomplished the not inconsiderable feat of finding somewhere, they pushed their way through the throng and walked back down the hill to arrive at the shop, it was after ten, but they found the showroom still locked and barred. Nor was there any answer to their ring.

'Damnation!' Mayo's strong point wasn't forbearance. 'Now we're going to have to hang around with no car to sit in, or else come back. Fancy a cup of coffee?' He'd sacrificed his usual solid breakfast to an early start and needed a boost to his blood sugar. 'He won't be closed for the day, surely? Unless . . .' He didn't finish. Better not to underline the doubt that must have occurred

185

to her as well, that he'd made a mistake, and Franklin had made a run for it, after all.

'There's someone inside,' Abigail said all at once, her ear to the door. 'I can hear them moving around.'

What followed was the sort of nightmare that Rayner Bliss had imagined in his worst moments. The least of it was the banging on the door and the shouted demands of 'Police! Open up!' Much worse than that was the arrival of screaming police cars and the forcible entry into the shop by means of hydraulic rams and God knew what else. And what seemed like dozens of uniformed men in blue. And being hauled from the shop through a crowd of goggling onlookers into a waiting police car, his head forcibly ducked, shoved into the back seat and driven off at speed.

The inglorious end of what had promised to be the beginning of the rest of his life.

The humiliation didn't seem to matter as much as the fact that he was free. All he wanted was a hot meal and a drink, and never to see the inside of any antique shop again in his life. As Lavenstock came into view, his heart sank even further. He wished he'd never heard of the place – it looked humdrum enough, ordinary, respectable, but under the surface? No way would he have come near had he known what it held for him. At least you knew where you were in the disreputable London borough where he'd been born. There you didn't expect life to be anything more than poor, nasty, often brutish and frequently short. He'd been the clever one of the family and at eighteen he'd gained a place at a redbrick university. He sometimes pondered why he hadn't made the best use of the escape, but the family tradition of not working when you could live without had proved too strong. Instead of going on to take the law degree the whole tribe of them were expecting him to employ for their personal advantage at some future date, he'd jacked it in after his first term. Still had a hankering after the legal pro-fession, though, and he'd landed a job performing lowly, un-demanding clerking duties in a solicitor's office, until sacked for certain misdemeanours. He sighed. It seemed to be his fate to be entangled with the law, one way or another.

'Can't I have a sandwich or something? My belly's flapping against my backbone,' he complained, immediately his particulars had been taken, 'and my God, I could murder a cup of tea.'

'You'll survive,' answered the desk sergeant unfeelingly, neither of them noticing the solecism, but since Mayo didn't want him collapsing on their hands half-way through the interview, a man-sized helping of sausage, fried egg, beans and chips, two fried slices and a mug of hot, sweet tea presently appeared.

'Get that down you, and God help your cholesterol,' said the uniformed constable who brought it. A pimply youth. They didn't used to worry about that sort of thing at his age. It made Bliss feel old, though he'd seen the time when he, too, would have shuddered, for different reasons, at such a meal. Not now, and anyway, compared with the prison food he might well be consuming shortly, it was ambrosia. 'Sod the cholesterol,' he said, diving in with his knife and fork. If that was the only thing he had to worry about.

Later, he was wishing fervently that it was, when the heavy food on a totally empty stomach was playing havoc with his guts. That, and his claustrophobia, brought on again by the smallness of the interview room and the number of people in it, made it difficult to concentrate. He wondered what they'd say if he asked for a packet of Rennies, and decided against it. They were none too friendly as it was, now that the first amusement at his ignominious capture had worn off.

An inspector, a sergeant and a superintendent conducting the interview, no less. Bliss should have been flattered, but it only brought the increased certainty that they were out to get him. He'd already been repeatedly questioned and he couldn't see what more they wanted. He'd no intention of making life difficult for them, only easier for himself. It had been a fair cop and all he was interested in now was damage limitation: 'What'll happen to me if I tell you everything?' he'd asked, early on.

'It's more what'll happen to you if you don't, sunshine,' Carmody had returned.

From previous experience, that was what Bliss was afraid of. With resignation, but not without a certain pride, as if he'd masterminded the Great Train Robbery and was expecting praise and admiration for it, he admitted his part in the scheme. How he'd acted as intermediary between Stefan Kaminiski and Tadeusz Siemek –

'Posing as J.J. Halley, solicitor?' interrupted Kite, for the benefit of the tape.

Bliss glossed over this as quickly as possible, knowing they were bound to come back to it, but not inclined to dwell on it unless he had to, and went on with his account of how he'd traced 'Vanessa', how he'd persuaded Paul Franklin to be a party to the scheme because he could be of help in the disposal and authentication of the picture, once they'd got hold of it. How Franklin had found someone to translate all the letters into Polish – not that he'd needed much persuasion.

Patiently, the details were taken down, not so patiently, he answered the questions. 'How long's this going to go on, then?' he demanded truculently after a while, attempting bravado. 'I've told you all I know.'

'As long as it takes,' Kite said blandly, looking quite prepared to sit there for the next twenty-four hours, if necessary. They'd been waiting to get this joker into that chair for a long time, and he wasn't going to rush the job. He wasn't renowned for his patience any more than Mayo but, like him, he could summon it up when he had to. 'Let's talk about Tuesday, the twenty-first of September.'

'Again?' Bliss sighed, and repeated what he'd said yet once more. They'd been to the races in Warwick, he and Steve, on account of they were going to meet Paul Franklin after he'd closed his shop, in order to discuss tactics before meeting Tadeusz Siemek for the first time on the following day. Steve had got lucky right away and won a couple of nicker with a bet on Secret Agent, in the two o'clock, the first race. The horse's name had tickled his sense of humour, he thought he couldn't go wrong with a name like that. Secret Agent, all this wartime crap we'd been hearing about, see? Well, anyway, he'd been right, hadn't he? It had come in first.

'What happened to the money he won?'

'How d'you mean, what happened?'

'Not everything was burnt in the fire. There was no money in his wallet.'

Bliss turned the colour of cold porridge, either at the thought of Steve's only partially consumed remains, or at the mention of the empty wallet. Not displeased at his discomfiture, Mayo, sitting opposite him, watched for further reactions. He was an oily character, you couldn't imagine him taking anyone in for more than five minutes, but people were ever gullible, or greedy, where money was concerned. They believed what they wanted to believe. Bliss wasn't a man who was naturally at a loss for words, these being his trade, so to speak, but he was badly shaken and the effort of maintaining his veneer of respectability was too much as it became uneasily apparent to him where the interview was heading.

'Here, what are you insinuating?' he protested as Kite's question got through to him. 'There wasn't any money! I'd tried to persuade Steve to quit while the going was good, but he wouldn't listen. Silly bugger placed all his winnings on a donkey with three wooden legs in the next race. Night Music. Unplaced,' he added morosely. He'd also lost more than he could afford, but wasn't admitting it.

'So Steve didn't have any money in his wallet?'

'Might've had the odd fiver I suppose, not a lot more.'

'What was it you had this big argument about?'

'Who says we had an argument?'

'Come on, Bliss, you were in the bar, in a public place. We've plenty witnesses.' One, at least, and there'd be more.

Bliss was silent, his mind obviously working, weighing up the implications of this while the tape whirred and an expression of pain crossed his face. He held his hand prayerfully to his stomach, and belched.

'Well, all right then, we did have a difference of opinion. There we were, not due to meet Franklin till six, both of us cleaned out, and Steve goes, "Why don't we shoot over to Lavenstock and see this Pole this afternoon? Get it over with? What's the point in hanging around here in this dead and alive hole all afternoon? We can be back in plenty time to meet Franklin." I didn't think the idea was so hot and told him so. No good comes of upsetting plans at the last minute. Upshot was, we had a few words. He lost his rag – very quick-tempered, our Steve was, sometimes.'

'Why did you want to see Tadeusz Siemek?'

'To find out what the hell he was playing at! He'd been over here two weeks and it seemed he'd done sod-all about approaching the Haldane woman. How long were we going to have to

189

wait before he made his mind up to talk to her? "Time he shifted his arse," Steve said, and I had to agree to that. "Plus Franklin's pussyfooting around on this. What's it to him, how long we have to wait, what's a thousand or two either way matter to him? I'm not sure we can trust the bastard."'

Bliss paused reflectively. 'Well, neither was I sure, come to that, and I wasn't into trusting the Pole too far, either. He'd always been lukewarm, seemed to me, I thought it on the cards he might decide to back out at the last minute. So in the end I agreed with Steve, and we drove over here.'

'So what happened when you got to Bessemer Street?'

'Nobody there, was there? No answer at the front door, and the back entry gate bolted shut. So Steve bunks over and unbolts it, finds the back door's open, well, not locked anyway. We go in and the house is empty, nobody at home. "What now?" I'm thinking. "We're no better off." "I know what I'm going to do," he says, "I'm going to have a kip on that sofa." He was well tanked up and that seemed like the best idea he'd had all day, to sleep it off. I told him I was going out for some cigarettes and he said to bring in a six-pack. He'd had enough, but you didn't argue with Steve when he'd had a skinful. In a right vicious temper, he was, that day. Well, I found an off-licence on the main road, and when I came back, he was lying there, bloody dead! And that's jonnuck!'

Silence descended. Kite let it carry on long enough for Bliss to realise just how much his explanation was suspect. 'Dead when you got there? Can't you do better than that?'

'How many more times do I have to say it? He was dead, I tell you!'

Mayo was looking at those pudgy hands. Carmody had reported Yvonne Prior as being scornful of Bliss having the bottle to strangle someone as fit and macho as Steve, but who knew what strength rage could give to a desperate man? If the row had flared up again ... And yet, there was that air of desperation about Bliss that comes when you're telling the truth and no one is believing you. Mayo reminded himself that Bliss was a con man, it was his stock in trade to convince people of the unlikely. He could lie in the Pope's face and make him believe him.

'I panicked then ...' He paused and wiped the sweat that had gathered on his forehead. 'I tell you, good and proper. Then

I started to think. The Pole, Siemek, would be questioned, he'd come forward with the whole story and bingo! I knew the barman had noticed that argy-bargy with Steve in the bar at the racecourse – him and who else, I wondered. My dabs were all over the bloody house, plus, somebody might've remembered seeing me in the off-licence. So I thought, Christ, why not put a match to the whole shebang and nobody'll ever find out.'

'You think big, Bliss, I'll say that for you. Come on, exactly how did you do it?'

Looking up, Bliss caught Mayo's intent, veiled look. It seemed to put him off and he hesitated, but only for a moment. He'd had plenty of time to rehearse what he was now telling them and was soon back into his stride. It was lucky he'd parked his car round in the pub car-park, he said, second nature, of course, not to have left it in full view. He'd pushed his way through the broken-down back fence, cut a length of clothes line, soaked it in petrol and threaded it from the body to the back door. Lit the fuse and retired in haste.

'What then?'

'How d'you mean, what then? How should I bloody know? You don't think I hung around to see what would happen? I just got the hell out of it, fast as I could!'

It was always dark on this side of the building, overshadowed by the grim Victorian presence of the Town Hall opposite. The lights flickered, on early this dark afternoon, with clouds scattering across a lowering sky. Despite his bravado, Bliss looked nervously towards the window as the wind flung a sudden scurry of rain against it.

'Carry on,' Kite prodded.

He licked his lips. 'Drove over to Coventry, didn't I, picked my belongings up, and back to Warwick. I'd nowhere else to go and Franklin agreed I could stay there, in his shop. Well, he didn't have much choice, did he?'

Mayo, who had no patience with meaningless rhetorical questions, came in. 'Didn't he? I don't know. You tell us why not.'

'*Why not?* Because he was in this as much as I was. Up to his neck, he was . . .' Bliss's voice trailed off under that assessing look, the silence that followed his reply.

'Who do *you* think killed Steve Kaminski, if it wasn't you?'

'I don't know,' Bliss answered shiftily.

'What would you say if I told you he wasn't dead when you set fire to the house?'

The wind bounced off the solid, impervious Victorian bulk of the Town Hall and back across the road, buffeting the twentieth-century standard issue police station until it shuddered in protest. 'I'd say you were trying it on, mate! He was dead, right enough.'

'The post-mortem shows he was breathing when the fire started. It was breathing in the fumes that killed him.'

'Is that right?' he answered cockily. But his hand shook when he drew on his cigarette. And his face was ashen against his sandy brows and hair, his reddish brown eyes, swivelling, gave him the vicious look of a cornered ferret. And those eyes said yes, he *was* capable, in certain circumstances, of killing, especially if it was to save his own miserable skin.

'At the very least you're facing a charge of arson with intent to conceal a murder. At the very best, you're looking to go down for life, Bliss.'

At that inappropriate moment, the door was opened and Mayo turned his head sharply to see Abigail standing there, making signs of apology as she indicated she needed to speak to Mayo. He rose and left the room, knowing she wouldn't have interrupted unless it were important. That he was right was apparent as soon as he saw her face.

'That pile-up on the M6, the one with the Dutch truck. They've identified the car driver who was killed as Paul Franklin. So Jago Haldane wasn't lying when he said Franklin drove away from his flat . . . nor that he'd been drinking, either. In that condition, half drunk and having just been thrown down the stairs, it's surprising he lasted as long as he did without having an accident.'

Mayo drew his breath in a long hiss. First Edgar Haldane, now Paul Franklin, maybe Cecily Haldane. *And then there were none.* The unworthy thought that he was losing all his witnesses intruded before he could help himself, but where did things stand now, with only Bliss's word for what had happened? God, what a shambles this was turning out to be! After all the unravelling, all the apparent complications, when it came down to it, this hadn't been any ingenious crime needing brains and intelligence to carry it through, but a tawdry little scam, amounting to

192

no more than most other murders – a series of blunders, lost tempers, with little or no regard taken for a person's right to live.

And like all such, it had exacted more than its fair toll of human misery. Piotr Kaminski's son dead, Cecily Haldane lying at death's door, Paul Franklin and Edgar Haldane, both dead ... where was it going to end?

For it hadn't ended yet. Bliss's confession to starting the fire had answered one question, but left unanswered the other: who'd made the attempt to strangle the life out of Steve K. – and very nearly succeeded? Unless Bliss was a better con man than Mayo gave him credit for, it wasn't him. Tadeusz Siemek, who might have had a possible motive, had a cast iron alibi. Had it, then, really been Paul Franklin? One thing was certain. That was a question that was destined to remain unanswered.

Cecily had been told that Edgar was dead.

They'd told her lies at first, that he had flu, he couldn't come and see her and run the risk of spreading infection in the wards, but even in her state she wasn't fooled. Knew it from her daughters' red-rimmed eyes, from Jago's short, abrupt visits, and began to fret.

The doctors consulted over the dilemma, weighed up the pros and cons and in the end reluctantly decided that she ran less risk by being told the truth than if she were kept in the dark, worrying. But go carefully, they said, she's still not out of the wood. Her faculties and memory were returning little by little, but too great a shock could even yet prove fatal.

It fell to Mavis Snell to hold her hand, speak, and pray that she'd been understood. The task of dealing with the bereaved was not one she welcomed, but was necessarily one that wasn't unfamiliar to her. She had found elderly parishioners were, for the most part, better able to cope with the immense grief of death than younger people, especially if the one who had died was of their own generation. The sorrow was no easier to bear, but the shock was less. Death comes to us all, each day from birth being a progression towards dying, and ultimate acceptance is gradually learnt on the way. She felt that, though Cecily gave no sign, she was telling her something she already knew.

No one had yet found the courage to suggest that Cecily should be told about Paul.

It was of Paul she thought, constantly, and sometimes with an unexplained terror. She couldn't yet recall what had happened immediately prior to the accident, but she was getting there. She remembered sending for him, and why. But not what had happened after that.

All that silly business about the painting! If only they'd asked her, she could have saved Jerzy's son coming all the way from Poland. How could she make him understand? She'd always suspected the Klee was a fake, and had known it for certain ever since that trip she and Edgar had taken to America, when they'd seen the original in New York, in the Museum of Modern Art. But she'd been unable to throw away anything Jerzy had given her, especially that, which he'd asked her to keep, just before he was shot down. *He* had believed it to be an original – or so she had thought, until one day when she'd pulled it out of the cupboard where she'd stowed it away, and looked at it with new eyes. And had seen that what she'd previously thought to be some sort of backing stitched behind the hessian on which the picture had been painted was actually large sheets of oiled silk paper, on which were printed official-looking documents with stamps and signatures ... Perhaps, if they were what she'd thought they might be, it had been worthwhile for Tadeusz to come here, after all.

'Do you want to see him, Ma?' Julia had asked at some point, during one of those long sessions when she sat by the bed, holding Cecily's hand, softly talking. About everything, and nothing. The garden, parish affairs, the friends who were asking after her. And then, telling her that she and Mark had made up their quarrel and were to be married, after all these years, and wasn't Cecily surprised? As if Cecily hadn't always known things would come right between them in the end!

'You know who Tadeusz is, don't you, Ma? Jerzy's son? Are we doing the right thing, bringing him to see you? It won't upset you, will it?'

Cecily had tried, harder than she'd ever tried before, to speak intelligibly. She must have made herself understood because here he was, now, with Mark and Julia, walking up to the bed and taking her hand and her heart was beating in great, hard, thumps. Tall, thin, dark, with high cheekbones. And that smile!

Julia had told her, to save her from the shock, how like his father he was supposed to be, but for the first moments after her eyes lit on him, she couldn't make a sound. She was eighteen again, up to her eyes in love with her dashing, glamorous Pole, no one else existing for her among the hundreds of airmen and women who lived crowded together in the huts on that bare windy airfield. Something very special between them. Eighteen, and half mad with a mixture of love and dread while she waited for him to return safely from yet another mission, relief washing through her, exhilarated to the point of intoxication, when he did. Never a thought of the future, the careless present was enough. Time was precious, make the most of it while you can. Laugh, and love, and let tomorrow take care of itself . . .

He laughed when I told him I was born in Camberwell. 'There's a butterfly whose name in English is Camberwell Beauty,' he said, 'purple and yellow, called that because it was first seen there.' What an odd, unlovely place to have a butterfly named for it! From then on, I was Vanessa to him. Vanessa, a butterfly, a Camberwell Beauty. So silly, I was never a butterfly – nor a beauty either, though perhaps I was then, in his eyes.

And then, the awful, aching emptiness, when the worst happened, and he didn't return. 'One of our aircraft is missing.' Such banal words to cover so much grief and sorrow. The end of life for me, too, I thought, though there was already another life stirring inside me.

Nobody can realise, today, what it meant then to have a child and no father for it. Easy enough for me to have invented a husband who had been killed. But I always hoped . . . hoped that one day he'd return. Meanwhile, how was I to support myself and a child, and care for him while I did?

Vee, dearest Vee, looked after Paul and then later, after Jerzy wrote to me and told me he was married, legally adopted him. Since she and Walter weren't able to have children of their own, it was a sensible solution. I was glad of it. But like all sensible solutions, it took no account of the heartbreak involved. I understood he had to do the honourable thing by that Polish girl, and I never wrote back and told him about Paul. Nor did I ever tell Edgar, either. About everything else, yes, but not that he was my child.

195

Paul. My firstborn child. How could you ever have raised your hand to me?

Alarm bells began to ring, needles oscillated madly. Feet pounded along the corridors. Then the blips on the monitor screen levelled out, registering nothing.

16

Unsolved cases, Mayo hated them, those that had to be closed without any real sense of finality. Conclusive evidence, that was all that mattered in the last analysis. Conjectural conclusions were, and never had been, any use to him. Firm, corroborative evidence that linked the perpetrator to the crime was all he was interested in. Anything else left his professional self dissatisfied and the private part of that same professional self, the one he showed to no one – except, on rare occasions, to Alex – profoundly angry.

He was angry this time. He might have his suspicions – and he did, he did! – as to who the culprit was, the person who had deliberately attempted to kill Steve Kaminski, had left him for dead, but there was nothing incriminating, and suspicions alone weren't enough to go to court with. Bliss, who swore he was innocent of trying to kill Steve, only guilty of attempting to get rid of anything that might throw suspicion upon his innocent self, had destroyed any hope of finding hard evidence by setting fire to the house. Tadeusz Siemek had a cast iron alibi, and in any case was out of the frame as far as Mayo was concerned. Paul Franklin was dead, without anything against him to suggest he had tried to kill Kaminski, and only Jago Haldane's word that he had attacked Mrs Haldane.

A man had died as a result of actions that stopped short of deliberate murder, but the story wasn't complete until he had nailed the perpetrators and delivered them for punishment. Cynicism draped itself like a cloak around his shoulders. He wasn't normally bitter and twisted, but weighing all this up in his careful way, the harsh conclusions he was coming to were forcing him to believe this would be one of those investigations that would be shunted away into some dusty limbo and never resolved.

The letter which came for him three days after Bliss's confession he read in silence, with a sense of sadness and inevitability. It was the missive Edgar Haldane had penned before he drove up to Baylewell and it read, Mayo thought, almost as if Edgar had known it would be the last journey he would ever take, that bourne from which no traveller returns.

It was enclosed in an explanatory letter from the Reverend James Denby, briefly describing the circumstances in which it had been given to him, and speaking of the request from Canon Haldane for it to be forwarded if necessary. 'He insisted on staying in the church that night. I wish now with all my heart that I had not agreed. I really ought not to have left him. He looked ill, but I put this down to the worries about which he had spoken. His letter will, I believe, explain all that. God rest his soul in peace.'

So much blame and remorse. James Denby, castigating himself for his lack of decision. And the canon's family, bewildered by this pilgrimage, or whatever it was, to Baylewell, which he should never have attempted, blaming themselves without justification for not having suspected the heart condition he'd been warned about, but robustly ignored. His doctor had advised him to take things easy, retire perhaps. He had smiled and disregarded the advice, kept the knowledge to himself.

His letter was written in an old-fashioned hand, sloping, well-formed letters with curly loops and tails that owed something to the lost art of copperplate. How long before the basic skill of handwriting was lost altogether in favour of e-mails, faxes, telephone calls? No time for such elegancies, no need for it, Mayo kept being told.

He tried to believe that was true, especially when confronted with the indecipherable scrawls passed on to him by some of his younger, educated-by-computer officers. But all that was a very long way from his mind now as he considered the import of the message conveyed in this neat and scholarly script.

It was put together in a precise, dry fashion, with an objectiveness that made it all the more shocking. It should not have been possible, Mayo thought, reading between the lines, for one good man to be brought to feel such despair and humiliation. Such failure in himself.

That day the ambulance had taken Cecily away, Edgar wrote, he had followed and stayed by her bedside until he was politely told there was nothing he could do for her. So he had left her in the expert care of doctors and nursing staff with their machines and monitors, with tubes and wires connecting her to a fearful array of other equipment. He had come back to the wrecked sitting-room, and automatically had begun to pick up the scattered contents of her desk. What he found stunned him enough to put everything else, even the urgent matter of informing the police of the attack, out of his mind.

It had almost leaped out at him, the letter from someone signing himself as Tadeusz Siemek, with an address in Bessemer Street. It was quite clearly a request for a meeting between Cecily and the writer who, it was also clear, was the son of someone Cecily had had an affair with during the war. Whether Edgar had ever suspected this, or had known about Paul, was something he did not say. Mayo asked himself again whether Cecily had told him, or if he had guessed, put two and two together? Whatever, when Edgar read Tadeusz's letter, he had jumped to the conclusion that it constituted some form of blackmail, that the prepared coffee tray had evidently been in expectation of this Siemek's arrival, and what had followed had been the near death of his beloved wife.

Without stopping to think, he had jumped into his car and driven over to Bessemer Street and battered on the door. Boanerges, son of thunder, calling down fire from heaven. An old nickname, an old failing, that temper of his, a besetting sin, except when it was used against the wicked, which in fairness to himself he had to admit was usually the only time he let rip.

And this was, overwhelmingly, one of those times.

What followed after the door was opened was a disgraceful scene, he admitted, a brawl, in fact, which Edgar, afterwards, deeply and bitterly regretted, appalled by its culmination. It was evident to him that the man was Siemek. The name of Cecily Haldane had not seemed new to him, nor her connection with Jerzy Siemeck.

After some high words, Edgar had gone for him. He was a big

man, he had been a rugby forward at his theological college, and even now, he wrote, he was proud of being as fit as many a younger man. Scarcely knowing how it had happened, he had the other fellow round the throat, taking him by surprise, shaking him and throttling the life out of him. It was only when he went limp and lost consciousness that he knew he had almost killed him. Not quite. As Edgar stood looking down at him, the man he thought to be Siemek groaned and opened his eyes. Edgar left the house, got into the car he'd parked outside, and drove off.

And then . . . and then, he had heard on the local radio of the fire, and the man's body found in the ashes. Dear God, Siemek must have passed out again, the fire had started and he'd been unable to get out! Worse was to come, when he read in the local paper that the man was not, after all, Tadeusz Siemek, but someone called Stefan Kaminski. He had not only killed, he had killed the wrong man.

After he'd read the letter once more, Mayo sent for his two inspectors. The case had had one unexpected benefit, it had at least brought about some sort of truce between them.

Abigail read the letter first, and a heavy silence hung over the room while Kite also read it. 'Well, that's it, then,' he said, looking up. 'That wraps it up.'

'Does it?' Mayo sat immobile at his desk. His hands rested on the desk's polished surface, like dead weights. He felt a sense of helplessness settle on him like a lid. 'First time I've ever had a posthumous confession. Pity we can't use it. A confession's no damned good without evidence to support it.'

The other two sat silent, acknowledging that with Mayo, there was a time to speak, and a time to be silent. That this was one of the latter. Even Kite contained himself, though there was a lot he wanted to say.

The sound of an aeroplane intruded into the room, its engine noise still loud only minutes after take-off from Birmingham airport, reminding Abigail that Tadeusz would even now be on his way back to Poland with his children, those precious deeds safely stowed in his luggage. Mission accomplished – even if not accomplished as planned. The title deeds, Tadeusz said, would be returned to the rightful owners and would, with luck, underline their claim to the country house which had been confiscated by the Germans and not returned to them after the war. Whether the claim would be successful or not was less certain. It was a common enough story, and many others had failed in similar attempts. Half a century after the war had ended, the situation was still the cause of much wrangling and bitterness. Had Jozef ever known it was a fake Paul Klee he had encouraged his son to smuggle out of the country? Did he know the deeds were concealed behind it? Whether he did or not, the fact that they were there at all threw grave doubts upon Jozef's right of possession. The story of how he'd acquired the painting now seemed to Tadeusz more than suspect.

It was all a very long time ago, but there was still the chance for retribution to be made, ghosts to be laid. Wanda would help him lay them. An unexpectedly warm, sympathetic relationship had developed between them. She hadn't gone back to Poland with him, but she'd promised, at least, to visit. And behind the promise was another. Perhaps.

Beyond the window, the plane disappeared into a bright blue autumn afternoon, leaving only a vapour trail behind it, and Mayo said at last, tipping his chair back, shoving his hands into his pockets, 'I wish I could believe it, but it's all lies. The content's substantially true, I think, everything happened as he said, except that the perpetrator wasn't Edgar Haldane.'

'Back again to X?' Kite ventured after a pause to digest this.

'X? Well, can you see a man of Canon Haldane's character doing such a thing – storming along to Bessemer Street and battering the door down, demanding vengeance, all on the flimsiest of evidence? I can't. Not to mention the unlikelihood of an old man like him overpowering Steve Kaminski – nearly fifty years younger and tough with it, never mind what he says about taking him by surprise.'

'On reflection, neither can I,' Kite said, 'but people do unbelievable things.'

'Not this time.'

'Then who?'

Again Mayo was silent. Finally he said, 'Mrs Faber.'

The other two avoided looking at one another, thoughts unsaid, the air thick with them. Kite instead looked at Mayo, wondering if he could be serious, and saw he was.

'I want to see Mrs Faber. Either here, or at her home, whatever pleases her. See to it, one of you, will you?'

He happened to be in the corridor, whose windows overlooked the car-park, when she drove in. His hand on the doorknob of his upstairs eyrie, he watched as she swung round and backed her four-by-four expertly into an awkward space. Ten out of ten.

She was wearing a sheepskin coat which she surrendered to Abigail in the heat of the office. She stirred two spoonfuls of sugar into her tea and took two of the Bourbon biscuits Mayo offered. He'd put her firmly in the twinset and pearls slot after seeing her the other evening at the vicarage – but today she had on a baggy, concealing sweater over trousers, her hair was carelessly tied back. For all her heavy build, she looked in good form. Strapping, you might say. Not at all the sort you'd want to meet in a dark alley on a dark night, at any rate. He fancied she looked paler, though that may have been his imagination. Recalling how overwrought she'd been before, he wasn't looking forward to the next ten minutes. Hysterics he'd never known how to cope with.

'Show Mrs Faber the letter, Inspector, will you?' he asked Abigail. Abigail handed it over and the other woman read it through in silence.

When she'd finished she looked up, obviously very shaken, her big brown eyes wide with horror. But she recovered quickly and handed the letter back, saying dismissively, 'What rubbish!' Her hand was shaking, however.

'It's possible, you know, Mrs Faber,' Abigail said, watching her carefully. 'Despite his heart condition, your father was a very strong man.'

'I'm not saying he wasn't. I'm talking about the impossibility of him acting like that. You didn't know him.' Condescending, putting Abigail's back up, making her think it was as well Kite was kicking his heels in court today, and not here to make his thoughts plain. Never able to abide being patronised, Kite. 'He could get angry, yes,' Olivia went on, 'but as for physically attacking anyone! That's quite absurd.'

'Then why do you think he wrote this letter?'

201

'I have no idea,' she said, picking up her teacup and draining it.

Mayo opened a manila file on his desk, shuffled through the papers, found one that was particularly interesting and scanned it. The marble Victorian mantel clock on top of a filing cabinet, one he'd repaired and brought from home to keep an eye on, gave a wheezy cough and struck the hour. He consulted his watch, got up and adjusted the hands, returned to his desk. Olivia Faber shifted impatiently, looked pointedly at her own watch. 'If that's all, I have things to do.' She was showing a different, more assertive personality here, away from the bosom of her family, as if freed from the necessity to be agreeable, as was expected of a daughter of the vicarage.

The silence went on. 'Where were you, Mrs Faber, on the afternoon of the twenty-first of September?' Mayo asked at last.

'The twenty-first of September?' Frowning. Puzzled about a day that must be engraved on her memory, Abigail thought.

'The day your mother was attacked,' Mayo reminded her.

She stared. 'I was at the hospital, of course.'

'Not all the time. You said you were with your brother from three to four o'clock.'

'Naturally, I meant apart from that! They sent us home from the hospital about half-past two. Julia went to the office to collect her belongings, Jago drove Father back to the vicarage, and then went back home.'

'None of you stayed with your father?'

'He could be very stubborn, and he insisted on being alone, so did Jago. He was very upset. He and my mother have always been very close.'

It was hardly a satisfactory answer, but he let it go. 'I see he works in London, normally lives there, doesn't he?'

'Yes, but he's been staying in his friend Rodney Brightman's flat since July. One of the new ones on Canal Wharf.'

'Not very convenient for him, I'd have thought?'

'It so happens, however, that it was, for the time being,' she said shortly. He waited, and at last, sighing, she explained. 'He's been as much in America as in London lately, and he – he had things to occupy him here in Lavenstock, so it was easier to commute to London.'

202

'And we know what it was that was occupying him here, don't we?'

She threw him a nasty look and then turned sharply away. Her hair caught on the neck of the big roll collar of her sweater, dislodging the ribbon that tied it back. Impatiently, she pulled it off and the hair, thick, dark and luxurious, fell around her face, softening it and making her look younger and altogether more vulnerable. She had no need of make-up with her complexion, and she wore none. She looked fresh and rosy as a country apple. 'I was speaking of his girlfriend,' she said coldly.

'Dani Lepszy, yes. The girl you introduced him to. Nice girl, Dani. Very fluent in Polish – must have come in handy when he needed to have that correspondence translated.'

She gave him a quelling-the-natives kind of look. 'That was *why* I introduced them, if you remember, Mr Mayo. Jago needed someone who could speak and write Polish, and I remembered my daughter Natalie's friend. That's all it amounted to.'

'Weren't you curious about why he needed this translation?'

'Why should I be? Greshams is an international auction house, he's regularly in touch with people all over the world.' Very different from all this, said the glance that swept disparagingly around the uninspired but perfectly adequate office of a senior police officer. She was lucky, he thought tartly, that he'd decided to talk to her here and not in one of the bare interview rooms equipped with hard chairs and formica tables, filled with the lingering smell of millions of stale cigarettes, institutional coffee and the whiff of despair left by dysfunctional humanity.

'Didn't you ask why he didn't use Greshams' professional translators? I assume they have them, a big international auction house like that?'

'Of course I didn't ask him. It was none of my business.'

'You didn't ask because you knew, isn't that more like it?'

'Look here, what are you trying to get at? What are you insinuating?'

'I am *saying*, not insinuating, that you knew all about what was going on. I think you knew the whole story about the Paul Klee painting, and what your brother and your cousin were up to.'

She stood up. 'I don't have to stay here. I've told you –'

'Please sit down, Mrs Faber. You've so far told us only what

203

you wanted us to know. Let's see if we can't find out what we need to know now.'

She looked round a little wildly, saw the impossibility of walking out without her coat and the unlikelihood of it being handed to her just yet, and sat down.

'Some more tea?'

She nodded, her mind working as it was poured. She took the first sip before answering. 'All right, yes, I did know about the picture! Jago told me how it had been supposedly brought out of Poland by someone who was killed in the war, and entrusted to some other person, who still had it. He and Paul simply wanted to trace the rightful owner and get it back to him. I swear – I *swear* until the other night, I had no idea that person was my mother. I wouldn't have believed it if I *had* been told.'

'Mrs Faber, I wouldn't put you down as naïve. You have a lot of influence over your brother, wouldn't you say? You're very fond of him.'

'I wouldn't say influence . . . we understand one another. Of course I'm fond of him.'

'Was that the reason you encouraged this wild scheme?'

'I didn't consider it wild. It would have been a feather in Jago's cap, to have come across an undiscovered Klee, wouldn't it?'

'I'm sure it would,' he said blandly. 'How long does it take you to drive home from Lavenstock?'

She blinked. 'Twenty minutes, sometimes half an hour, depending on traffic.'

'So how did you get back in time to be with Jago from three to four?'

She looked wary but answered coolly enough. 'He rang me on my mobile when I was half-way there.'

'So you just turned and drove back?'

'I *just* turned back because he sounded so upset!'

'In a panic, do you mean? Asking you to come to him immediately? That was it, wasn't it? And when you arrived, he made you promise to swear you'd been with him for the last hour. He needed an alibi, having just attempted to strangle a man, whom he'd left for dead.'

'*Jago*? This is ridiculous!'

'Mrs Faber.' Mayo tapped Edgar Haldane's letter. 'You say

204

your father couldn't have done as he said and tried to kill Steve Kaminski – and for what it's worth, the inspector here and I agree with you.' Abigail nodded dutifully, wondering if this was a nudge to her to take more part in the questioning, but decided it wasn't. He was well into his stride with Mrs Faber, knowing where he was leading, beginning to put the pressure on, and Abigail knew how easily a witness could be deflected by an irrelevant question. She sat back with her notebook.

'But if we substitute your brother for your father,' Mayo was saying, 'then immediately the story becomes believable. I think it was Jago who found the letter, stormed along to Bessemer Street and half killed Kaminski, thinking he was Tadeusz Siemek, who had kept the appointment with Cecily and quarrelled with her. Remember, he knew about the Klee, a possible source of dissension between Tadeusz and your mother – something your father never knew about. Jago's quite capable of tackling someone like Kaminski, given the incentive, but if your father had ever seen that young man – a tough character by anybody's standards – he might have though twice about claiming to have overpowered him.'

'And how is my father supposed to have known all this about Jago – and why was he prepared to fabricate such a pack of lies, take all the blame?'

'I can't tell you – I can say only this is what I surmise must have happened. I don't suppose he *did* know, for certain. Unless Jago confessed to him, which I very much doubt, but he must have been pretty sure. Your father was a shrewd judge of character, I'd guess. And knowing he could die any time, he thought the sacrifice of his own character didn't matter, as long as he averted suspicion from Jago.'

And maybe, Mayo thought, maybe the old man had even sought to hasten his own end by that long, tiring day, though weren't clergymen supposed to regard that as a sin? Well, it had happened, and he'd escaped being questioned over his 'confession'.

'You *surmise* what happened,' Olivia said, her voice brittle with sarcasm. 'In other words, you've no proof whatsoever.'

How true, Mrs Faber. No proof of the sort they needed: beyond reasonable doubt. Julia had told Mayo that her father had found his lost spectacles in the chair in which Jago habitually sat. Julia thought it was Paul Franklin who had put them there: he had sat in the same chair when he had come with what she had, in retrospect, seen as the rather spurious excuse to visit her mother in hospital. She thought it a stupid and unnecessary thing to have done, perhaps an act of bravado which might, possibly, have linked him to the attack on Cecily. But Edgar Haldane wouldn't have known that Paul had sat there. It was much more likely that Edgar had believed it to be Jago himself who had quarrelled with his mother over the Klee before rushing off to Bessemer Street to wreak vengeance. 'You've no proof,' Olivia repeated.

'We've a witness who saw a blue car outside the house in Bessemer Street at the right time. Jago runs an old blue Morris Minor whereas your father's Rover is a maroon colour.'

She couldn't have known how shaky this was as evidence, but he'd voiced the thought passing through his mind, more as an afterthought than anything, and there she was, her face crumpled, gone to pieces.

'His car?'

It could have been any blue car, but she knew it had been Jago's. He knew he had her now. He could allow her time to compose herself before asking more questions, but it was she who spoke first.

'I had no choice.'

We all have choices, he thought. Moral imperatives that influence our actions, the choice to act, or opt out. To rely on practical experience, backed up by scientific proof, or to go by gut feelings, the sort he'd had about Jago Haldane from the first moment of meeting him. Gut feelings, he reminded himself, were not the good copper's tools for bringing criminals to justice. But he'd seen too often that when a loved one was involved, the instinct to protect was overwhelming ... He looked more kindly at her ravaged face. Perhaps she really hadn't had a choice.

'Robert said I would have to tell you.'

'Robert?'

'My husband.'

So there was someone else who knew, apart from Jago Haldane himself. Another family member, but perhaps someone with a sense of probity, who wouldn't find it quite so necessary to protect Jago.

'Mrs Faber,' Abigail said, 'would you like to revise your statement?'

Jago Haldane, while his sister was, unknown to him, being questioned by the police, sat with a pen in his hand, staring into space.

He felt hopeless. Twice he'd tried to kill a man; once he had failed, though Paul was now dead, all the same. Steve Kaminski, Paul. Not to mention his father's death, his mother's. There was only one end to it all, and oh God, this time he had to succeed, but this time he had no impulsive rage to carry him along. He was angry with himself, yes, and full of shame, but neither angry nor shamed enough, perhaps. He was afraid he couldn't do it, gin bottle, sleeping pills regardless. There were reasons why not, reasons that were insidious: his sisters, the thought of causing them more pain than anyone had the right to inflict . . . and perhaps, even more than that, his career, in ruins.

After all, what had he done? *You have taken a human life.* Ah yes, his father might tell him that, from the grave, but he could feel no guilt, only an overwhelming sense of colossal failure. Above everything else, that his father had actually believed him capable of using violence against his own mother . . .

He looked down at the letter he was trying to write.

I'm sorry, Liv. You've always been the best of sisters, but I shouldn't have asked you to lie for me. All I can say is that I never meant to kill that man, Kaminski. I am not excusing myself, but I want you to understand how it was . . .

I had become very uneasy, even before Ma was attacked, about how we were going about the business of that Klee, maybe that was why I chose not to involve myself any more than was necessary, in case things went wrong. Paul had been vague about how they were going to persuade Ma that this Tadeusz Siemek was the rightful owner of the painting, and to hand it over to him, and I'd begun to have grave misgivings. I should have approached Ma myself, I know that now. If I'm being honest, I think I must have suspected from the beginning that something wasn't quite right. But it was only after I drove Father home from the hospital, not knowing whether Ma was ever going to be able to speak again, that I knew for certain. We began to try and put the room to rights and I picked up the letter which had come from Tadeusz Siemek at the Bessemer Street address, and saw that he'd arranged to see Ma that day. And suddenly, I saw what I thought had happened and knew I had to act.

I didn't stop to think. I left the house without even saying a word to Father, though when he wrote to me, through James Denby, he told me he realised afterwards, when he picked Siemek's letter off the floor, what I must have done. He thought – yes, he believed it possible! – I had been the one Ma had been expecting, that she'd shown me the letter and we'd argued over it . . . and the rest.

The rest . . . well, the rest of it did happen almost exactly as Father imagined, except that I didn't kill the man I thought to be Tadeusz Siemek as a result of an argument. I simply shoved him back into the house when he opened the door, took him by the throat and told him why I was killing him. He tried to speak, but he was dead within seconds. I got in my car and drove off. I only learned later that he was Kaminski, but by then it scarcely mattered. The only thing I haven't been able to make out is how the house caught fire. I got away with it because of that fire. I have even wondered, sometimes, if it was you who did that, Liv . . . but no, you wouldn't have done that, even for me.

James Denby is going to send Father's letter to the police, if he hasn't already done so. In his letter to me, Father told me what he intended to write. A futile gesture. No one will ever believe it, nothing will stick.

Is that what he intended? No one could ever accuse him of lack of intelligence. Nor of being under any illusions about me. Was it his way of making me confess? If so, he didn't know me as well as he thought. I haven't the guts.

My decision is made. I shall never tell anyone what happened. I intend to burn this letter and then – the gin bottle, the pills, the car engine switched on in the garage. This time, I shall make sure.

Goodnight, Liv. Sleep well.